POISON NIGHTS AND TWILIGHT ALCHEMY

CANDACE ROBINSON
SGD SINGH

To all those who dream of magic

Crowmare Sea
Sorcerer's Keep
Rust Fields
Nightmore Forest
Abyss Canyon
Silver Birch Straits
Shadow Springs
Forest of a Thousand Sorrows
The Duke's Manor
Lake Elera
Alder Bay
Village of Whispering Holly
Thyone Pass
Raven Wing Inn
Town of Moonglade
Dogwood Glen Swamp

Dulce

Shadows danced like joyous skeletons beneath the silvery glow of the full moon. The garden, dressed in obsidian, ivory, violet, and cerulean floral blooms, swayed in the night as the carriage drew closer to its destination. Wreaths of sage and honeysuckle along the entrance gate greeted the newlyweds, and Dulce sighed in merry contentment. *Home.* No longer was she the manor's sole heir—that honor would now be shared with the handsome man seated beside her.

Cornelius William Hale. Known before today as the most eligible bachelor in every village of Moonglade.

Their conversation had been sparse after the long day

of lavish wedding festivities in the town common house. Cornelius had insisted on inviting everyone in Moonglade, near and far, but hours of feasting, dancing, and greeting many she didn't know, especially in a dress weighing nearly as much as herself, left Dulce's feet aching, no matter how showered with flattery she'd been.

Dulce peeked at Cornelius out of the corner of her eye, his smile gentle while he held her hand in his. She should feel like the luckiest woman in the world. Not only was her husband handsome, but he was also kind and generous. Cornelius had pursued her with charm and grace, his humor winning her friendship. And although Dulce had to admit to herself that she didn't love him *yet*, she had accepted his marriage proposal.

To turn down a proposal from such a perfect man would have broken her parents' hearts, if they had still been living.

Besides, it must not be denied that Cornelius was clearly the one Vesta had meant when she'd read Dulce's fortune in the tea leaves last spring. There could be no doubt.

"The man who will own your heart entirely, and you his," her housemaid had said, her eyes glazed over in that way they got, "is the one who will lift you from a most unfortunate and muddy circumstance."

Hadn't Cornelius been the one who'd helped her up when she'd tripped in the garden only days later? Anyone would deduce the same. It had to be true, because look, here she sat. His bride. Owning her heart entirely would just have to come later.

Cornelius's thumb tenderly caressed Dulce's hand, pulling her from her thoughts and reminding her that they had nearly reached the manor.

Oh dear. Dulce's heart pounded with sudden panic. *The wedding night!*

The moment she knew completed every union would be approaching rather soon. Too soon. Dulce's hand grew clammy within Cornelius's as she thought about what would surely be expected of her within the next hour. They'd hardly kissed a handful of times, chaste kisses that were lovely but admittedly had failed to make her weak in the knees like the heroines in the poems she loved. Even though most of those ended in beautiful gloom.

The carriage jostled toward the manor's ancient bristlecone pine, its gnarled trunk like so many open arms, and Dulce smiled, her worries fading at its familiar sight, the memories it conjured. Her mother had loved this tree and used to take Dulce to sit beneath it almost every day while she read her tales of brilliant alchemists. Vesta would stand watch, scolding Dulce to be careful as she climbed within its smooth branches, demanding she get down before she broke her neck.

"You're being rather quiet, darling," Cornelius whispered in her ear, his breath warm on her neck. "Are you not happy?"

Dulce smiled as she turned to meet her husband's vivid hazel eyes. "I am. I'm only tired from so much celebrating—that's all."

He took his hand from hers and draped his arm around her shoulders, pulling her close against him. "It was a beautiful celebration though, wasn't it? I especially loved the glazed venison. And the orchestra was moving."

His words didn't quite calm her nerves, but Dulce smiled again and nodded all the same.

Giving her hand one last squeeze, Cornelius adjusted his cravat, a smile in his voice. "We're home."

Dulce peered from the carriage window as the horses halted before the manor that had been in her family for generations. Deep green ivy crawled across its entranceway, tiny sapphire flowers blossoming within the vine's depths. Metallic dragonflies, blue and green moths, and copper butterflies flew throughout the garden. Several of the bushes were cloaked in shining gossamer where spiders had spun their silk. Ever since she was a girl, Dulce had instructed the servants never to disrupt the arachnids' homes.

The carriage door opened to reveal Sylvan, his gray hair disheveled from driving them home, and he bowed with a wide gap-toothed grin. He'd apparently waited for her wedding day since the day she was born and couldn't stop smiling and congratulating her.

"Your father and mother would be so proud, Miss Dulce," he'd said, his eyes full of jovial tears just before the wedding ceremony. "I just know they would."

Dulce had warned him not to drink too much plum brandy, and he'd only laughed.

Cornelius stepped in front of Sylvan, dismissing the servant for the night, then held his hand out for Dulce. A gust of cool fall air blew past her, and she shivered, gooseflesh sprinkling across her arms.

"Thank you, Sylvie," Dulce said. "I do believe Mr. Hale and I have all we need for the next two days."

Generally, Sylvan and his grandson Lucas remained at the manor along with Vesta, but Cornelius had kindly suggested giving the entire staff a few nights away at the town's best inn—the Royal Lion—while he and Dulce learned to be husband and wife. The servants certainly deserved some time to themselves after the hard work they'd put in over the years, especially after Dulce's parents passed.

Sylvan hadn't liked the idea though, taking it more as a critique of his professionalism, which Dulce found endearing, though ridiculous. There was no better housekeeper in the world.

"If you need anything"—Sylvan wrung his hands—"we'll happily return and be at your service immediately," he promised.

"All right, I'll remember that." She grinned, knowing there would be no reason to take a horse into town and ruin their holiday.

As the carriage pulled away, Cornelius scooped Dulce into his arms, and she gasped, her dress billowing in the wind. "Mrs. Hale," he said, carrying her to the door. "Now it's just the two of us."

"Yes." She laughed softly. "At last." No more room full of strangers or her parents' old friends.

Cornelius carried her over the threshold, a proper bride and groom, and Dulce couldn't hide her smile. Two lanterns illuminated the stone foyer with its many plants and ornate rugs. Once on her feet, Dulce lit the candles around the sitting room until her beautiful groom was bathed in a warm orange glow.

Her gaze meeting his, Dulce's heart thrummed against her ribcage, singing its own sweet lullaby. Was this the moment she would fall in love with him? Should she grasp her husband by the hand and lead him to their bedroom where they could mold their bodies together beneath the silken sheets? Perhaps now would be the perfect time to loosen the buttons of her wedding gown, to cross the room and unfasten his trousers.

Dulce blushed at the thought.

Surely it would be more proper to converse first? Her tongue suddenly felt heavy in her mouth, no words escaping her. Dulce trusted her own judgment—she hadn't made a mistake in marrying him. She would be a good wife to Cornelius, and she *would* fall in love with him. Hopefully very soon.

"How about I brew us each a nice hot cup of lavender tea?" he asked with a smile. "Then we can … talk."

His smile really was lovely. Dulce inwardly sighed and pressed a hand against his firm chest. Really, Cornelius was the most considerate of husbands, recognizing her nerves and being happy to soothe them.

"That sounds perfect," she said. "Thank you."

No matter what ailed her, lavender tea was akin to a cure.

"You just relax, darling." He guided her into the nearest chaise lounge and wrapped a shawl around her shoulders. "That's better. I'll return shortly."

Dulce released a long, relieved breath yet couldn't relax. She brushed her palms down her ivory gown, the poofy sleeves tickling her skin, as she stood and sat at her father's piano. He'd taught her how to play when she'd begged him at four years old after hearing one of the songs he'd created. She still loved the piano as much as reading dark and dreary poems. Pressing her fingers to the ivory keys, she played a gentle, moody melody, and thoughts of the first time she'd met Cornelius in the market at Vesta's palm reading booth drifted through her mind.

Every Saturday, Dulce would visit the market to choose fresh fruit, look at the latest dresses through the shop windows, and stop by Vesta's fortune-telling booth to keep her company. Vesta had always been more like family, treating Dulce like her own daughter.

Dulce enjoyed the reactions of Vesta's eager customers. It never failed that someone would come along praying Vesta could provide them with a romantic match. One spring morning, a tall, alluring man approached the booth—Cornelius. Dulce had been wearing a simple black dress that day, and she'd looked easy to mistake for a commoner sitting behind Vesta's booth. Holding a recently repaired horse bridle, she had recognized him at once from one of the summer solstice parties.

"Oh." He leaned on the table, ignoring the cards strewn across it. "I hadn't realized the market palm reader was so breathtaking. This meeting must be good fortune." Cornelius gave her a lopsided smile, his rich hazel eyes sparkling.

Dulce arched a brow. "I'm sure you say that to all the girls in the market."

"No." He straightened, answering in all seriousness, "Only this one."

Dulce halted her movements on the piano keys and thought about how gentlemanly Cornelius had been toward her during their courtship. He would arrive nearly every day just in time for afternoon tea, treating the staff as wonderfully and courteously as her father always had, which was another reason she'd accepted his proposal.

She pushed up from the piano and drew the lacy

window curtains aside, peering out the glass into the garden. A fox burst from a hydrangea bush in the moonlight and darted past the conservatory, its jolly yips reaching her. An owl hooted in an alder tree, and she caught the rustle of its snowy wings.

Turning from the window, she studied the sitting room. Once her parents succumbed to illnesses alchemy couldn't even cure, Dulce had left nothing changed in the house, keeping everything the same, as her mother had it, holding onto their memory for as long as she could. Until about a year ago, when she began, one by one, to change out some of the household items at last. But never her mother's vases or paintings. Marigolds and daisies, her mother's favorite, always filled the vases, removed only when the flowers withered, replaced by fresh blooms.

A throat cleared behind her, and Dulce whirled to find Cornelius holding out a cup of tea toward her. She scolded herself for nearly forgetting his presence, so lost in memories as she was.

"Thank you," Dulce breathed, grasping the porcelain handle. She blew against the tea's aromatic steam while Cornelius took a long, slow sip from his cup.

"Drink up." Cornelius smiled. "A man could grow impatient to take his bride back into his arms. Especially the most exquisite bride to ever live."

Heat crept into Dulce's cheeks, and she pressed her lips to the cup, drinking down the delicate lavender tea.

Its floral flavor didn't linger in her mouth as usual. Instead, a slight bitterness, a flavor at once alarming and familiar, intensified.

Dulce tried to gasp, but her throat tightened, and her tongue became numb, swelling, the flesh filling her mouth until she choked.

The room swayed, and she reached out for her husband, yet Cornelius's dreamy smile only grew, turning insidious as he stood watching her. Making no move to help her.

"That's a good girl," he purred.

Her husband had done this. She'd married him, and he was killing her. Murdered on her wedding day.

"You poisoned me," Dulce managed, choking, her legs weakening, her feet sliding against the carpet. Pain filled her insides, twisting.

Mother's favorite silk carpet, she thought stupidly when its amber and lapis-colored fibers loomed closer.

Cornelius didn't move to catch Dulce as she collapsed, her mouth dry, her lungs screaming for air.

She attempted in vain to pull herself up on shaking hands, only to meet Cornelius's indifferent stare. He almost looked intrigued by what he'd done, tilting his head to the side like a curious raven while she struggled.

"Indeed, I did poison you," he cooed. "Death is a wonderfully convenient part of life, isn't it? Rest assured—I will grieve yours more spectacularly than any groom before me."

"Why...?" Dulce slurred.

"Why?" He crouched just out of her reach, smiling with apparent delight.

"My fortune," she rasped. "It was yours..."

"Money? You think this is about money?" Cornelius chuckled. "How vulgar, my dear bride."

"You filthy bastard," she ground out.

He chuckled and rose, placing one shining shoe on her back and pressing until she fell to the floor.

Blackness cloaked Dulce's vision then, buzzing filling her ears … until there was nothing.

Reed

The saying goes, bad luck is when perfect timing and a lack of preparation meet reality. Growing up in Dogwood Glen, Moonglade's neighboring slum, Reed didn't believe in luck. Believing in luck would only get you empty pockets at a gambling tavern. No, there were those born with privilege and those born in squalor, who made their own privilege.

Tragedy and struggle just happened, sure as the sun rose and set. It was nothing personal.

Dogwood Glen had once upon a time been a quiet village filled with dogwood trees, their flowers decorating its swampy forests in white lace. Today it was nothing but a maze of muddy lanes between ramshackle huts of rotting wood. Lanes that grew narrower by the day, a stench-infested serpent winding its way past the masses of those born in squalor. Sure, the occasional tavern made of slightly less rotting wood could be visited—if one didn't mind a fight with an unmuzzled codpiece of a drunkard and questionable cuisine. And on Sundays the market, full of shouting vendors, smelled slightly of decaying fish.

The Glen was surely not what it used to be.

Reed left Dupont's apothecary that afternoon wondering if he should change his stance on luck. It was beginning to seem he might have the worst luck of all the unfortunate moldwarps in the Glen. One thing after another went wrong, until it felt as if his brand of bad luck had particularly good timing. If a fresh leak in the roof wasn't enough, his brother Philip let himself be pickpocketed out of the rent by walking through a crowd of reeky children at play, an activity any dimwitted toad knew to avoid, and then—in a fit of regret over the loss, no doubt—he went and got himself sick by insisting on hanging around Dankworth's, knowing full well the pestilence had taken the tavern's main chef only the week before.

Admittedly, it was hard to be too angry at his brother while the poor man lay whey-faced and sweating on his bed, his tongue the color of a putrefying aubergine well past its date. He could scarcely drag himself to the chamber pot and hardly eat more than a few bites of treacle porridge.

Still. Now Reed had two problems to solve. The rent money, such as it was, had to be paid in no more than twenty hours, or the Leper's ruffians would start collecting fingers. Or ears. One of them preferred noses, he'd heard, and Reed touched his own protectively at the thought. He was rather fond of his nose. His second problem was acquiring the remedy against the pestilence, a tonic that must be administered before Philip's eyes filled with blood, a sure sign the plague's victim had reached the point of no return.

The only known cure was a mysterious concoction of herbs Reed had just discovered was by no means cheap, thanks to the Glen's bull's pizzle of an apothecary and his colossal greed.

Reed thought of his brother and tried not to panic. Philip was the only family he had left. The only family he had ever known. The two of them survived—that was what they did. They made their own luck. Losing their parents, along with everything they had, the brothers had scraped by on whatever they earned in the smoky taverns and sunbaked fields of Dogwood Glen. They had clawed their way to a roof over their heads that they could call their own, clawed their way to something resembling respectability. Reed would not lose his brother now. Not when Philip still had dreams, aspirations, to one day teach at a school outside the Glen, which proved how completely opposite from each other two brothers could be.

Reed wracked his brain for some solution, forcing himself not to turn around and re-enter the apothecary and punch Dupont in his puke-stocking of a face, the grasping clotpole.

The farms weren't hiring yet. No one was building anything either. He could work for the blacksmith, or lend a hand at the butcher's again, a job he detested, but so did everyone else. He could bake bread at Rohwedder's, if he wanted to work before dawn. But all of these options would still mean waiting to save enough for Philip's remedy, and waiting was not an option—it would mean his brother's death.

He knew of no job that would pay on short notice, no employer loggerheaded enough to hand out advanced pay, not if Reed wished to prevent him and his brother from falling deeper into the Leper's debt.

No job but one.

Reed would just have to fight for the coin. What were bruised knuckles and a few broken ribs, all things considered.

Passing through the market, Reed heard nothing but talk of the beloved librarian who'd died tragically from the pestilence the day before. How her family couldn't afford her a proper burial.

Old Mrs. Mason was even crying about it, her considerable bosom heaving like some spongy sea beneath her many chins, and Reed halted for a moment to eavesdrop.

"Tansy was the kindest lass here in the Glen," she sobbed into her stained handkerchief. "No one gave as much time to helping the children here as her. She will be greatly missed—that I can promise you. Greatly missed."

"She deserved a funeral to make even the sprites cry," Miss Atkinson called while she stirred something in a bowl, her skeletal arms moving like branches in a strong wind.

"Like the funeral Oscar attended in Moonglade this morning," Mrs. Mason sniffed. "He wasn't invited, but he delivers horseshoes to one of the shops near the manor where the funeral was held. The shop's owner is a cousin of the widower, and the dead bride was an *heiress.* Alexandra Josephine Bancroft. Her husband will inherit everything she owns."

What a name, Reed thought, rolling his eyes.

"Oh, Reed!" Mrs. Mason exclaimed, noticing him. "She was around your age. I believe only nineteen."

Plenty of women died in the Glen around nineteen and far younger every day, but he only nodded.

"Oscar mentioned the widower will be fine," Leopald chimed in beside Mrs. Mason. "Apparently there are many a wagtail lass glad to see the swollen parcel of a husband of hers back on the market. Cornelius Hale is akin to a prince to the women in Moonglade." He fell into a fit of coughing as his wife smacked the side of his head.

"Don't forget Oscar also said the bride looked beautiful as the spring day when they buried her in her mother's garden," Mrs. Mason continued. "Wedding gown, jewels, and all. So very regal."

Reed shook his head. *Such a waste of jewels.*

"She was called Dulce," Leopald added proudly, as if he were close to the heiress himself. Reed tried not to roll his eyes again. If anyone from that house ever set foot in the Glen, he'd bet a year's rent they wouldn't last a day. The smell alone.

"That poor, poor man…" Miss Atkinson lamented.

Reed had heard enough. They were more worried about this rich heiress than the beloved librarian they were originally mourning.

He gave a final nod to Mrs. Mason before leaving. His last fight had saved her husband from the pestilence, and she would not soon forget it. Reed could usually expect to receive some of whatever it was she cooked every Friday evening.

But it isn't close to Friday now, he thought with a pang of hunger.

Past the tangle of huts, Reed walked in blessed silence along the river's edge, the stench of its murky water pushing in the opposite direction by the morning's northerly breeze. He kept an eye out for anything edible and found a batch of penny bun mushrooms concealed in the weeds, fungi he promptly gathered into his jacket's deep pockets. Next he discovered, nearly hidden behind a box hedge, that the whortleberry bushes were at last full of fruit. Reed filled the small sack he carried in his other pocket, hoping as he did that he could make it back home before the berries were crushed.

With the Leper's clay-brained toads, one never knew.

"Well, well, well," Tobin called in his lazy drawl when Reed approached the Leper's arena. "If it isn't his fen-sucked majesty Mr. Reed himself. Come to grace us with his royal, pribbling pompous presence."

"Tobin." Reed nodded, ignoring the drivel that always spewed from the man in a generous stream.

An unremarkable building from the outside, the arena was made of worn dark oak with no signage and surrounded by the only trees and dry land left in the Glen. Inside, the building's central feature was a fighting ring of stretched canvas and bloodstains, its railing of knotted branches and frayed ropes encircled by half-broken benches. Its secondary feature was the many tables to make bets on the fights. The Leper lived somewhere within the structure's shadowy hallways, but few knew where.

The arena was the only place the Duke's enforcers left alone when they scoured the land for treasure and bribes, all the while pretending to crack down on crime. A fact Reed found interesting.

"Or maybe," Scott answered, standing slowly to lean on the porch's worn railing and look down at Reed, his greasy hair falling over his shoulders, "our pretty ivory-headed pumpion has decided to come work for us. What do you say, eh? Are you through mewling about with *respectable* pignuts who refuse to pay a decent wage?"

"Will I still have to wear one of those lumpish hedge-pig bonnets?"

The trio crossed their arms in unison, which maybe would have been intimidating but for the ridiculous hats the Leper made them wear. Red velvet Breton caps with gold ribbon. Most offensive hats to ever offend, especially on a pack of stuffed puttocks as these three.

"I need a fight," Reed called before they could defend their boss's mangled fashion sense. "Today, now."

"No can do," Tobin stated, scratching his chin. He actually appeared regretful—a sentiment Reed happened to know was beyond the man's very limited emotional capacity. "The boss says no fights for a fortnight."

Ford spit something green over the railing and said, "We're all in mourning for Tansy, you see. It's a shame I didn't get to tumble her first."

"She was betrothed," Scott corrected, looking offended.

"Shut it," Ford snapped. "No one cares."

"How much do you need?" Tobin called, his eyes dancing with the only real thing Reed knew he felt. Greed.

"You know we're always here to help out a fellow Glenny, right? You can pay us back in a fortnight. After you win, that is."

With interest. These plague sores would make sure Reed had no choice but to work for them. For the Leper.

The notion of that turned his stomach, and it wasn't just the hats. He reached into the sack he held and ate a handful of whortleberries, pretending to be grateful for the offer.

Reed thought of Philip, slowly dying in their dilapidated hut unless he stopped it, along with his own fingers, his ears, and his nose, all things he very much wished to remain intact. There had to be another way.

He turned to leave, waving at the trio.

"I'll think about it," Reed lied.

He knew what he had to do. The solution to all his problems had been given to him not long ago. A bride lay buried in jewels only two short leagues away. Her house would be in mourning, black drapes drawn across every window. Nightfall was nearing.

It was a hanging offense, graverobbing, this was true enough. But Philip was dead if he did nothing, as good as dead if he began working for the Leper, his dreams crushed to ashes.

There was no choice.

Reed had a grave to rob.

Dulce

"*Observe the four teacups in front of you, duckling,*" *Mama said softly. "See them as north, south, east, and west.*"

Dulce studied her mother as she placed four porcelain teacups in a square formation along the dining table, their sides painted in delicate pink roses, their borders shining swirls of gold. The curtains were drawn back, morning sunlight spilling into the room. It reflected off the liquid within the cups and sent glowing images across the crystal candelabras above them.

Ever since Dulce's fifth birthday two years ago, her mother had made her play the Tea Game each morning after breakfast.

"*You will take a sip from the cups and tell me which of the four tastes different.*" *A mischievous smile playing across her lips, Mama* dropped a mint leaf into the steaming cups before propping her hands beneath her chin, watching Dulce. "Are you ready?"

Dulce rubbed her tiny hands together and sat up straight in her chair, frowning as she concentrated on the teacups.

"Will I get a chocolate again if I guess right?"

Mama always surprised her when she won the game, and chocolates were Dulce's favorite.

"Mr. Fox might allow you two this time if you choose correctly." Mama winked and slid the jar of chocolates closer to the teacups. "I have it on good authority that he thinks you're gifted."

Dulce bit her lip, wanting desperately to win those two chocolates. Lifting the doll beside her into her lap, she peered down at Mr. Fox and whispered into his furry triangular ear, "I might need your help." She hovered her doll above the steaming brews, letting Mr. Fox inspect them one by one. The liquid within each cup was generally the same color every morning, just as they were now. Mr. Fox sniffed each one, but he told her nothing. North was where she decided to begin.

Dulce brought the first teacup to her lips, taking a slow and steady sip, finding it floral though slightly bitter, with hints of earthy apple and smooth sweet undertones. Tasty.

"Chamomile," she declared matter-of-factly, resting the cup back against the table. "With honey."

Mama remained silent as she always did, waiting until Dulce completed her guesses.

Dulce lifted the southern teacup and found it held a flavor that matched the northern one exactly. Pursing her lips, she tried the western one next. Flowery and sweet, yet not completely. A hint, albeit small, of something sharper coated her tongue, a new kind of bitterness, not belonging to the daisy-like family of Asteraceae at all. Dulce was almost certain this was the brew she would choose, but just to be precise and thorough, she brought the final teacup to her lips and took a sip, only to find no sign of bitterness or anything out of the ordinary from the first two.

"The western tea is different," she answered proudly and tapped the porcelain with her forefinger.

"How certain are you?" Mama hedged, always attempting to make Dulce think further, to second-guess her decision.

Dulce knew she wasn't wrong. "I would wager Mr. Fox's life on it."

"Ah, that must mean you're incredibly sure of your choice."

"I am."

Mama sat in silence, contemplating the cups for an agonizing moment, and then grinning, she grasped the jar of chocolates and dropped two glorious squares into Dulce's tiny, awaiting palms.

"You did well, duckling," she said. "You are much better at this game than I expected for someone of such a young age. I'm proud of you."

Dulce beamed with pride at her mother's words as she chewed happily, savoring the first of the two chocolates. She rested the second in Mr. Fox's lap and planned to savor it. "Can we play in the garden now?"

"Of course," Mama replied. "But first, while you eat your chocolates, I have something to ask you. I think you're old enough to learn more about our little morning Tea Game."

Dulce sat up straighter, her attention arrested at once. Her mother had always refused to tell her why differentiating between teas was so important.

Mama was serious, with no hint of mischief in her eyes now. "This will be a secret between you and me. One you must promise not to tell anyone," she said. "Do you understand?"

"Not even Papa?" Dulce always told Papa everything, especially when he was teaching her new songs on the piano.

"Papa is the only exception." Mama laughed, draping her long, dark hair over one shoulder. "Because he knows about this secret already."

"What about Nanny Vesta and Sylvie?"

"Nanny Vesta and Sylvan are both trustworthy and know most of this, yet not the entirety," Mama assured her gently. "Sometimes we must keep things to ourselves to protect those we love. Like carrying a burden for them, something too heavy that they don't need to carry themselves."

Dulce thought hard. "Like the time Papa cleaned up Sylvie's spoiled cabbage and replaced it with fresh ones from the garden before he returned from the market? No one told him because Sylvie would feel bad for Papa's spending money and doing work he thinks only he should be in charge of."

Mama ruffled her hair with a smile. "Exactly like that, yes."

"I understand." Dulce pressed a finger to her mouth and glanced at Mr. Fox. "It's a secret."

Her mother took in a deep breath and let it out gradually.

Dulce chewed on her lip. She had never seen Mama this serious.

"I've been poisoning you, duckling."

Dulce blinked, hugging Mr. Fox tightly as her tiny heart thundered inside her chest, nearly cracking her ribcage.

"You want me dead, Mama?"

Her mother stood, rounding the table, and knelt beside Dulce, her silk skirts making that wonderful Mama sound they always made. She took Dulce's hand in hers, her golden-brown eyes unwavering. "I would never harm you, my love. I'm giving you these poisons because I want you to be strong. There are dangerous people in this world, people who would try to hurt you because of who you are, and the wealth you will one day inherit. Poisoning is their favorite method of reaching their greedy and grasping ends. If poison cannot hurt you, it will instead protect you. Do you understand now why this game is so important?"

Dulce didn't understand, but she slowly nodded anyway, trying hard to imagine anyone wicked enough to poison her. Were the monsters in the storybooks real? One thing she understood was that she trusted her mother completely.

"I started with small doses, introducing your body to various poisons," Mama continued. "Only the teeniest drop each fortnight before gradually adding a little more. This is why at first you felt tired and needed to take a morning nap—do you remember? This slow building of tolerance against them will help you gain immunity from poison." She stood. "Now that you're old enough, I'm letting you decide for yourself. Do you want to continue?"

Dulce nodded eagerly. A body tolerant of poisons sounded positively magical. She would become like the mongoose, able to resist even a viper's venom. Impervious as a honey badger or hedgehog. There would be no poison-peddling assassin that could defeat her.

"Our games will grow more challenging, duckling. Especially since you're a witch. Like me."

"A witch?" Dulce blinked, squeezing Mr. Fox's arm.

"Yes. A secret that we keep to ourselves from the villagers in Moonglade. Your grandmother once sent me far away to hone my skills as a child and through most of my adolescent years, yet I will teach you myself, without the cold and harsh ways of old."

Dulce mulled over all the surprises that had been revealed. "I want to learn more."

"And you will." Mama smiled. "Now, let's go out into the garden and play, shall we? We'll resume our secret games tomorrow."

Dulce jumped to her feet in delight. "You hide, and I'll count!"

The garden was bathed in sunlight, marigolds and daisies in full bloom, and Dulce ran through the door, Mr. Fox in tow, forgetting to eat her last bit of chocolate slowly.

A dull ache thrummed at the back of Dulce's head, radiating across her temples, and she opened her eyes to utter and complete darkness. Darkness as she'd never experienced it before, a thick blanket of onyx seeping down to her bones.

Rubbing her temples, she went to sit up when her head struck something hard.

"Ow," Dulce croaked, her voice muffled as she touched her forehead, then trailed her fingers across the surface above her. Smooth folds of silky material over something hard.

Dulce rapped her knuckles against it, feeling its dimensions, a foot beyond her head and to each side.

Cold realization crashed into her like a raging storm.

She was buried alive.

Cornelius had done this. He had poisoned her with … hemlock, yes. There was no mistaking its grassy-lemon-dirt flavor, even beneath the sweet lavender and heaps of sugar he'd added to the tea. Dulce had been so overwhelmed by the upcoming wedding that taking her daily dose of poisonous berries or teas wasn't as consistent.

Alchemy was something she'd once cherished, yet she hadn't performed any spells since her mother's death three years before and had only kept up the tradition of eating poison berries and drinking toxic teas. Being a common witch had been a side of herself she'd let die with her mother, a side that ached to live again now. However, there was no spell she knew that would break

24

her from this coffin. Without proper ingredients, that was. Which she didn't have at the moment.

How could she have been so foolish as to think Cornelius an honorable man, to judge him so wrongly? How could she not have seen the deception in his heart? If the bastard even had a heart.

If her mother were alive, she would've warned Dulce about him, with his slimy, over-the-top gentlemanly behaviors and simpering, false kindness. Dulce had been so blind. An utter and complete fool. Cornelius had barely even kissed her a handful of times, and she believed him to be in love. Most men would've tried to unfasten her dress when they'd been alone, to kiss her passionately in the gardens. But she had assumed he'd held her in too high of esteem and had wanted to wait for their wedding night.

This never would've happened if she hadn't believed he was to be her true love after Vesta's fortune. The tea leaves had to have been meant for someone else entirely—Vesta's readings were never wrong.

The scent of earth caressed her senses, and horror churned within her. She was truly underground! Buried. Believed dead. Did Cornelius know she was still alive when he'd had her buried? Was he laughing right now, imagining her slowly suffocating to death?

The vile snake. He had never wanted her.

Dulce padded her hands around the coffin, searching the darkness. There was nothing useful buried with her. Only a silk pillow and what felt like a mountain of petunias. Petunias from *her* garden.

She still wore her wedding gown, her pearls that Cornelius had so lovingly placed around her neck before the entire town, and the family ring on her middle finger. The ribbons in her hair she wanted to strangle him with. Dulce imagined him artfully crying as his new bride was laid to rest, the villagers offering him their heartfelt sympathy, and she seethed with fury.

A low growl escaped her, and she squeezed the clump of flowers resting against her chest until the petals were crushed. If Dulce's mother hadn't helped her become immune to poisons, she would've surely been dead instead of falling into unconsciousness for … how long? Her estimation was three days based on the strength of the poisonous flower.

What if Cornelius had decided to murder her in a different manner? She wouldn't have woken from a rope around her throat or a blade in the heart. No, the ruthless serpent wanted to end her life in a manner that would leave him blameless. Oh, how sad Vesta and Sylvan must have been…

Cornelius would pay for this. Dulce vowed to make certain of it.

If she ever got out of this grave, that was…

Dulce pressed her palms against the coffin's lid and pushed with all her might, but to no avail. No rope had been fastened near her hands so she could pull on it to ring a bell and alert someone that she was alive below ground, like she'd read about in grim poems. Was she buried where Sylvan or the others would hear her?

She was truly trapped.

With each passing second, Dulce realized she wouldn't live long. Not with the air inside her coffin running out.

Perhaps a blade to the heart would've been more

merciful after all.

Dulce refused to shed a single tear for her failed marriage and the bastard who had deceived her while she pounded against the dreadful coffin, hoping against hope that someone would hear and help her. She pounded until her fists ached with bloodied bruises. Until exhaustion and thirst swept over her as the air thinned and her strength waned.

No longer could Dulce fight against her eyelids closing, and when she finally gave in to sleep, she swore she heard digging, felt the jarring impact of a metal shovel against her prison.

Dreaming of an impossible escape, even as she surrendered to death…

Reed

If the drunks at Dankworth's were to be believed, graverobbing wasn't a crime, but rather an art form. There were rules to obey, procedures to follow, and details to observe. The most sacred of which was: one must never, ever visit a grave sooner than nine days after burial. Nine to symbolize the nine months the dead grew before birth, nine to remember life renewed. Also, the time of offerings—bread, water, and lighted lamp to welcome departed souls back to earth for the night—would be over, which clearly indicated the graverobbers' welcome.

Reed had never been able to ascertain what exactly

would happen if this rule was broken, but it was clearly something very unpleasant. He guessed it involved curses, bad luck, and probably death by haunting.

Three things he fortunately didn't believe in.

The first and most unbreakable rule established, the drunk would move on with his lesson. *Once a grave is selected*, he would explain, certain precautions had to be taken. *First, make sure to tie a black ribbon around your arm in a display of mourning. This shows any watching spirits that you have respect and gratitude for what you'll take.*

Secondly, and very important no matter how squeamish you might feel about it, kiss the forehead of the deceased the instant you see them. This will ensure they don't haunt your dreams.

Reed thought if a person was squeamish, they should take up another line of work, one that didn't involve rotting corpses. He discovered pointing this out usually enraged the drunks, however, and let them ramble on about technique instead.

A body snatcher only needed a pointed spade and a 'resurrectionist cane'—a four-foot iron bar with a hook at one end—a tool easily hidden beneath a cloak. This was perfect for cracking open the head end of the coffin, attaching the sharp end beneath the dead's chin, and pulling them out. A single body would fetch a pretty price if one knew the right physician to sell them to…

Reed knew of no wealthy physicians in the Glen and had no interest in hauling a body around even if he did, especially since he had no cart. Besides, though he was willing to steal jewels off a dead heiress, this method of stabbing into her sounded barbaric.

Did rich people nail wooden coffins shut? Or would the dead bride be buried in some kind of stone casket? If that was the case, he had no hope of prying it open alone.

The sun was beginning to set by the time Reed checked on Philip, borrowed tools from a farm he knew wouldn't miss them anytime soon, and made his way toward Moonglade. His brother's condition was not noticeably worse, and he'd managed to eat some of the berries Reed offered him, along with warm water with stewed mushrooms. Reed tried to assure him everything would be okay by morning, but he could see Philip didn't believe him.

"After I'm gone," he'd said, his voice barely above a whisper, "get as far from here as you can. You'll find a better life for yourself, Reed—you're too smart for this place."

Reed had only nodded, though he had no idea where he would go or what he would do. He wasn't smart—he was only reckless.

Once Philip was better, they could take whatever money was left and travel the world on grand adventures, finding peace and happiness away from the filth of the Glen together.

Reed walked hidden within the tall grass alongside the road, ducking down at any sound of horses, staying out of sight as he traveled. Oscar was journeying to the south, but there were other ways to find out the precise location of the dead bride's manor. When Reed reached Moonglade, he planned to ask the oldest barkeep in the emptiest tavern about the heiress.

Sure enough, a lonely tavern stood atop a hill just outside the village, its dusty porch looking down on the crowded streets of Moonglade. As the sun set, lanterns glowed one by one before the storefronts, their warm light shining through the tree-lined lanes while passersby hurried on their way between a blur of carriages. Someone played a lute, its delicate chords drifting along the warm breeze in melancholy harmonies.

Reed secured his tools beneath his tattered cloak and entered the tavern, the picture of an innocent country bumpkin.

"One pint of your finest mead, my good man," Reed called cheerfully as he settled onto the worn stool in front of the solemn barkeep with a large gray mustache. The man stood wiping mugs of foggy glass using a towel that looked the worse for wear, ignoring him.

Reed kept his white hair hidden beneath the hood of his dark cloak, knowing it would be memorable to anyone asking after strangers in the unlikely event his crime was discovered. His formerly dark hair had turned white after his fifth birthday when he'd fallen ill with the same fever that claimed his parents, and it had never regained its natural color. Philip insisted it made him more strikingly handsome, but Reed felt his unruly white hair was an unfortunate thing for the criminally inclined to possess.

"Word in the villages is a recently wed couple is in search of stable hands," Reed said, sipping his drink with a cough as if it were the first of his innocent life. "I wonder if you might direct me to the home of the Hale's?"

The barkeep glanced at Reed's hands, then resumed wiping glasses and placing them along the shelf.

"Good with the horses, are you?"

So. He was the suspicious type. Reed would need to move along quickly, but not *too* quickly.

Reed held up his clean hands and wiggled his fingers,

offering the man what he hoped was a non-suspicious smile.

"I walk the horses to the blacksmith more than I do the mucking out, most days." He took another ungraceful gulp from his mug. "But lifting bales of hay for bedding, fetching water at all hours of the day, and preparing the bran mash after a hunting party was my main duty. Well, that and grooming. The grooming never ends, does it? But a job is a job—I had no complaints."

The barkeep nodded in approval, though Reed could see he was still untrusting. For one thing, he hadn't given up the dead bride's abode.

"Rumor has it"—Reed leaned in—"the newlyweds only have four horses in their stable. Four! Can you imagine? What a dream it will be to get the job. Why, half the day to sleep away the idle hours…"

The barkeep at last looked at Reed with a sympathetic gaze, even refilling his nearly empty mug.

"I'm sorry to tell you this, my boy," he said, "but that house is in mourning. The bride is dead, buried just this morning."

Reed slammed his mug against the worn counter, spilling mead along the wood. "*Dead?*"

"I doubt if they'll be keeping a running estate," the man continued. "Not for a while. My guess is those horses are already gone, them and the rest. Wouldn't look good to be carrying on like normal for the rich, no sir. Goes against tradition, doesn't it? Especially with the mistress so young and childless…"

"Would it be all right if I inquired all the same?"

"Doubt anyone will answer at the gate," the barkeep told him, shaking his head sorrowfully. Then, meeting

Reed's hopefully heartbroken expression, he added, "But I don't suppose there's any harm in trying."

Finally. Reed was beginning to wonder if he'd need to make himself sick with mead before the spleeny old geezer gave up the fobbing residence.

"If you follow that road for the better part of an hour, you can't miss the place." He pointed to the only visible road in sight. "Largest manor in Moonglade, half hidden behind a wall of ivy and honeysuckle vines."

"A stone wall?"

"Its obsidian gate is one of a kind, decorated in golden pomegranates and unicorns."

Reed had to remind himself not to roll his eyes at this. What ridiculous anomalies the rich were. Golden fruit and nonsensical creatures all over their gorbellied gates, while the rest of the malt-worm population nearly starved. If he had ever felt an ounce of guilt over robbing the dead bride before, he certainly felt none of it now.

Reed finished his mead, paid the man with profuse thanks, and left—his digging tools held firmly against his side. The sun had set by the time he reached the market square, and it was easy to stay out of sight as he followed the narrow alleyways parallel to the tree-lined avenue through the town, the buildings becoming scarcer and the houses ever larger while he made his way up the hill. The night air was crisp, autumn approaching fast, and he was glad of his cloak. Here amongst the houses of the rich, there were no pedestrians, only the odd carriage, and Reed stayed within the shadows of the sycamore trees and yew hedges that decorated the neatly cobbled lane as it stretched beneath the stars.

When he at last came to a wall that dwarfed all the

others before it, he knew he had reached his destination, even without seeing its famed gate. Honeysuckle vines covered it in a massive wave of flowers, their fall berries shining silvery in the moonlight along dense foliage, completely disguising the wall of stone beneath them. Reed followed the wall until the gate's entrance was in sight, lamps lit above it, illuminating the drive, and then he turned around, following the wall back the way he'd come.

There had to be another way in, an entrance for the reeky peasants to do their jobs and vanish from sight.

"Hello," Reed drawled, finding exactly what he was looking for.

A door of rough pine hidden by vines, its rusted handle hanging half broken from its hinges, saving him time picking the lock. It opened with a soft creak, and Reed froze in the darkness, waiting for any sounds of alarm.

None came.

Time to find this grave, dig up my treasure, and get back home.

The garden proved to be a vast, sprawling affair. Mazes of boxwood hedges, a lake surrounded by willows, their hanging branches waving gingerly in the moonlight, rolling hills that he discovered led up to the rear of the manor, stone and iron that stood imposing and regal even at this late hour. A light within an ornate fence of jagged barbs and artistically twisted metal, its spikes enormous, caught Reed's eye as he approached the back entrance of the home. The lamp glowed amongst well-tended flowering shrubs, towering roses, and headstones. He knew that *here* he would find his gravesite.

The cemetery gate wasn't locked, merely decorative,

and Reed slipped past it silently, waiting in the darkness behind a fringe tree for any signs of occupancy inside the manor. If anyone remained, they must've retired amongst the seemingly infinite rooms within the opposite side of the place. No hint of smoke escaped the manor's many chimneys, no sound of activity reached the garden, and though its windows were covered in black cloth, no sliver of light shone from its countless panes.

Reed stepped from the tree and passed through the extravagant garden, studying a few headstones before finding the grave clearly belonging to the dead bride. It was piled high with a variety of white flowers, their velvety petals not yet withered.

He extinguished the lamp. If the heiress's soul actually did need this to light its way back, well, that was just bad luck for her, wasn't it?

Back in the shadows of the fringe tree, Reed chewed on a piece of already beginning to stale bread—left out for the dead—and waited in silence for anyone to notice the precious light had gone out. But even after twenty long minutes, no one came.

Returning to the bride's resting site, he struck the earth with his spade and began to dig.

It was surprisingly easy work, perhaps because the grave was so freshly dug, and after a few hours passed, his spade revealed the coffin within. He had half a mind to pass this information on to the professional grave robbers, but then he remembered rule number one and decided against it.

The craftsmanship of the coffin itself was more luxurious than anything Reed had ever seen. Made of what he was fairly certain was pink ivory—a material he'd only seen in the Leper's own billiard cue—its surface was decorated in copper peonies and crocuses, silver lavender and delphinium, all surrounded by golden herbs.

"Shame I can't sell the whole bawdy thing," Reed muttered, prying it open.

The coffin's lid fell back, and Reed stilled. If he thought the casket was beautiful, it was nothing compared to the beauty of its inhabitant. He remembered in that moment the gravedigger's practice of kissing the forehead of the dead upon first sight, and though he had thought it revolting at the time, he had to almost force himself not to lean forward and press his lips against those of the bride's.

"Right," he whispered, shaking his head to bring himself back to his senses. "Stop gawking like some loggerheaded varlot and focus on the job at hand, Reed. The dead are lost to the maggots…"

The heiress had been buried in her bridal gown, all fine white lace and silk. Her name had been carefully embroidered into the bodice in blue thread, as death traditions demanded. *Alexandra Josephine Hale "Dulce."* She adorned three strands of luminescent pearls around her slender neck, and her thick dark hair was decorated in gleaming gemstones beneath a veil of embroidered gossamer. Her pale hands were clasped at her chest, and on her middle finger, she wore a ring of carved gold, its center occupied by a design of white diamonds encompassing the largest ruby he'd ever seen.

Determined not to look at her enchanting face again, Reed reached for the ring, and, avoiding touching her skin, he pulled. But the jewel refused to pry loose.

"Right," he whispered again, twirling the blade he

always carried in his boot as he hesitated. "Will you let your brother die because you're too much of a qualling canker-blossom to cut one fobbing finger off one fobbing corpse? It's not as if she needs the thing now, is it? No."

He made the mistake of looking up at her face again and swallowed deeply. She had, impossibly, become more beautiful, clouds passing over the moon to reveal cheeks tinged a gentle pink in the starlight.

Reed took a deep breath, lifting her hand, and brought his blade to the base of the ring, squeezing his eyes closed, determined to finish what he'd started.

"My beloved mother left me this ring upon her death," a woman's voice passed through the silence, and Reed yelped in a decidedly unmanly fashion as he fell back, dropping his blade. "Tell me. What right does a stuffed plague sore such as yourself have to it?"

The corpse's eyes were open, two gleaming tourmalines in the moonlight, as lovely as the brightest stars in the night sky. Reed gaped at her, filled with horror and shame.

The heiress was alive.

"You're not dead…"

"Clearly," she snapped, pulling herself upright with obvious effort. "And you're a graverobber. A roguish, milk-livered graverobber."

"Clearly," Reed said with a bow. How does one even apologize for almost cutting the finger off a corpse who wasn't a corpse at all just to steal and pawn their belongings? "Rest assured, Your Ladyship, I wasn't planning to sell your organs. Only your jewelry."

The heiress frowned, hands on her middle. She had

apparently never heard of the practice. "And you seek thanks for that, do you...?"

Reed busied himself with dusting off his clothing and collected his blade, then started to climb from the grave.

"Thank you," she stated, and he was surprised to find only sincerity in her expression.

Reed sighed and raked a hand through his hair. "I'm sorry, I was desperate to save my ill brother—he's all I have left. I'll take my leave now."

"Wait."

He turned back, one hand reaching for the ledge of the grave. To his surprise, the heiress held out the ring to him.

"Take it," she uttered. "From one orphan to another."

Reed looked from the ring to her face, curious what game she played.

"Promise to tell no one I'm alive, and you can have my jewelry."

"I don't understand." Wasn't her husband heartbroken over her death? Wouldn't he be overjoyed to discover that his young bride was alive?

"In addition," she exhaled, closing her eyes again. "I can't seem to move my legs at all, and I would greatly appreciate some water."

He simply stared at her and smirked. The rich giving orders. As they always would.

Meeting his gaze, she unclasped the pearls from around her neck with obvious effort and held them out to him along with her ring.

"I was nearly dead until you dug me up," she said. "I have you to thank for my life. Will you help me?"

He was all too aware that time was running out for his

brother, just as it had been for the heiress only minutes prior.

"Very well, Majesty." Before she could protest, he lifted her in his arms and climbed from the muddy grave as she clung to him. Her body felt warm and impossibly delicate pressed against his, and the sweet scent of lilies filled his nostrils. He'd meant to startle her from issuing further orders, but as his gaze met her golden-brown eyes, Reed felt tempted once again to kiss her perfect lips. He was most assuredly losing his mind.

Her pristine gown now soiled, he released her gently upon the garden's manicured grass and handed her the gourd of water from his belt.

Accepting it with shaking hands, she drank in giant gulps, and he noticed she was shaking, gooseflesh rising against her pale flesh. He didn't waste a moment to remove his cloak and drape it over her shoulders.

"Take them, Reed," Dulce insisted, and he started at the sound of his name coming from her. She then stood with admirable determination, holding the jewels out to him once more. "Save your brother. And speak of my living to no one."

Dulce

Reed took the jewelry from Dulce reluctantly, his brow arched as though she would reclaim them, and she felt a pang of sympathy for the strange young man with peculiar white hair. Her gaze met his and lingered there, his deep chestnut eyes widening just a fraction as her fingers remained against his for a heartbeat too long. His brows were as black as a raven's wings, and with thick dark lashes and a slender build, he was quite handsome, truth be told.

Dulce folded his hand with finality over the jewels and left his warm touch. The pearls were nothing but a wedding decoration, a memory she wanted to forget from a marriage she wished she'd never chosen for herself. The ring was different—it had belonged to her mother, a special family heirloom. While she cared deeply about it, she didn't cherish the jewelry as much as the intricately carved music boxes with the dancing figures inside that lined the shelf in her bedroom. Treasures her mother used to gift her on each birthday, sixteen in total. It was something she'd missed the most after her mother's passing. Dulce's temper rose at the thought of Cornelius taking possession of them. Her *husband* better not have touched a single one, or his fingers would go missing before she finished with him.

If Reed hadn't been trying to thieve from her grave, she knew within her heart of hearts she never would've been found. And while Dulce should've been vexed with the thief for attempting to steal from her "corpse," it was his actions that had saved her.

"Can I ask you something?" Reed inquired as he placed the jewelry in his pocket and busied himself with filling her grave once again. "Well, two things."

"You may ask." Dulce shrugged, stretching her stiff legs and arms, her muscles protesting after their confinement. "Whether or not I answer is another thing entirely."

He angled his head to the side, regarding her for a moment before resuming his task. "How do you know my name?"

Half dead from lack of air by the time her coffin fell open, Dulce had known with chilling certainty that there was no use in fighting. She would've lost. Even if he had come to steal away her body for coin, she would've been useless against him. No, her only chance had been to wait, to breathe, and hope that her strength returned before it was too late.

"Ah, that." She laughed softly. "I thought it wise to pretend death, since my strength had left me. Did I do well? I was sure you could hear my racing heart." Everything Reed had spoken she'd heard, including his desperation to help his brother. His name. *Reed.* It suited the ivory-haired young man, somehow.

Dulce's cheeks heated as his eyes fell to her chest for a split second before he focused on his task with renewed haste. *Foolish thing to say.*

"You did very well—I never guessed for a second that you lived." He winked, returning the pile of flowers to her grave, followed by the lamp and bread, presumably as it had been before. Dulce shivered at the thought, then stretched her neck, the pain fading from her muscles in slow increments.

Reed stood looking at her now, a frown only improving his features as he offered her a handful of berries, which she readily ate, their juice spilling over her dress in delighted destruction.

"Why do you want no one to know you're alive?" he asked. "Not even … your husband?"

"An impertinent question indeed." Dulce smiled. Keeping her gaze on the gathering fog, she said, "Don't you think it's past time you go home now? Before you're missed? You still have a brother to save, no?" She removed the tattered wool cloak he'd placed upon her, a gentlemanly act of kindness. And even though Cornelius had always seemed kind, he'd never once given her his coat when she'd shivered.

"Fair enough." He bowed his head with a

mischievous grin, and Dulce was surprised to find herself once again charmed by the thief. "Perhaps you will tell me when we meet again. Good day, *Majesty*."

"It's Dulce," she said, and he only smirked before sauntering toward the shadows, his dark cloak billowing in graceful, tattered folds behind him as he disappeared into the foggy darkness.

Left alone, Dulce regarded her grave—anger rolled through her while she stared, remembering all too well the horror of being buried alive. The ridiculously lavish casket Cornelius must've used her own money to make a mockery of grief with. The clipped flowers from her gardens that should've never been cut. She swore revenge on her traitorous, most rankish compound of villainous dirt of a husband for his loathsome deceit.

The night fog thickening, her manor more obscured from sight with each passing moment, though its southern wall remained mere feet from her, Dulce lifted her muddy silk skirts and studied the other headstones around hers. Her mother's. Her father's.

Taking a deep breath, she hiked through the trees in satin slippers as she made her way through the gardens to the other side of the manor, a light mist drizzling down upon her until she reached one of the apple trees and ate two pieces of fruit, her strength returning in earnest.

Dulce fought the urge to tear off her wedding gown. Would Cornelius even still be inside the manor, or had he retreated somewhere else?

She frowned. Why would he murder her if it wasn't for money?

Crows cawed above her when she stepped from the shelter of the apple tree, their cries reverberating through the misty night as though warning her of danger.

"I could've used your warning before I ended up in a casket," she muttered. "But thank you all the same."

The fog rolled its alabaster hands throughout the gardens, ivory and onyx Dracula orchids hidden from sight, and as Dulce reached the north side of the manor, it towered before her, its slate stone glistening beneath the moonlight and flickering stars. Not every window was draped in darkness, as tradition demanded, but instead, warm light shone from the sitting room near the entrance.

Dulce slinked through the fog of the gardens, remaining unseen in case anyone happened to look. She wasn't certain if her trusted staff remained within, or if it was Cornelius alone who shirked the appearance of grief. She imagined finding him relaxed on her settee, sipping hot brandy in contentment, as though he hadn't poisoned his new bride.

No, you loathsome, poisonous toad, your dead bride has a little surprise for you.

Inching closer to the windowpane, Dulce discovered two figures standing within, and she stilled. It wasn't Vesta, Sylvan, or his grandson Lucas who accompanied Cornelius—it was a woman Dulce had never seen before. She stood a little above his large frame, her tall height akin to a goddess in poems. Her face was half turned from Dulce, but her luxurious long ruby hair fell in thick braids and curls over her shoulders. Cornelius fawned over her like a drooling dog as she laughed, the sound resembling chiming bells through the window. He leaned forward, one arm draped around the woman's slender waist, his other hand curved around her backside.

Unsurprising. Murdering adulterer.

Movement caught Dulce's eye at her mother's bristlecone pine tree, and she noticed an ivory horse tied to it. The beautiful stallion must belong to the unexpected *guest*.

As Dulce turned back to the window, she found the scoundrel threading his fingers through the woman's long ruby hair and backing the stranger into *her piano* while kissing her. Not in a chaste or loving manner, but instead rather sloppy and revolting, as though he were some sort of swamp beast drinking the woman's oxygen with his dishonorable tongue. Relief filled Dulce that she hadn't fallen for the pribbling lout. But still, she had accepted she could one day come to love him, and she grew humiliated, frustrated with disappointment at herself for trusting him, for believing that he'd been the one to give her a bright future. To pull her from...

Dulce's breath caught. Unfortunate circumstance... Unfortunate and *muddy* circumstance...

It couldn't be.

No, a desperate grave robber was most certainly not meant to be her true love. Dulce shook away the ridiculous thought.

The front door opened with a bang, followed by laughter, and Dulce crouched low, her hands trembling while she held her breath. The ruby-haired woman stepped out into the foggy night first—Dulce's heart quickened when Cornelius walked behind the stranger toward the bristlecone pine like a lovesick pet.

Pathetic bastard. She longed to see him beg for his life.

Dulce tightened her fists, hoping Cornelius wasn't about to depart with his lover.

The woman didn't reach to untie the horse from the

tree, though—instead, she pressed her palm to the bark. Cornelius stepped back in apparent reverence as the woman spoke, almost singing, her words obscured at this distance. This was clearly some sort of incantation, one that Dulce didn't recognize. As Dulce watched on with bated breath, lavender light spilled up from the ground surrounding the tree. The bristlecone pine glowed a soft white and flowed into the woman.

A witch. Like Dulce. Only she wasn't common, and this was no parlor trick—this woman was powerful.

What was the witch taking from her tree? This was unlike any alchemy she'd ever witnessed or wielded.

Finally the woman stepped away from the tree, and the night fell back into darkness, only the light from the manor illuminating the fog.

"Will I see you again soon?" Cornelius whined, nearly begging. "The servants won't return from the Royal Lion for another week when I send a carriage to fetch them to pack up their belongings."

"Not for a while, darling," she said dismissively, untying her horse. "Important business demands my attention elsewhere."

A crestfallen expression marred Cornelius's loathsome face and she laughed, letting him kiss her again. Then, with a sweep of her alabaster fur-lined cloak, the witch mounted the stallion and took off into the night, not sparing a glance back at Cornelius.

Dulce could've confronted him at that moment, yet she wanted to toy with him. Just as he'd toyed with her. She hadn't planned on revealing to him that she was a witch since she'd thought she had put that part of her life behind her. And she was more than pleased that she'd waited since she was going to uncage her inner witch very soon.

Once her husband was out of sight, Dulce darted toward the conservatory. She turned the padlock and entered the large space, breathing in the scents of intoxicating florals that permeated the air. Mountain laurel, oleander, foxglove, monkshood, and every other poisonous plant imaginable took up one side of the conservatory. On the other were plants of various berries that could easily be consumed without death. And lining the back wall, shelves cluttered with jars and vials of countless colored liquids created from plants. After Dulce gained a tolerance to poison, her mother had taught her how to perform simple spells using alchemy. Since her mother's death, she hadn't created any new concoctions, but she hadn't disposed of any either.

She grabbed a jar from the shelf, its yellow liquid mixed with monkshood, rosemary, mint, and salt. Ignoring their bitter taste, she drank the potion down and, like an old friend greeting her, let the appearance of death unfold.

Dulce lifted a small mirror from the shelf and watched as she worked with the alchemy to transform herself. Her black hair thinned, patches disappearing to manifest bald spots. She smiled, revealing rotting teeth, while her smooth, milky skin wrinkled, a piece of her forehead curling back in a gruesome wave of blood to exhibit her skull. Smoky moths danced in her hair—onyx dragonflies rested on her shoulders. Blood-red beetles and pea-green worms crawled down her muddy dress. Her flesh turned grayish, her lips a shade of ice blue. Bone shone through her fingers as she plucked a spare key to the manor from one of the jars.

Peering at herself once more in the mirror, she giggled. "Perfect." Dulce missed this, missed the way magic felt flowing through her, floating around her.

She would now play the role of the decaying corpse Cornelius would've had her become.

Leaving the conservatory, Dulce found that light no longer shone in the sitting room but now radiated from the second-floor window of her bedroom.

She unlocked the front door, its bolt barely making a click. The house felt empty, draped in darkness. Every mirror covered in white cloth, every clock stopped. Her chest tightened for Vesta and the others, and she wondered how her staff was faring after her funeral. How would they react when they learned she was alive?

Removing her muddy slippers, Dulce maneuvered silently through the familiar house and ascended the stairs in darkness, the wood cool against her bare feet.

When she reached the landing, sounds of movement came from her open bedroom door. She stood watching Cornelius as the absentminded fool removed his shirt. *Her* silk blankets were rumpled, and the foul stench of sweating bodies invaded her senses. She would burn her favorite blankets and all of his belongings along with them.

"My *dear*, handsome, husband," Dulce purred, and Cornelius whirled to face her. "It seems we missed our wedding night."

He turned deathly pale, horror etched across his face. His lower lip wobbled comically as he gawked at the illusion she'd created before him.

"Darling," he rasped, "you're all right. Such

wonderful, joyous news!"

He was tall, his bare chest sculpted, his abs defined, his arms muscular. A man any woman in Moonglade would want. Dulce only wanted to poison him the way he had poisoned her. She yearned to shove the mixture of night irises and aged elderberry down his throat until his face and insides bloated with pus.

"You poisoned me, dearest," she cooed, stepping into the room, her muddy dress swishing. "I thought you loved me. Tell me, why did you kill me? If you tell me, only then can I rest in peace."

"I… I had no other choice," Cornelius stuttered, backing away from her, tripping over his discarded shirt and nearly falling. "I had to! I was threatened—that's right. You would have suffered much worse were it not for me. I made sure you died quickly and painlessly because I love you. Try to understand, darling."

Dulce tsked, shaking her head slowly. Insects and worms fell to the floor in soft plops. "You pressed your boot on my back to make certain I died because you *love* me? How quaint."

She gripped his vile neck in one cold hand, and Cornelius wept and blubbered most satisfyingly.

"Now tell me the truth," she demanded. "Otherwise, I'll haunt you for all eternity. As your *wife*. You can make love to me while worms and maggots feast on you."

Cornelius turned whiter than the bones peeking from beneath Dulce's exposed flesh.

"I-I love someone else!" His voice cracked with hysteria, and she nearly laughed, releasing his neck. "That's why I gave you the poison. She needs the land— I don't know why. It's valuable to her and she insisted on having it. You have to believe me—that's all I know. Will… Will you leave me alone now?"

"No, I think I've changed my mind," Dulce purred, blocking his way from the room. "Who is this woman? I know she's a witch."

Cornelius spun, rushing across the room to throw open the attic door and bound up the steps. Dulce trailed behind, ever so slowly, singing a gentle song that had played at their wedding. She held back laughter as Cornelius cried and whimpered like a weak bladdered babe.

When she reached the top of the staircase, Cornelius was frantically shimmying through the small window that led up to the roof.

Glancing out into the misty darkness, she turned to watch his boots disappear with the rest of him while he scrambled onto the parapet. There wasn't anywhere else for him to go. Would he spend the night on the slippery roof, hoping daylight would banish her ghost?

Dulce shook her head, grinning to herself. He'd been so smug as he killed her—now look at him.

A piercing scream filled the air, followed by eerie, deafening silence. Dulce froze, knowing Cornelius must have fallen.

She rushed down the flights of stairs and into the night in search of him. At the back of the manor, ironically close to her grave, Cornelius's unblinking eyes met hers. His body hung impaled by the enormous spikes along the cemetery garden's iron fence, his blood streaming from his suspended limbs to pool amongst the misty grass.

Reed

Shuffling along the empty lane, exhaustion consumed Reed, though the night remained young. He'd hiked across the countryside, dug up a grave—only to find its occupant *alive*—then filled said grave in again, and now he had to trudge back home. It all seemed some sort of fever dream. The heiress though... She was surprisingly generous. And certainly attractive. Reed recalled the vision of her beautiful face, her golden-brown eyes filled with unspoken emotion, and found his curiosity piqued. Why did Dulce hide the fact that she lived, instead of announcing it?

No. Now was not the time to dream of mysterious

married heiresses who gave away their jewels to graverobbers. He must return to Philip and save his brother before it was too late. And after that? Well, the whole world was open to them—they could go wherever they pleased, far away from the dreary Glen.

Reed didn't have to walk for long before a wheat merchant's cart passed him on the road, its half-sleeping driver unaware of his new passenger. The steadfast mule pulling it voiced no objection to the added weight as it plodded along in the foggy night.

Only shopkeepers sweeping and tidying their spaces and maybe the few drunkards they traveled by saw them at all, and as the cart left the sleeping town, nothing but quiet spoke. The road back to Dogwood Glen was mostly deserted, save for the odd carriage. Reed was relieved for the rest after so much walking and digging, and he tried not to fall asleep while he sat hidden between two sheaves of wheat, the bound stalks tickling the exposed skin of his sore hands with the night breeze. Reed wondered how his brother was faring, dreading the thought of his condition having worsened in the hours since he'd left him.

When the cart approached the outskirts of his village, Reed alighted unnoticed, blending into the shadows of a row of beech trees, and returned the tools he'd borrowed to their owner, knowing full well what losing them could mean to a struggling farm.

It seemed in the lonely and silent darkness that the whole world slept, but Reed knew this wasn't so.

The Pikeman never slept.

Reed turned toward the Glen in general, and its swamps in particular, taking the familiar path through its mossy branches, a path he'd known since he was a boy and could follow even in darkness. He imagined he could smell his destination already.

The only pawnbroker of his kind, Nickolas 'The Pikeman' Davies would exchange virtually anything for coin. Anything at any time of the day or night. Not far from the road, only minutes into the shelter of the swampy outskirts of the Glen, the lights of the pawnbroker's butchery illuminated the ghostly bald cypress, their moss-covered branches waving mournfully above murky water in the fog as Reed passed their smooth columned trunks. His boots were now covered in filth. The stench of the place was no longer just in his imagination.

The reek of rotting meat permeated the night, and he ignored the glowing eyes of roving dogs to ascend the worn and half-decayed stairs to the butcher's porch. Three men appeared from the depths of the establishment like moving shadows, one of them stepping into the light with a crooked grin.

Ellis. A beefy man with the most unfortunate nose Reed had ever seen.

"Reed," he growled. "What can we do for you on this fine night? Just got through with a new shipment of mutton. Or is it something … *warmer* you're after?"

Reed arched a brow. The day he turned to the offerings of a fleshmonger for romantic companionship was the day he'd rather vomit blood until he wished he were dead. Not to mention catching the clouted pox.

"I seek negotiation with Mr. Davies," Reed said with a bow, removing his cloak's hood. The Pikeman relished his little *traditions*. And didn't like to be called the Pikeman. Rumor had it he'd once forced a merchant—

who'd said the word after too much drink—to eat a rotting opossum that had drowned in the swamp, causing the man to nearly die of dysentery.

Ellis sighed in resignation, tilting his head for Reed to follow him, and added, "You're no fun, you know that?"

"We must have different definitions of *fun*."

"I'd be interested to know what yours is." Ellis wiggled his eyebrows in a decidedly revolting manner and chuckled to himself as he led Reed inside. They moved between the rows of strung-up slaughtered hogs, their blood pooling into a rusted trough beneath them. Past tables piled high with slabs of meat and rotting sheep heads, where cages holding scarred dogs, disheveled roosters, and even one bear cluttered the hay-strewn floor.

Outside, they crossed a bridge of rickety wood, the air only marginally fresher, to another much smaller building, a crooked hut built on stilts atop the murky waters of the swamp itself. Sounds of violence emanated from its many open windows. Some unfortunate scut had failed to hold up their end of a bargain.

Ellis didn't hesitate but simply strolled forward, opening the door—a bloodied man hanging from the mossy beams was just another night in the Pikeman's employ.

The Pikeman turned lazily to them, a crazed smile splitting his bony face at the sight of Reed. He was at least two heads shorter than Reed, his teeth mostly blackened.

"Don't mind the décor," the Pikeman cooed. "Or, you want a crack at him? Might be good practice for the next fight, eh? Eh?"

The Pikeman had won big on one of Reed's fights and

had taken a liking to him ever since.

"Thank you, Mr. Davies," Reed drawled. "But maybe some other time. Tonight I'm in kind of a hurry, if it's all the same…"

"Right!" The Pikeman slapped Reed on the back with a high laugh that woke an unconscious man slumped in a chair in one corner. "I heard about Philip. Sad, sad news. Still! Death comes for us all sooner or later, doesn't it?"

Snatching up a bottle of a foul-looking brew, the Pikeman led Reed into yet another building, this one empty but for a small desk on which sat a large candle of green wax, and two rickety wooden chairs that Reed knew to be the most uncomfortable things ever slapped together by a drunken craftsman.

Reed set his treasure on the table, Dulce's delicate features filling his mind once again. To think these valuables would've been left to rot along with her had he not been there to dig them out in time. He shook away the haunting thought. Focused instead on the jewels, the ring's enormous ruby winking in the candlelight, the pearls' decadent shine comically out of place in such humble surroundings, and stepped back, waiting.

The Pikeman rushed to sit as he hurried to settle quartz spectacles over his eyes, their sunken orbs now appearing twice their size. He focused solely on business while turning the jewels over in his stained, skeletal hands, studying them intently, all hint of mad laughter vanished from his gaunt face. Reed knew the Pikeman could see past any forgery through the mysterious lenses and pitied any foolish enough to attempt cheating him.

Reed waited in silence, doing his best to hide his impatience. The good thing was the Pikeman never asked questions about where anything crossing his desk came from.

"I'll give you two hundred gold units for the lot," he said with finality, returning the glasses to his blood-splattered pocket.

It was more than Reed could have hoped for. Ten times as much as he would need to save his brother. The ring alone would earn him more than he'd ever had in his life.

"Done," he agreed.

The apothecary had gone to sleep but always kept a boy on the lookout for desperate customers—a service he got at two pence a night. Reed roused him with a prod of his filthy boot as the boy lay slumped in the shop's entry, sound asleep. The night was more than half over by now, the fog so thick Reed could hardly see past his own outstretched hand.

"He'll want you to wake him for this," Reed said, and the boy hurried off into the night to wake the greedy toad.

The man stumbled in, thick purple bags beneath his eyes, and his gray hair wilder than a tree swallow's nest. "What is it that you couldn't wait until morning?" He glowered.

"I'm here for the plague's cure." Reed drew out two coins from his trouser pocket. "I can pay."

"Ah." The man's lips curled up into a wolfish smile. "The price has gone up, I'm afraid."

Of course it had...

"Can't get good comfrey these days," he muttered, twisting a key and searching through a hidden shelf. "And feverfew isn't fresh unless you get it from the traveling nomads…"

Reed wouldn't waste time haggling over the price of his brother's cure, though it made his blood boil to know the apothecary had charged half the price the year before. With Philip this close to death, there was no time to waste, and with coin he hadn't earned himself, it seemed not worth the bruise to his pride.

He shoved four coins into the man's anticipating palm, then waited as the owner leisurely drew three vials containing pale golden liquid from a cabinet. Reed ripped the remedies from the man's grasp before rushing out of the apothecary to his brother.

Philip lay pale and trembling in darkness when Reed finally returned home, the candles all having burnt out long ago, the fireplace gone cold, nothing but ash.

"Philip, it's me. Reed. I got your cure," he announced, his chest heaving.

His brother didn't say a word, only persisted in a non-lucid state, and Reed's heart lodged in his throat. What if he was too late?

He hastily lit another fire, promising himself he would buy enough wood to keep the drafty hut warm all winter if Philip remained too ill to travel.

Wrapping his brother in every blanket they owned, he propped him up to force the bitter-smelling herbs down his throat, refusing to let even a single drop spill. Reed kept his gaze fixed on the clock, and by the consumption of the third vial, Philip regained some of his usual color and warmth, though still marred with sores. After a few ticks of their father's old clock, his brother's trembling at last ceased.

The cure was *working*.

And yet, his brother didn't wake.

Reed drew a chair to Philip's side and sat in silence while time passed before finally telling him of how he'd met a beautiful girl who'd helped him save his brother's life. He embellished the tale, making himself the hero who boldly rescued her from being trampled by a runaway carriage. Instead of a desperate thief who'd snuck onto her property to dig up her grave.

"A girl you say?" Philip croaked, startling Reed. His eyes were open, and he even tried to smile.

Reed laughed in relief. "One that's too good for either of us."

"Speak for yourself, white hair," Philip crooned, his voice almost clear. "I'm practically royalty with these good looks. And stop looking at me as if I died."

"You nearly did…"

"But I *didn't*." His voice was stronger now, his smile bright. "I have my brother to thank for that."

"I expect nothing less if I'm ever at death's door." Reed winked.

Philip grew serious, taking Reed's hand and squeezing it. "I swear it," he whispered. Philip observed Reed for a long moment, then sat with a wince. "Now tell me more about this girl. Does she happen to have a sister?"

"You're clearly in no position to—"

Heavy pounding on the hut's rotting door rattled the entire building, and Reed's wild stare met Philip's alarmed expression.

Before Reed could grab something to barricade the

door, it swung open with a heavy bang. A towering enforcer with a dark curling mustache appeared in the doorway. "Reed Hawthorne," he bellowed as two more uniformed men pushed their way through the broken door and lifted Reed to his feet, seeming to enjoy nearly pulling his arms from their sockets. "You are under arrest for the crime of graverobbing, an offense punishable by death."

Dulce

Dulce sighed, ridding herself of the corpse spell she'd played on Cornelius by pressing three sage flowers into her mouth, their pungent flavor unpleasant against her tongue. "Dead by your own cowardice before I got the chance to kill you myself, dearest husband."

She took in her surroundings—Cornelius's broken body, his chest pierced by the iron spikes of the fence guarding the cemetery, his crimson blood gathering below him, shining like a thousand rubies beneath the silvery moonlight. The manor loomed behind her, empty as a mausoleum.

Dulce stepped toward Cornelius's suspended body—

his expression no longer twisted in fear but blank, his eyes devoid of life. Leaving him there to rot was not an option, and she could never hope to dislodge him herself. Besides the stench and unhygienic consequences his decaying corpse would soon invite, someone was bound to take notice of the master of the manor splayed atop a fence like a stuck pig at a carnival.

She remembered Cornelius telling the witch that the servants were still at the inn. Thankfully, the establishment wasn't dreadfully far. She would let them sleep through the night, then find them at dawn.

Until she discovered precisely who this witch was and what danger she posed, Dulce would continue to remain a dead bride to all but those she trusted most.

Turning her back on Cornelius's gruesome remains, she entered her home and went into the kitchens, where she found an abundance of what must've been a leftover funeral feast Vesta had made in Dulce's honor. She fell to devouring roast capon, croquettes of fowl, asparagus, wild rice, and fresh berries—including a single mistletoe berry, promising herself to not miss her daily dose of poison again—in an untidy manner until she was full to bursting. The poison she barely felt, only a slight blurring of the room for a moment before everything was as it should be.

Boiling water in a large basin, she next filled a hot bath, and, discarding her destroyed gown into the fireplace where it shriveled into flames, she washed away the mud caking her skin, luxuriating in the lavender water until it turned cold.

When at last Dulce wound up one of her music boxes and lay down on her freshly made bed, sleep didn't come for her. Perhaps after too many hours of unconsciousness, she simply wasn't tired. So she went downstairs and sat at her piano, playing a haunted melody over and over until just before the sun rose.

She slipped on a simple deep maroon dress, then grabbed a vial from the conservatory and disguised herself with the contents, changing her hair from black to a mousy brown, her nose slightly misshapen, her eyes shrunk, and her jawline squared. Her mother would've been proud that she was finding her way back to magic. It only took a near-death experience to reclaim her witch, to realize how much she missed alchemy.

Dulce hitched a plain mare to the carriage and drove to the inn. She might be the mistress of the manor, but once her parents passed, Sylvan had taught her many things in case she was ever to need the knowledge. Even as a child, she would often ride beside Sylvan in the front when he went into town on errands.

The sun was hidden behind thick clouds, the sky streaked with gray, the perfect dreary morning Dulce loved. She passed the market shops where, at this hour, only servants milled about on the day's business, the shops' owners preparing for early customers.

Near the end of the town's square, beyond a park, the Royal Lion slipped into view. Turrets, mirroring the hue of pearls brushed the sky, and burgundy curtains hung in the windows. Dulce drew the horse to a halt near the inn's entrance and fiddled with her brown braid while slumping her shoulders forward, trying to appear anything but an heiress.

The scent of cinnamon cigars encompassed her as she stepped over the threshold and into the opulent lobby.

Clearly Cornelius had been trying to keep up the appearance of a generous lord by continuing the staff's stay here. Dulce smiled knowing Sylvan would feel most uncomfortable sleeping in such pompous surroundings. A young couple sat at one of the dining tables, eating a hearty breakfast in silence while a woman stood behind a tall desk of carved mahogany, her face absent of the smile she'd had when Dulce last visited to have tea with some of her mother's friends. When she'd looked like a well-dressed heiress and not a servant.

"Morning, Miss," Dulce greeted the older woman, producing a letter in her husband's hand on her stationery. It was simple to use alchemy to do the trick when she already had a letter in his handwriting. "I'm here to retrieve Mr. Cornelius's staff on his request."

The woman peered at her as if she smelled something foul, but Dulce placed three gold coins on the desk, and she perked up, eagerly snatching them.

"They are in rooms twenty-two and twenty-seven on the second floor," the woman said, adding, "And tell Mr. Cornelius I'm extremely sorry for his loss."

Dulce nodded solemnly and hurried to ascend the marble staircase at the end of the hallway. Paintings of musical instruments encircled by fruit on thick velvet lined the corridor in dark frames. Voices arguing could be heard behind one of the doors she passed.

Near the end of the hall, she knocked on room twenty-two and waited until the door swung open to reveal Sylvan, a line forming between his thick gray brows as his red-rimmed eyes met hers. "Yes?"

"Gather your things at once and meet me downstairs," she instructed in a high voice through her nose. "Mr. Cornelius requires you and the others to return to the manor with me."

He hesitated until he read the note she handed him, then nodded. "Of course."

Telling herself not to run, she did the same at Vesta's room, nearly hugging the woman the instant she saw her pale, grief-stricken face.

In case there were any prying ears about, and to avoid a public outbreak at the shock of it, Dulce would wait to reveal her identity to them until they were safely back at the manor.

It didn't take long for Sylvan, his grandson Lucas, and Vesta to join her outside, almost as if they too knew they would not stay at the Royal Lion long. Their expressions remained melancholic, dark circles rimming their eyes as Dulce held the carriage door open for them and drove them home, her heart pounding anxiously. She was impatient to tell them she was alive and ease their sorrow, though she held her tongue.

Sylvan's wife had passed, Lucas's parents succumbed to illness shortly after his birth, and Vesta had become a kind of second mother to the orphan, who was still an adolescent.

Reaching the manor, Dulce waited for her passengers to alight and face her.

"I need to tell you all something," she said, her own voice coming out strange, sudden tears threatening to spill from her eyes. "I'm not a servant. It's me. Dulce."

Vesta frowned. "That is a wickedly cruel thing to say."

Dulce ate a few sage blossoms, the spell dissolving, her face and hair becoming her own, and the three of them gasped. Besides her parents, they were the only ones who knew she was a witch like her mother.

"Oh, Mrs. Dulce!" Sylvan rasped. "How? We saw you with our own eyes, dead as a deer at festival feast, you were!"

"Pale and cold too," Lucas added, shivering dramatically at the memory.

Vesta rushed forward, hauling Dulce into her arms and squeezing her tightly. "Is it really you?"

"It's me," she breathed, embracing the woman in return. "I'm alive. And we have much to discuss."

Released from Vesta's embrace, Dulce told the people she trusted most in the world what had transpired between her and Cornelius. How he'd poisoned her, how she'd woken in the casket below ground, and how a young thief had saved her from meeting the cold fate Cornelius dealt her.

"That craven son of a boil-brained flesh-monger!" Vesta bit out between clenched teeth. "Where is he? Why, I'll—"

"He's dead," Dulce answered, not the slightest hint of sadness came at the fact.

"Please tell me you poisoned the villainous measle," Lucas said brightly.

"Unfortunately, no." Dulce tsked. "I was robbed of the pleasure."

She continued with the rest of her story, of the powerful witch, and of how Dulce had frightened Cornelius to the point that he'd been foolish enough to climb to the roof and fall to his death.

"Serves him right!" Lucas balled his hand into a fist and held it up. "If I'd been here, I'd have—"

"A witch was here?" Sylvan asked, his throat bobbing.

"Using magic, you say?"

"Do any of you know her?"

Vesta shook her head. "Mr. Cornelius never mentioned anyone like that in our presence, nor did we see any woman with ruby hair at your funeral."

"The witch did something to Mother's tree with her magic," Dulce continued. "It was as though she were taking life from it. And before Cornelius's death, he told me that this land was valuable to the witch, yet he didn't know why."

Sylvan's gaze met Vesta's, and something knowing passed between them.

"It's time to show her, Vesta," the old man said. "Take her inside while Lucas and I dislodge Cornelius's body."

Lucas didn't look the least bit enthusiastic about the concept but nodded.

Vesta wore an expression she'd never seen on her before, and Dulce's pulse thrummed with anticipation. They had hidden something important from her.

"Show me what?"

Vesta's face softened. "You would have learned the truth very soon anyway. On your next birthday, to be precise. But now it seems you are to learn your mother's secret sooner. Come—follow me."

She led Dulce into the manor as the men disappeared to find Cornelius's body.

Dulce's mind raced. What secret would be revealed within the manor's walls? She knew every inch of her home and all of its contents. What new piece could be given to her?

She followed Vesta down several carpeted hallways

until they reached the cellar door. Vesta lit a candlestick, and her gaze filled with warm compassion. "Are you all right, my little Dulce? How is your heart?"

"I didn't love him." *Truth.*

"That doesn't mean you didn't want to."

"Perhaps, but that changed the moment he poisoned me." *Instantly.*

Dulce took a deep breath, fighting back the tears pricking her eyes. Not because she was forlorn about Cornelius's death, but because by trusting him, she had put her loved ones in possible danger too. "Anyway, I only married him because of your tea leaves."

"My tea leaves are never wrong," Vesta clarified, shaking a finger at her. "Your true love will come."

The white-haired thief drifted into Dulce's mind once more, and she shook her head, banishing this most ridiculous thought. She would never see him again.

"Love is the least of my concerns."

"For now," Vesta declared. "However, we have an important task ahead of us to focus on." She guided Dulce down the cellar's stone staircase, its familiar scent of peonies enveloping her. Her mother had always sprayed a mixture of peonies down here to keep the musky smell of earth out, and even though it had been three years since her mother passed, hints of the scent still lingered.

When they reached the cellar, nothing peculiar caught Dulce's attention, even when she looked back at her memories of playing there as a child.

Everything was the same. Shelves of yarn, bolts of fabric, and embroidery threads lined the stone walls. Worn tables of oak stood beneath wide chandeliers of half-melted candles, knitting needles in brass canisters across their surface. The comfortable chairs with their silk cushions worn, thick carpets of wool displaying animals she had loved to make stories of while her mother crocheted on a winter afternoon, and the massive hearth.

Vesta carefully put the candlestick along the floor and pulled a chair from a corner to a nearby shelf. She climbed onto the chair and ran her hands across the top of the shelf until she found a thin braided rope and tugged on it.

The sound of scraping stone against stone echoed behind Dulce, and she whirled around, gasping. A wide slab of stone slid aside, leaving a cavernous opening within the cellar's wall.

Perhaps Dulce didn't know all the manor's secrets after all.

"Your mother learned about this room on her twentieth birthday," Vesta said, carefully stepping down from the chair, "just as her mother before her. I don't know the precise answer to what this land holds, but I do know you are to protect it. All firstborn witch daughters are."

Vesta disappeared into the shadows of the mysterious room and returned to face Dulce. She held a tome of leather and gold reverently. "See if you can find something in her spell book," she started. "Though I guarded this room, I vowed to your mother that I would never read this, only do my duty to make certain it and you were safe until your twentieth birthday. When I thought you had passed, I was sure I'd failed."

"No, Vesta, you didn't. I'm here." Dulce rushed forward to grasp the older woman's shoulders and gently squeezed them. "Mother made sure I could never be poisoned."

Pushing the spell book into her hands as tears streamed from her eyes, Vesta gently stroked Dulce's hair just like she did when she was a child. "Your mother was a very wise woman."

"She was." Dulce suddenly laughed while embracing Vesta, such happy relief washing over her. She was alive, something she didn't know she'd taken for granted.

"Take your time in here," Vesta said at last, lifting the candlestick from the floor and placing it within the shadowy room, preparing to leave Dulce alone. "I'll check on Sylvan and Lucas."

"Thank you, Vesta. For everything."

Alone, Dulce stepped hesitantly into the new room, the scent of peonies even stronger within. Shelves lined the walls from floor to ceiling, filled with jars of every shape and dimension. Both dark and colorful candles, mysterious metal objects, and cauldrons the size of her palm to the size of a tub. Dulce placed her mother's spell book on a lone table covered in embroidered silk. The tome appeared ancient, its pages yellowed and frayed, the leather binding peeling.

She lit a few more candles around the room, noticing that not a speck of dust lingered on any surface. Resting her candlestick on the table beside it, she opened the tome, and what appeared to be a regular-sized book expanded into something much larger with many more pages than the human eye would've seen. Here wasn't just any common parlor book—this was a true alchemy spell book, one any witch would certainly treasure.

Studying the first page, Dulce scanned through spell

after spell, fascinated instantly. Growing things from seeds in a matter of moments, levitation, shifting, dream-walking. As she read one page after another, she found nothing about drawing magic from land. Not until she reached the middle of the book where a folded letter had been placed, its crisp paper much newer than the tome's. It was written in her mother's familiar hand.

Dearest Dulce,

I'm sorry I couldn't be here for you longer, but I am part of the land now. Land that you will protect. My ancient bristlecone pine is yours, a Tree of Life, one of five secretly scattered across the territories. Each represent a point on a star. They are the key to everything, to life itself. If their power is ever disturbed, even just one, their roots will begin to lift, altering magic. They would eventually become stone, the plants and animals the same, our land's vital water turned to brackish death, and the air will be filled with a poisonous fog as the sun itself dies, leaving nothing to flourish.

You must not let this happen. You must protect our land, our single tree, as generations have done before you, my beautiful, brave girl. It will come as no surprise to you that you don't come from a line of common witches, but great ones. I didn't want magic to be forced upon you during your younger years as it was on me, perhaps that was selfish on my part by not showing you this book sooner. But I wanted you to slowly learn to love magic and not have it be a burden on you. However, I'm now regretful that I won't get to see you truly grow into your magic completely after your twentieth birthday.

Everything you need to know is already in your heart.

Dulce's hands shook as fresh tears rained down her face. It was as though she could hear her mother's voice speaking to her in this very room. She missed her so much she was sure her heart would break. She wished she'd told her all the things she hadn't gotten a chance to, thanked her for all the times she'd failed to. If she were there now, she would tell her that she'd taught alchemy to Dulce in the perfect way, that she had loved it, and still very much did.

Her mother wanted her to protect the bristlecone pine, but that only reminded her how another witch had done something to the tree the night before with magic.

Dulce slammed the book shut and fled from the room, not slowing until she reached the ancient tree. The gentle giant towered over her, its great twisted bark a comforting sight in the drab daylight.

Her lips parted in horror as her gaze met the earth surrounding the tree. The land lay cracked in wide jagged wounds, a web of injuries, oozing tar like open veins.

Reed

"Y ou two fine gentlemen ever heard the one about the two cows and the old goat-herder with the giant pizzle who caught the hog pox?" Reed poked his elbows into the burly enforcers sitting too close at his sides.

They showed no reaction.

"See, it all started when the cattleman tried to pass off one of his hogs as his wife…"

Reed thought the enforcer on his left was fighting a smile, but he couldn't be sure.

With the night long gone and the sun concealed somewhere, the barred carriage sped over the uneven road, jostling its passengers against him in a most unwelcome way. His second journey in less than a day, but at least these horses were much swifter than the merchant's mule.

"His wife, truth be told, had somewhat of a swinish look about her, especially around the eyes. Definitely in the hips."

The enforcer on his left turned to the window, while the other stared straight ahead, his expression as unreadable as stone.

"Anyone ever tell you two you're no fun?" Reed decided the enforcer on his right didn't deserve to hear the rest of the story and instead hummed a tune, the raunchiest bar song in the Glen. Enforcer Left definitely knew it, now visibly trying not to laugh.

Reed had learned long ago to appreciate small victories. He was arrested, probably on his way to the gallows. However, anything could happen.

His brother was safe from the plague and healing. That was what mattered most.

Reaching Moonglade—after a journey in which he succeeded beautifully in annoying two enforcers—Reed was dragged across the town's cobblestone prison yard and down several uneven stairs, where he found himself unceremoniously thrown onto a pile of foul-smelling straw. The sound of clanging iron echoed off stone as the cell door slammed shut, bolts driven home, and unease crept into his mind like swamp fog. The room had a wide view of the jail's office—deserted but for one portly guard busy with paperwork at his desk—and was equipped with four cots, a water spigot, and an actual hole in the ground for a latrine. Luxury accommodations compared to any jail in the Glen.

Peering up at his cellmate, Reed smiled wide, all swamp fog lifted.

If the enforcers planned on detaining him indefinitely, they shouldn't have put him with the Pikeman.

"Your loot was hot," the Pikeman grunted, looking pleased about it as he lounged along one of the cell's cots, picking at his teeth with a bit of straw. "I won't ask where you got it 'cause I was bored anyway." He spat, meeting Reed's gaze. "Back home, it's nothing but compulsion, compulsion, compulsion all the time. Lots of crying and begging. I could use a break. Stretch my legs a bit. But I said to myself, I said, if I'm to be taken in by the Duke's enforcers, you'll be joining me."

Reed knew better than to think the Pikeman had given his name up to enforcers out of anything but his own volition, but at least that explained his arrest. He still wondered how Dulce's jewels had been found so quickly. Could they hold some kind of magical tracking properties inside them? He'd heard rumors of that sort of thing— rubies owned by witches, infused with magic, and gold created in an alchemist's lab. He'd always thought it all a bunch of pribbling, superstitious lunacy. Magic wasn't real. At least, not in the filth and misery of the Glen.

"It shouldn't be long now." The Pikeman sighed, lying back and regarding the ceiling as if he'd miss the place. "A friendly word of advice if you don't want to return my payment in full. You've got about … three minutes to prepare for acquiring its replacement."

Reed glanced around, searching the place for any sign of valuables.

"There." The Pikeman jerked his chin at an iron box in the far corner. "Reckon that'll hold a pretty loot. Teach 'em to leave us Glen folk alone."

Reed stood, rolling his neck and shoulders, wondering where the Pikeman's men would wreak their havoc from. He'd heard many tales of the Pikeman's love for chaos, and he wasn't too keen on learning of it firsthand.

The walls of the cell appeared to be solid stone—the bars thick as his wrists. High above though, the ceiling was nothing but wooden beams across what was clearly a thatched roof, its layers of water reed and longstraw peeking between mossy sedge grasses.

Reed lowered his gaze to meet the Pikeman's grin.

"What did you do to the jewels?" Reed asked. "If you don't mind me inquiring."

"Are you suggesting it was my interference that brought the law to our doorstep?"

"Well, I mea—"

"You'd be quite right." The man laughed maniacally, still lounging along the cot as if he had all the time in the world, not bothering to put on his shoes. Reed arched a brow at his long and filthy toenails. "I cleaned them in the usual way," he continued with a shrug, "with boiling peppermint water. That ring put up quite the fuss at that. Don't include that fobbing bauble in my payment. The pearls I'm happy to take back though. Ah. Here my boys are now…"

The Pikeman stood on his bed, his shoes tied before Reed could blink, and the ceiling burst into flame. The lone guard at the desk showed no reaction, too immersed in his work to bother with a couple of degenerate Glen scum, the cell's low walls protecting the flames from his view.

A braid of silk fell like a twisting serpent through the

smoky clouds above to unwind at the Pikeman's side, and the pawnbroker secured one foot into its knotted base, wagging his fingers at Reed before using both hands to grasp the fabric.

"You have ten minutes to bring my payment to the Rowan Inn's alleyway," he said with a wink. "After that, you're acquiring quite the pretty interest. Don't waste time having too much fun."

"Wait!" Reed shouted as the Pikeman was lifted into the air. "You're leaving me here? At least give me something to pick the locks with!" The enforcers had already confiscated the knife in his boot, so he'd been left with nothing of use.

The guard at the desk finally noticed the smell of burning thatch and rushed from the room, shouting.

"I'm sure you'll figure something out!" the Pikeman called down to him, followed by a chorus of laughter.

"Ruttish, plume-plucked, measly wagtail puttocks," Reed muttered.

A beam cracked like a sinking ship's wails overhead and tumbled to the cell floor with a crash, igniting the straw along it. Reed lifted the cup next to the water spigot and banged the metal against the bars.

"Fire!" he yelled. "Somebody, help! Even Gallows' prisoners have the right to humane execution! You paunchy bunch of full-gorged ratsbane maggots! *Fire!*"

The roof fell in at an alarming rate now, smoke descending like fog, choking him, the cell a fountain of sparks and flame as beams continued to rain down.

Reed soaked his scarf in water and wrapped the sodden wool around his face, protected from the worst of it by the time the guards' lumbering steps pounded on the stairs, one holding the keys to his cell. Hiding under the cover of smoke, he waited for the lock to disengage, and, when the man slid the bars back, Reed hurled himself forward and smashed the metal cup into the guard's face. Snatching the keys from his limp fingers, Reed spun to elbow the second guard in the throat as the sound of fire bells rang outside the gaping roof.

Surprised by his attack, the first guard held his broken nose and stumbled forward into the cell, a falling beam narrowly missing his head. Reed kicked his choking companion forward to join him, pulling the bars back into place and locking the cell once again.

"Oye!" the first guard screamed in rage. "You won't get away with this, you roguish lout! I'll have your head, you graverobbing scum! There's nowhere you can hide, do you hear me? *Nowhere!*"

Reed did hear him of course, but he paid no attention, focused instead on the metal box in front of him. *One problem at a time*, he told himself. *Get free of the Pikeman's debt, then get free of the law.*

"You'll hang before the next sunset, that's a promise!"

That was quite the threat when Reed was no longer the one locked behind bars.

The other guard regained the use of his voice, and croaked, "Where's the second maggot trash gone off to?"

"Maybe he burned," Broken Nose offered.

"Nah, the smell isn't right."

Reed ignored them and at last managed to get the box open, prying apart its hinges with an iron crowbar left in plain sight beneath a window next to a broom. Inside, he found a red velvet pouch, the Duke's own crest embroidered across it in golden thread. Untangling its delicate cord, Reed discovered a treasure that was quite something to behold.

Every conceivable coin in the land—presumably confiscated by corrupt enforcers from drunks and gamblers—as well as jeweled knives, silver spoons, and even a golden engraved baby rattle. Dulce's pearls and ring stood out amongst the rest, their luster far exceeding the worn rabble surrounding them.

The harsh crackle of flames signaled he needed to leave soon.

Reed stood, letting the box fall shut. Scanning the room, he discovered what he wanted immediately. The paperwork-conscious enforcer had left his hat and coat in his haste to raise the alarm. Reed spared a few seconds to trade his cloak for these, hoping their oversized dimensions would go unnoticed as he tucked his white hair beneath the cap.

He was running out of time to meet the Pikeman.

Tying the velvet sack and stuffing it securely beneath his jacket, Reed pocketed the ring. He couldn't say why, exactly, since he didn't mean to ever sell it. Perhaps it was because Dulce had mentioned how her beloved mother had left it to her upon her death. Maybe even then the idea of seeing the heiress once more was forming in some shadowy part of his mind.

Slipping into the alleyway behind the jail, Reed walked at a leisurely pace until he reached the guard stables. The animals were alone, seemingly every groom and stable boy having run off to help put out the fire, and only one mangy dog announced Reed's presence.

Not bothering with a saddle, Reed placed a simple bridle over the nearest horse—a bay gelding—and led the creature out through the hay delivery doors.

Not a soul noticed him.

Two blocks from the jailhouse, Reed mounted the horse from the crumbling steps of a cloth merchant's shop and raced into town, praying the Pikeman still waited at the inn.

He did, much to Reed's relief. Being in the Pikeman's debt was a fate almost worse than death, if one believed the gossip. Something Reed was inclined to do, after everything he'd just witnessed.

"I told you he'd come." The Pikeman laughed, his hand out for payment to three of his men. They grumbled, their faces hidden in the shadows of their dark cloaks, as they paid the bet they'd lost against Reed's escape. Reed grinned at them as he dismounted, the velvet sack swinging cheerfully while he sauntered toward the Pikeman.

Reed was a wanted man now, but that didn't mean they should feel any kind of sympathy for him. Sympathy meant weakness, and weakness would only get one killed in the company of animals such as these.

The Pikeman stood before a nondescript trader's carriage, two plain and scarred horses, perfectly ready to disappear back into the Glen, where no man, woman, or child would ever dare to give up his location.

Reed threw the sack of treasure to him, and the pawnbroker caught it neatly. Looking inside, his eyes sparkled with satisfaction.

"Good boy," he said. "Our business is concluded."

Reed bowed his head a fraction. The Pikeman had gotten at least three times the coin he'd given Reed—of course the weedy-snouted bastard was satisfied.

As if sensing Reed's judgment, the Pikeman announced, "Take Rusty's cloak," snapping a finger at one of the men—presumably Rusty—who tossed the garment at Reed. He opened the carriage door, preparing to leave, and the others scrambled to find their places on its exterior. The horses stamped their hooves, impatient to be on their way as the Pikeman called, "Let me know when your next fight is, and we'll make another pretty penny, eh?"

A cracking whip split the air, in a chorus of hooves on cobblestones, and they were gone.

Reed stood in the deserted alleyway, and the fog thinned, revealing cobblestones littered with rotting cabbage, onions simmering in puddles of filth. He threw aside his enforcer disguise. Securing the cloak over his shoulders, its fur-lined hood over his white hair, he thought about what he should do next.

The Pikeman would have the full support of the Glen, fear of the man and his volatile insanity demanded this.

Reed wouldn't be so lucky.

He had nowhere to go. If he went back home within the next fortnight, it would only put Philip in danger. His brother needed to mend his weakened health and continue to work in peace until he was strong enough to travel. Reed owed him that much, at least.

Every enforcer within a day's travel would be searching for him—it was only a matter of hours. He had to get out of sight, and quickly.

There was only one place to go. The one place the enforcers would never suspect he would return to.

Dulce's manor.

Setting the horse loose to graze in a field of black

prince snapdragons at the bottom of the hill, Reed made his way to Dulce's manor on foot, keeping his steps within the cover of hedges and trees. Reaching the stone wall, he snuck through the door as he'd done the night before and slipped into the garden unnoticed.

The sun shone down, its warm rays dispersing the thick fog, turning the branches of an enormous weeping willow to glowing green as it kissed the sparkling waters of the lake. Crows watched him from the branches of an elm when he passed, song thrushes singing in the crisp breeze while flowers, dark in nature, bloomed along the hedges and vines. Reed thought it must be a dream to live in such a place.

Approaching the looming manor, the enclosed cemetery in sight, Reed froze.

Two men, one elderly and one appearing no more than sixteen, dragged a dead man across the grass by his bare feet, his torn-open middle trailing his insides like rubbery worms. The grave Reed had carefully refilled lay once again open, a pile of dirt and rock at its side. The men didn't notice or care when the dead man's head bounced over a stone with an audible *crack*, instead carrying on their hushed conversation as they tossed the body into the waiting grave.

Maybe coming here wasn't such a good idea after all…

Dulce

With trembling hands and tears pricking her eyes, Dulce dropped to her knees and spread her fingers along the earth, trailing the cracked lines in the dirt. Gray dots erupted across the tree's exposed roots, its sickness spreading. The witch's magic had infected her mother's tree, a Tree of Life—its death was beginning. However, the ancient bristlecone pine had not been destroyed yet.

She peered up at the sky—darkness didn't reign over her world, though the sun was very much hidden behind the dark clouds of the slate gray sky.

Dulce pressed her hands on one of the roots, its small pulse thrumming against her fingertips, the tree's energy slowly being siphoned away by whatever curse the witch had cast. A struggle within the tree stirred, a sense of sickness flowing through its network. Soon, the timber would die—and so would everything else in the land.

How long did they have before it was too late? Her mother's letter didn't mention where the other four trees were located, but she had an inkling the witch knew.

"I wish I had known sooner, Mother," she whispered.

Grasping the skirts of her dress, Dulce ran through the deep burgundy hollyhock garden, leaping over small bushes dotted with plump blueberries, and rushing like a madwoman to the back of the manor.

Her staff lingered in the family cemetery, safe and sound, unaffected by the panic that threatened to overtake her. Vesta hummed a happy tune while picking weeds and placing them into a wicker basket, while Lucas dropped down into the grave where Dulce was once buried. A loud creak of the casket reverberated as the young man shut the lid.

Sylvan wiped the back of his hand against his sweaty brow, his smiling gaze meeting hers. "I know this villainous lout doesn't deserve it," he explained, "But this was the easiest place to bury Mr. Cornelius quickly until you know the witch's motives." He reached down to the grave and helped his grandson out.

Vesta frowned, lowering the wicker basket. "I don't believe the pompous boar bladder deserves to be buried on Dulce's property at all. Even temporarily."

Dulce's chest heaved, and she stepped toward them. "You're quite right, Vesta. A murderer doesn't deserve such honor, even in death. But since we're short on time, this will have to do. Temporarily, of course."

Sylvan and Lucas collected their shovels from beside one of the headstones and began filling the grave with dirt.

Dulce's breath quickened as her panic rose. They needed to focus on the reason why she'd hurried to find them. "There's something wrong with Mother's tree," she announced. "I found a letter in her spell book, and—"

Her words ceased falling from her lips when she caught a glimpse of a few locks of white hair floating near one of the hazel trees. She recognized the color instantly and knew precisely who they belonged to. Why had the thief returned? And why was he sneaking around like a sly fox? Was her jewelry not enough? Had he returned to creep into her manor, consumed with greed, determined to take more of her things?

In a low voice so that only Vesta could hear, Dulce said, "One moment. I'll return shortly." She then left the servants and circled the garden's laurel hedges until she stood just behind Reed, his gaze fixed on the cemetery, where Sylvan and Lucas continued to cover the grave and Vesta returned to her task of plucking weeds. Reed no longer wore his tattered cloak from the night before but another, more luxurious version of the garment. She wondered if he'd stolen it or used some of the money he'd traded for her jewels to purchase it. Perhaps he didn't have a brother at all.

"Returning so soon?" she cooed.

Reed cursed under his breath and spun to face her. "You're a stealthy one."

"And it would seem you're not." Dulce pursed her lips.

He smirked just before his face softened. "Your

husband tried to murder you?"

"Ah. A thief and a snoop." She folded her arms, regarding him. Reed seemed genuinely concerned over what he'd heard. Shocked, even. "If you must know, yes. He tried to poison me."

"And so you stabbed him, repeatedly." He nodded in understanding that truly wasn't understanding at all.

"On the contrary," Dulce started, wondering at how flippantly the thief spoke of murder. "I only gave him a little scare. It was his own cowardice that got the fool killed."

"Sounds as though he deserved it anyway." Reed shrugged, frowning up at a Pesquet's parrot that squawked.

"Yes, well…" The thief was even more handsome in the daylight, but Dulce had more important matters to attend to that involved life and death. "Why are you here, Reed? Did you not get to help your brother?"

"No, Philip is healing perfectly, thank you. However, I, uh"—he folded his arms and leaned against the tree—"the thing is, I was arrested. Because of the jewelry you gave me."

Dulce gasped, her eyes widening. "Did you tell the enforcers I'm alive?" Sudden fear coursed through her at the thought of the witch learning that she lived. That the woman would know Dulce would try to stop her curse.

"I happen to be a gentleman of my word." Reed pushed from the tree with the heel of his boot, the movement graceful as a dancer. "But perhaps you can go to the jail and tell the enforcers yourself that I am no graverobber."

No graverobber indeed, she thought.

"I would love to help you." Dulce smiled. "But the thing is, I can't. Just yet."

"And why is that, Majesty?"

"Since you left, I have … learned of much more pressing matters."

His deep brown eyes fixed on hers, Reed arched a brow, his white hair falling across his forehead as he scowled at her, making him somehow even more handsome. "And may I inquire, if it's all right with Your Worship, how long do you estimate these pressing matters will take? Not to be an inconvenience, but with every enforcer in the vicinity after me, I find that I don't have anywhere else to go."

This man was a stranger, and yet, even though it meant danger to himself, he had kept her secret. He had saved her life by freeing her from her grave. He had helped her when she was weak and hungry, dying of thirst. She felt bound to him in a sense—she had to admit this, even if only to herself. And now, they were both in hiding. For different reasons, yes, but hiding all the same.

He had escaped capture and clearly knew more about the dangers of the world than she did.

Maybe, just maybe, they could continue to help one another.

"Last night after you left, I discovered a witch here with Cornelius. They'd gotten rather *close*, it seems, and she put a spell on my land."

"A witch." His gaze was full of skepticism as he ran a hand along his jaw. "Cast a magic spell."

"Yes. I saw her with my own eyes," she insisted. "I'm not mad—there's no reason to look at me like that."

Reed continued to look at her exactly like that.

Dulce warred with herself. Should she tell him everything she knew? If she wanted his help, she would need to trust him with something of the truth.

"There are five trees across the territories whose magic helps to give our world its vitality, its life," she confessed. "If their power is disturbed, which the one on my land has been, thanks to this witch, it will be very bad."

"Very bad…"

"Yes, there will be catastrophic consequences. If the trees turn to stone, life can no longer be sustained here in Moonglade or the neighboring lands. The foliage and animals will also become stone, our water sources will turn undrinkable, and our air unbreathable. The sun will disappear, shrouding this entire region in darkness. My tree's roots already show signs of sickness!"

Reed blinked, seeming to not understand what a dire situation they faced.

"Total annihilation." He nodded. "Got it. Not exactly what I was expecting you to say as your reason for not telling the enforcers you're alive and that you gave me your jewels, but… Wait, why *are* you hiding?"

"I need to find this witch myself. To make her reverse her spell."

"Ah, you have heard of the *enforcers*," he drawled. "Why don't you ask them? It would help us both out, wouldn't it, Highness?"

Dulce laughed without humor, her panic rising. This was a waste of time. He knew nothing of magic. Just as most in Moonglade didn't. Sometimes she didn't understand why she needed to keep her being a witch a secret, yet after reading her mother's letter, she knew why.

To keep the Tree of Life safe.

"Powerful witches can be capable of terrible things if they wield their spells in a way that goes against the laws of magic. The enforcers would be no better than Cornelius within mere moments, useless against her."

"Mm-hmm." Reed nodded, but she could see he still thought her mad. "Describe this *witch* to me—maybe I've heard of her."

Dulce narrowed her eyes. "She's incredibly tall, strikingly beautiful, her hair is the shade of rubies, and she rides a white stallion."

Reed's lips curled up at the edges, his eyes dancing with amusement.

"You *know* her?" She bit the inside of her cheek, hope filling her chest.

"Not personally, no." Reed tsked. "She's not from around here, but I saw her once in the Glen, outside the apothecary. Not a woman to be trifled with, if you believe the stories. They say she works for the Duke, a woman most fear. The apothecary unquestionably did. I'm fairly certain he pissed himself when she arrived. She has a reputation for making those who cross the Duke disappear. They call her La Bisou Morte."

"Death's Kiss?"

"Is that what that means?" Reed chuckled. "She's rumored to be the Duke's personal assassin, though you can't believe most of what drunks say, especially after they've lost a bet. No one knows her real name, and I hear she likes to keep it that way." He let out a low whistle. "One thing's for certain. Whatever she does, the Duke is behind it."

The Duke? He resided farther north in Alder Bay,

only a few days journey by carriage. "Would you happen to know where she lives, this Death's Kiss assassin?"

He shook his head. "Other than possibly in the Duke's town? No."

Dulce nearly threw her arms around Reed in gratitude for returning to her home.

Straightening, she folded her hands in front of her and said aloud to herself, "We'll need to travel to Alder Bay. I can't take my carriage or horses—they're too recognizable…."

Reed cocked his head and folded his arms once more. "What exactly do you mean *we?*"

"Someone has to stay here to look after the manor and the Tree of Life," Dulce said. "And, though it pains me to admit it, it would be unwise for me to travel alone. My task would benefit from the assistance of one more, a guard in a sense … daring and more worldly than myself—it would be utter foolishness to deny this fact." Before he could say anything, Dulce hurried on, "You say you have nowhere to go. I'll pay you. *Handsomely.*"

"Did you not hear me?" Reed frowned. "La Bisou Morte works for the *Duke.*"

"The Duke is a pompous ass who responds to wealth." Dulce waved a hand. "Greed and prestige drive him. These are obstacles we can work with if we must."

The sound of carriages approaching along the road filled the air, and Reed stilled. Company was drawing nearer to her manor with each passing second.

"The enforcers know it was your things I stole." Reed winced. "I should've realized they would want to discuss the robbery with the grieving widower. I suppose this won't go well, seeing as he's now lying in your grave."

There was no time to formulate an elaborate plan, so Dulce went with the first desperate idea that came into her head. "Come with me." She grasped Reed's arm and pulled him in the direction of the cemetery where her staff stood staring at her in surprise.

"Take Reed into the manor and hide him," she instructed Vesta, before the woman could say a word. She hurried to replace the flowers atop her grave. "He's the man who saved me."

That got their attention.

"Yes, Reed Hawthorne at your service." He bowed with a smirk even though they were running out of time.

"Mr. Hawthorne," Dulce continued. "This is Vesta." She then turned to the other two. "Sylvan and Lucas, since you're finished here, continue to pick weeds and look busy gardening."

"And you?" Sylvan furrowed his brow, appearing worried as the bell was rung, the sounds of horses at the gate. "Where will you be?"

"Ensuring that Cornelius makes an appearance shortly."

Reed glanced over his shoulder at her, his immaculate obsidian brow raised again as he followed Vesta, but she ignored him. Darting toward the conservatory, her fingers fumbled with the padlock, but she finally ripped it free. She leapt through the door and yanked open a cabinet, glass clinking against glass, until she found the jar she wanted. Tipping it back against her lips, Dulce swallowed the bitter potion.

"Come on," Dulce begged, her gaze trained on her hands as she focused on molding them. "Work faster."

A relieved sigh escaped her when her hands

lengthened, thickened, the now-revolting shape of Cornelius's fingers forming. Dulce lifted the handheld mirror, her reflection that of a man she once thought of as handsome with hazel eyes, chestnut hair, and chiseled features. She was the spitting image of her dead bastard husband.

Locking the conservatory, she hurried to meet the enforcer's carriage at her gate.

"Mr. Hale, I presume," a man with a dark curling mustache said, coming to attention before the carriage. "My name's Enoch, and I'm one of the enforcers." She thought he might bow, but instead he took off his hat, appearing sheepish. Another dark-haired enforcer remained atop the driver's seat, holding the horses' reins, his gaze straight ahead as if ordered to do so.

Dulce could look like anyone, but she couldn't speak as them, so this could pose a problem. She cleared her throat, and in the deepest, raspiest voice she could muster, she sputtered impatiently, "I'm unwell and not feeling myself. What is the meaning of this, this disturbance?"

"We'd like to inform you that your wife's grave has been disturbed."

She glowered. "Impossible. What nonsense are you spewing?"

"Two pieces of her jewelry were stolen," Enoch started. "The thief was caught, but he, uh, there was a fire at the jail and he … seems to have escaped in the ensuing chaos."

"Tales of your department's incompetence are none of my concern," Dulce snapped, much like the time Cornelius himself did when the horses' hay was delivered late once. "If you're here to petition my house for coin, you'll find me less than amused by your methods."

"Your wife's ring and necklace were destroyed in the fire." He sighed.

"Do not speak of my poor wife," she croaked, then let out a sob that sounded true as she imagined how her mother would reprimand her over allowing a family heirloom to melt in a fire. "A member of my devoted staff has remained by her graveside since the moment she was laid to rest and will continue to do so until further notice. If it's graverobbers you concerned yourself over, go and concern yourself elsewhere. That is all."

Dulce turned to leave, but the enforcer had more courage—or wits—than she expected.

"May I have a look at the gravesite?" Enoch asked, halting her movement.

"If you must." Dulce opened the gate with exaggerated sadness, sighing and muttering about harassment in the time of grief for good measure.

She led the enforcer through the gardens to the back of the manor where Lucas was gathering weeds into a basket beside Sylvan, the two shovels no longer in sight. Both men stood and nodded respectfully to the enforcer, removing their hats and staring at the ground, the picture of forlorn servants.

As the three of them watched, the man knelt in front of Dulce's grave and pressed his fingers to the dirt. He lifted a handful of soil, then let the granules drift slowly from his palm. She held her breath, praying he wouldn't demand that the body within be exhumed.

"May your wife rest in peace," Enoch finally said, standing.

Exuding indignation, Dulce walked the enforcer to his carriage in silence. As Enoch stepped inside, he studied her with a frown, and Dulce's heart hammered at the thought that he somehow recognized her, but he only shook his head before shutting the door.

Once the carriage vanished from sight, she hurried to the manor, still wearing Cornelius's form in case the enforcers were to turn around. "Vesta!" she shouted once she entered the comforting walls of her home. "They're gone."

The woman rushed down the marble staircase and her lips parted in bewilderment.

"What is it?" Dulce asked.

"Your lips are showing," she whispered as though the enforcers could somehow hear the secret exchange.

"Drat." At least the image of Cornelius had held long enough to get the enforcers to depart the property.

"I left Mr. Hawthorne in the attic."

"Thank you." As Dulce took a sage leaf from her pocket, she told Vesta the rest of the story about the witch—La Bisou Morte—her mother's letter, and what would happen if she couldn't find the woman to break the curse.

"You will break the curse." Vesta wrapped her in a warm embrace. "I know you can do it, Dulce."

"I'll continue to study Mother's spell book. There is still so much to learn." Perhaps there was an answer she would find.

"You are your mother's daughter," Vesta reassured her. "There is nothing you cannot do once you put your mind to it."

Dulce smiled wistfully and ascended the staircase.

Once she drew open the attic door, she found Reed peering out the window.

"That doesn't qualify as hiding," she called.

Reed spun to face her, his eyes wide as saucers. "I saw you down there. You used a *spell*."

"Do you believe in witches now that you know I'm one?"

"You've opened my eyes to magic." Reed trailed a forefinger across his lower lip, his smile crooked in a way that made Dulce avert her stare. "You pulled off looking like your husband well. At least from the glimpse I saw of his bloody corpse."

"Lumpish pignut is the preferred term," she clarified. "Now, have you seen enough that you'll accompany me to Alder Bay, or do you need more proof of magic?"

Reed contemplated the ceiling, the light from the window falling across his smooth neck, and she turned her gaze away once again. "In addition to payment," he said finally. "I want you to teach me how to alter my looks the way you did."

Dulce grinned. "Then we have a deal, Mr. Hawthorne."

Reed

Reed lay on a bed soft as clouds and thought about La Bisou Morte. How dangerous *was* she, really?

Dangerous enough to destroy the air, water, and land, according to Dulce.

But Dulce was also a witch, one who could alter her appearance if she wished, considerably dangerous herself.

Before today, if he'd given witches any thought at all, he would've said they were fabrications used to scare their children into behaving. Clearly, he knew very little of the world of magic.

All right, he knew nothing of it.

Which begged the question, how useful could he

possibly be to the heiress? Could an ignorant Glen-dwelling pauper whose only talents lay in beating a man to a bloody pulp really help to save the world?

"Not very fobbing likely," he muttered. "But you've got nowhere else to go anyway, have you?"

This sudden willingness to put your life in danger couldn't have anything to do with a certain pair of beautiful brown eyes, now, could it?

Reed waved the thought away like an irritating insect and ate the last piece of a chestnut apple pie Vesta had left on a tray for him. Its crust melted in a way that proved butter had been involved, and lots of it.

He'd had the first hot bath of his life. The first new clothing he'd ever donned. The first lambswool slippers he'd seen currently covered his feet. Though he wondered who'd worn them before him. Mr. Lumpish Pignut, no doubt.

Before Dulce could begin her quest to save the world from La Bisou Morte's corrupt spell, there was much work to be done. And most of it—he was told—did not require his presence.

First, the deceased husband would need to be seen publicly leaving town. Reed volunteered to help pack his things, but Vesta shooed him out of the room, insisting most of Cornelius's belongings were already packed, given that he'd only resided in the manor for a few days before the fool impaled himself. If Cornelius were still alive, Reed would've been hard-pressed not to push the deceptive toad off the roof himself, something he deserved after trying to murder Dulce.

Reed had offered to drive the carriage out of town—eager to try out a disguise—but Sylvan had looked disappointed in his cognitive skills.

"I am known around Moonglade to drive this carriage," he'd informed Reed. "Actions that divert from the norm will only garner unwanted attention."

"Like the lady of the house *dying* on her wedding night?" Reed pointed out. "I'd say that diverted pretty significantly from the norm."

Sylvan scowled at him as he piled more of Cornelius's trunks onto the carriage.

"You can make yourself useful by bathing," he'd grumbled as he returned inside. "You smell of swamp gasses."

"Thank you," Reed called after him with an exaggerated bow. "That was exactly my intention."

If he had known bathing could be such a phenomenal joy, Reed wouldn't have bothered attempting to be useful at all. The tub in his suite was the size of his and Philip's entire house, the water miraculously hot, the rosemary, lemon balm, and calendula soaps leaving his skin soft as petals. If it hadn't been for his hunger—and the knowledge that Vesta had delivered a meal to his room— Reed might've stayed in the bath for hours.

The bed of clouds, his entire body cleaner than he had ever felt in his life, his stomach full beyond his imagining, Reed slept.

By the time he awoke, the sun had set, its fading light casting deep shadows across the luxurious room, the gold filigree along the ceiling like the teeth of some giant beast in the gathering darkness.

At the sound of horses pulling a carriage along the drive beneath his window, Reed sat, wrapping his freshly washed cloak around his shoulders, and went to meet

Dulce.

He found only Sylvan driving an unpainted carriage led by a pack mule and a stranger on a massive Clydesdale horse.

The stranger called out to Lucas with a familiar feminine voice, and Reed realized the *man* was in fact Dulce herself. Instead of the young and admittedly handsome appearance of her late husband, she was now disguised as a stout older farmer type with a large middle. As she leapt from the horse, Reed heard her laugh for the first time, the sound like a summer day, sending a warm sensation along his ribcage.

"It's as I told Sylvan," she continued, "it only serves our purposes for the people of Moonglade to think Cornelius mad with grief. He *is* about to disappear mysteriously from his rooms and never be seen or heard of again, after all."

"Still," Sylvan grumbled, climbing down from the carriage and taking the mule by the reins, "that's no reason to practically give away your fine horses and carriage."

Dulce waved a hand dismissively. "The orphanage needed a new carriage. And Cornelius's kind charity will be a distraction from his otherwise lumpish loutery once anyone finally notices he's gone. I—speaking as an ill-sounding Cornelius, of course—told the staff at the inn not to disturb me under any circumstances, so that should buy us quite some time before anyone comes sniffing around the manor with estate questions."

Reed was left amazed at how easily one could get rid of a person—if one could only impersonate them convincingly enough. It seemed to him that magic could be used for all sorts of criminal enterprises, and he hoped the Leper never gained the use of it.

"Ah, Reed!" Dulce said in a comically low voice as she noticed him standing in the doorway. Smiling as she passed, she uttered, "We depart at dawn, prepare what you must! Leave the unnecessary!"

Reed turned to Vesta and wiggled his fingers by his head, whispering, "Do the … *changes* affect her brain?"

Vesta pretended not to hear him, answering only, "You will find your new wardrobe outside your room, *Mr.* Hawthorne. And see that you do not neglect to take the elixir provided for you. That hair will never do."

Reed pretended to notice his hair for the first time, exclaiming, "Oh, *never*, I quite agree."

Over dinner, an argument erupted concerning who would accompany Dulce on her journey north. All three of the servants wanted to stay with the heiress, a fact that Reed found spoke well of her kind and generous nature.

"I've painted the carriage and I'm ready to travel," Sylvan insisted. "There's nothing more to do here that Lucas cannot do in my absence."

"What about your gout?" Dulce asked.

"It's fine. It's nothing."

She lowered her silver slowly onto a plate of radishes and poached potatoes. "And if men come with estate questions, what will Lucas tell them? Do you think they will respect the word of a mere sixteen-year-old? Or a housemaid? No offense, Vesta, but—"

Vesta ate two peas. "None taken."

"It has to be you who gives them Cornelius's letter of explanation," Dulce said with finality. "And Vesta must nurse Mother's tree with my potions in our absence."

"We will return in less than a week," Sylvan tried, though Reed could see he'd given up. "No one will even notice—"

"We *hope* to return in less than a week, but we might not."

Reed watched the four of them, the servants all equally worried for Dulce as she continued her meal.

"I will not put Lucas in any danger," she vowed after a long silence, the determination in her gaze captivating Reed in the candlelight. "I promise you that, on my own life."

"I never questioned that, Dulce, I only—"

She reached across the table and took his hand in hers. "I promise it, just the same, Sylvie."

They left at dawn the next morning, their belongings piled onto the freshly painted carriage beneath waterproof oilskins, a foreign merchant's insignia decorating its side. A new knife was hidden in Reed's boot, courtesy of Dulce, and he was disguised as said foreign merchant, having swallowed the first of the bitter elixir, which turned his hair a deep brown that perfectly matched his eyes and nothing else. His appearance couldn't be altered further since he was new to the elixir.

"You'd be surprised how little one is recognized with a simple change of wardrobe," Dulce had told him, seeing his disappointment.

Dulce would travel as his wife—a position that would keep her in his presence and under his protection throughout—her enormous volume of striking blonde curls and bright green eyes setting her apart from the 'dead' heiress, should any who knew her notice them along the way. A black high-collared dress hugged her curves splendidly.

Lucas sat tall in the driver's seat, bundled in the fur-lined uniform of a foreigner's coachman, the Clydesdale resigned as their preparations to depart were completed.

Reed doubted any would notice them as they passed through the empty streets of Moonglade, the town cloaked in a thick layer of fog, and even the crows were still asleep.

"Will your brother be all right?" Dulce asked, surprising him with her kindness. She was genuinely worried about a man she'd never met, when most of the wealthy wouldn't spare a moment to care.

"He'll pull through—thank you for asking," Reed said. "I only wish he could leave that place and focus on his dreams of teaching."

"And you?" she inquired, her arms hugging an older tome to her chest. "Do you wish to leave as well?"

"Me?" He chuckled. "I'd wish to never fight for money again. Fight only for the love of it. Freedom from debt, that would be nice."

Dulce's lips twitched at the corners. "I've never attended a ring fight before."

"Ah, well, that's probably a good thing for a respectable lady such as yourself."

"Perhaps this respectable lady would quite enjoy one."

He chuckled again, then his gaze returned to her tome. "What are you reading?"

"My mother's spell book. I stayed up all night reading as much as I could, memorizing new spells for if we need them. These were spells I should've learned when I was younger, but my mother wanted me to have a different childhood than she did." Dulce shrugged. "It would've been useful to know beforehand, but I'm a quick learner."

"So what did one learn as a wealthy child then? Piano?"

"Yes, *piano*." She laughed softly. "But also I was fed poisons."

Reed sputtered, horrified, "Poisons?"

"It's a tradition in our family to start slowly at a young age, not only because I was a witch but because of the wealth and what one could do to someone to steal it."

"It sounds like a blessing from your mother then."

"Yes. Very much."

"I would say to teach me the way of poisons, but I don't have anything worth stealing," he drawled.

"I'm not so sure about that, Mr. Hawthorne. You're quite extraordinary." She smiled and opened her book to read.

Him? Extraordinary? Was a swamp rat anything worthy of praise? And yet, her words warmed him, filled him with a newfound confidence.

Soon they reached the rolling hills above the town, and Reed looked down at the Glen in the distance, its swamps and ramshackle huts shrouded in mist as the sun rose in the slate-gray sky, its light nearly obliterated by cloud. They stopped every two hours to allow the horse—whom Dulce named Golden Toffee—to feed and drink, to stretch their legs and to eat something of the dried fruit, bread, and nuts Vesta had packed for them. Reed thought he was already becoming too accustomed to eating well. He could almost hear his brother's taunts at how he'd *gone soft* in a single day...

Reed studied the sky over the Thyone Pass farther ahead. "Looks like a storm."

"They say once you enter the pass, you can't stop," Dulce said.

He shrugged. "They say a lot of things, mostly involving being eaten by creatures that probably don't even exist."

"There's an inn just before it. The Black Fox," Lucas told them, eating half a sandwich in one bite, clearly proud he knew something they didn't. "It's the last place to rest before miles of wilderness. Grandfather says we have to stay the night there, or else Toffee will get too tired through the Pass."

"I wonder if it's true what they say about the creatures that live within Thyone Pass?" Dulce whispered, as if the creatures might hear her if she spoke too loudly, and Reed ate more bread to hide his smile.

"Probably not." Lucas shrugged, speaking around another enormous bite of sourdough and ham. "Or we would have seen hunters' trophies of them."

"After reading through Mother's book and seeing what La Bisou Morte's spell has already done, I doubt nothing. Anything is possible," Dulce muttered, her hands clutching the tome.

Rain poured from the sky by the time the Black Fox came into view through the carriage window. Sitting at the base of the jagged mountains of the Pass, it was made entirely of tar-painted wood, three stories of ebony and glass, its design foreign in its elaborate carvings like wooden lace around pointed doorways and windowpanes. Glistening white gossamer cloaked every single shrub, and he wondered how many spiders were crawling within their branches and leaves.

As they drew closer, Reed felt that the inn itself was watching him.

Beckoning him closer.

A hunched man with a bushy peppered beard appeared out of the misty rain and waved their carriage forward to halt beneath the Black Fox's wide porch, its dark pillars carved with the faces of screaming children— or were they laughing? Reed arched an eyebrow at them before alighting, helping Dulce from the carriage as he imagined a chivalrous husband might, and Lucas dutifully retrieved their luggage packed for the journey before departing to sleep in one of the stable rooms, the party determined to keep up all appearance of normalcy.

"We don't get many guests these days," the man said as he led them inside, his accent unfamiliar to Reed. "Weather isn't fine, you see. I expect we'll get more rain before the night is through."

The inn's lobby was as dark as its exterior. Dulce shuddered in the cold, and Reed draped an arm around her.

The innkeeper hurried to light a fire in a hearth made of black stone, its height taller than any man.

"I apologize for the absence of our regular staff," he continued, opening a large registry and sliding it across the desk at Reed. "They found themselves unwell and didn't dare to risk our guests' health."

"Most thoughtful of them." Reed nodded, signing the registry *Mr. and Mrs. Jones Taylor,* the common name they chose to go by. "We will take your best room, if it's not too much trouble."

"No trouble at all." The man retrieved a key from the wall behind the desk, each one tied to a black tassel, the one he handed Reed having the largest tassel of them all. "Dinner will be laid out at half past seven, though I'm afraid it's only stew and bread tonight."

Reed smiled, accepting the key. "Stew and bread will do splendidly, thank you." It was certainly a much better meal than he was accustomed to in the Glen.

They followed the man—who insisted on carrying their luggage—up a staircase of more dark stone, the paintings lining the walls hidden in deep shadows, as if the artist only had shades of gray to work with. Dulce took his arm, murmuring, "You're quite good at playing the aristocrat, my lord."

Reed smirked. "Much obliged, I'm sure, Highness."

She fought a laugh, and the effect on her features was alluring, even in the cold shadows of the place. Reed no longer noticed the cold with her delicate hand on his arm.

Their room consisted of two beds large enough for an entire family in the Glen, their carved wood draped in canopies of black velvet, an armoire of that same ebony stone, a mirror surrounded by carvings of wolf-like creatures with wings, and a bath.

"I'm going to keep the spell book close," she said, resting her hand on her satchel. "I don't trust leaving it anywhere I'm absent from it."

He nodded, not trusting the inn in the least, and as she opened the luggage, sorting through a few vials, he asked, "So how did you get the name Dulce?"

She smiled at him over her shoulder. "Do I look more

like an Alexandra or a Josephine?"

Reed smirked. "Not at all. Dulce suits you rather perfectly."

"Alexandra comes from my grandmother on my mother's side, and Josephine, my grandmother on my father's side. But as a young child, my father said neither suited me, and I was too sweet for such stuffy names, so he called me Dulce." She grinned. "Although, after all that's happened now, I'm not certain my father would feel the same way any longer."

"On the contrary." Reed cleared his throat before he said something that sounded like a sappy poet. "Speaking of sweet things, I do believe there is a meal calling us downstairs."

The pair returned to the inn's lobby, finding the dining room by virtue of its being the only area with any light. Multiple candles cast a soft glow along the inky wallpaper of black poppies on gray, and the chairs, made of the same dark wood, were decorated in carvings like so many grasping hands.

Hands struggling to climb from graves, Reed thought. He glanced down at his stew and brought a spoonful to his lips.

"It's quite beautiful," Dulce said cheerfully, and Reed stopped eating to stare at her. "What?" She met his no doubt gaping expression.

"If you can call *haunted* beautiful," Reed whispered. He jerked his chin at the painting of a young girl with bluish skin standing alone in a forest of gray, her eyes full of sorrow as they seemed to *stare* into his very soul. "Just *look* at that painting, for one thing."

"Oh, it's most certainly haunted," Dulce agreed,

continuing to eat. "But why should that make it any less beautiful?"

Reed shook his head in fascination.

She took a small velvet bag from her pocket and fished out a white berry, then slipped it between her pretty lips. "I'd offer you one, but you'd die."

He smirked. "A tolerance to poisons. Quite the quality you have."

"Indeed." The edges of Dulce's lips curved up into a smile.

Reed finished his stew in silence, unable to halt his thoughts about what one went through to become accustomed to poisons.

On returning to his room through the inn's dark and empty corridors, Reed was surprised to find the water from the bath's greenish copper faucets was hot. He filled the tub and let Dulce bathe first, then sank down into its blissful depths himself.

Tired from a full day jostled in a carriage along rocky lanes, Reed slipped into the room to find Dulce had fallen into a deep sleep on her bed. He studied her heart-shaped face a little too long before blowing out the candle on his bedside.

Reed hoped absently that Lucas was comfortable in the servant's quarters, that Philip didn't worry too much about what had become of him. He tried not to think of Dulce, sleeping just two steps from him, her breathing soft, but as he closed his eyes, she was the only thing he could think about. With the light casting an eerie silver glow through the window, her face was the perfection of a priceless marble statue, and he was reminded of the first time he saw her, lying within her grave.

"Reed," Dulce whispered, waking him, the rain outside falling in loud torrents now, and he opened his eyes, seeing nothing but shadow. The creatures along the mirror seemed to move, and he blinked, his vision clearing.

"Hmm?" he managed, confused. Someone—Dulce—was most certainly climbing into his bed. A leg came up to rest over his, a smooth foot caressing his own. He was fully awake now, all too aware of her body against his back, soft and warm.

Dulce's breath was hot along his neck as she whispered, "Reed, I'm frightened." Her delicate arms wrapped around him then, and he froze. "Won't you hold me?"

Surprise, desire, and confusion all warred within him. Desire quickly won over the others, and Reed began to turn around, all thought vanishing, powerless against his longing to obey, to take Dulce in his arms and kiss her, just as he'd wanted to when he first saw her.

But instead, sudden pain halted his movement.

Dulce's hands were claws, her razor-sharp nails digging into his chest, blood welling in their wake. Her soft lips became teeth, ripping at his neck. Reed cried out in alarm, cursing into the darkness, as he threw himself from the bed, shoving Dulce from his side.

A ray of candlelight shone from the opening bathroom door, and Dulce stood frowning at him, fully dressed.

Reed blinked. "What—"

Movement in the mirror caught his eye, and the blood drained from his face. A woman as thin as a skeleton smiled at him from his bed, the depths of her hollow eyes appearing to laugh at his desire while rotting teeth elongated to form the sharp fangs of a beast.

Reed flinched away, whirling back to Dulce, only to find that the girl from the dining room's painting stood behind her in the bathroom's light, her clothing dripping wet, her skin that of a drowned and rotting corpse.

"I take it you see one of the ghosts standing behind me." Dulce plucked up her cloak from the bed. "We should probably leave. It's well past dawn."

"Am I going mad?" Reed asked, opening his shirt to inspect the skin of his chest. Though he could still feel the cuts along it, his roving fingertips proved there was nothing there.

Cheeks pinkened, Dulce turned away, and Reed hurried to button his shirt again. "No, you aren't going mad," she told him. "I believe they want you to themselves by the way they're staring daggers at me."

"Well, they can continue wanting. Let's get out of this cursed place." Reed hurried to slip on his boots, then threw on his cloak and hat without bothering to comb his hair. He snatched up their luggage and strode toward the door. With one last glance back before leaving the room, he found the woman still grinning at him from the bed, the girl still standing in the bathroom, her gaze full of sorrow.

"That was nothing a little blessed thistle and rue couldn't have prevented," Dulce said beside him on the stairs. "I can purchase some at the next apothecary we see so that ghosts can't appear at all."

He arched a brow. "I don't care if you buy all the thistle and rue in the world, we aren't staying anywhere with ghosts again. I'd rather sleep outside in the rain."

She rolled her eyes, a hint of a smile curling her lips. "As you say then, *Mr. Jones Taylor.*"

Dulce

"How was I supposed to assume that you didn't know ghosts are real?" Dulce asked as the carriage traveled away from the Black Fox. "Does the Glen not speak of such things?"

"We have other things to worry about," Reed said. "Like getting food into our bellies. But to be fair, yes, magic and ghosts are spoken of. I'd just never encountered either until I met you. So I suppose I have you to thank for that, Majesty." His tone ended the sentence on the edge of flirtation.

Dulce angled her head to the side, the corners of her lips lifting. "Is it Highness or Majesty that you mean?

You've used both."

"I mean *both*. Unless you prefer Your Royal Majestic Highness," he drawled, his deep baritone sending delicious tingles down her spine.

Get a hold of yourself, Dulce. "Anyway, I promise I won't let a single ghost appear to you in Alder Bay."

"Good. Otherwise, we may need to sleep in the same bed."

She blinked and straightened in her seat, trying not to imagine him shirtless, his bare chest pressed against her thin nightgown.

"To protect you," he clarified, a hint of amusement dancing in his gaze.

"Of course." Had she been wanting a different answer? *No, she was married only days ago. Nearly murdered by said treacherous man. But the tea leaves… Don't think about those blasted tea leaves!*

Dulce had only encountered one other haunted inn when she was younger. It had been on a family journey to the edge of Moonglade to visit her grandparents before their deaths, and her mother had cast the malevolent spirits away with thistle and rue.

She'd packed numerous ingredients for the journey in her satchel, her pockets, and a spare bag to keep in the carriage. But still, she'd been more focused on the witch than ghosts. "I should've been more prepared, yet I wasn't expecting the ghosts to fall head over heels for you either." The memory of his surprised expression made her smile, and he noticed, glowering, which only made her smile more.

"You're enjoying yourself way too much," he muttered. "When a stout old dead man climbs into your bed, we'll see who's laughing then."

Dulce rolled her eyes while fighting another smile and took out a dried elderberry from her velvet pouch, then placed its poison against her tongue.

Rain poured from the sky in heavy sheets as the carriage approached the Thyone Pass, and Dulce was thankful their horse had a thick coat of fur when the temperatures dropped. She attempted to memorize more new spells from her mother's book while casting her gaze every so often to Reed, who was sketching a cat atop a headstone in a weathered journal he'd found beneath the seat. The chestnut locks suited his handsome features just fine, yet the ivory hair felt more like him. The elixir they'd taken before leaving her manor would linger in their bloodstream for a good while. But for how long? The answer was to be determined. However, she'd brought a few other batches in case they were necessary.

The rocky path through the towering cliffsides to either side of them rose like waterfalls in the downpour. The Pass transformed to a river, conversation impossible in the noise, though Lucas, wrapped in his oilskin cloak, kept up a steady stream of shouted encouragement as Toffee soldiered on.

Sunlight hardly reached into the depths of the Pass, illuminating their way for only a few short hours on their journey north, and by the time the cliffs' end was in sight, night fell in earnest.

Toffee picked up her pace as if racing from the

clutches of the Pass, and Dulce watched from the carriage window to see glowing eyes peering back at her from the crevices of the cliffs. She nearly grasped Reed's hand when strange noises akin to screaming beasts mixed with the sounds of incessant rainfall reverberated.

At some point, she must've slept, because Dulce awoke to find Lucas folding a blanket next to a fire, while Toffee grazed lazily, a rope tied from her harness to the carriage, the landscape wide open pastures.

Reed slept next to her, his head against the window. A pleasant woodsy scent with a hint of rosemary wafted off of him when she moved closer to exit the carriage. She stared at his lovely features, his high cheekbones, his plump lips, a few heartbeats too long before leaving him to rest.

"It's not far now," Lucas told her, yawning, the sun rising along the rolling hills.

"You could've taken shelter in the carriage, Lucas."

"I prefer the outdoors." He shrugged. "Besides, I'll have quite the story to tell Azalea when I return."

"With a batch of flowers." Dulce grinned, knowing he was sweet on the girl who worked at the bakery.

"Perhaps." Lucas waggled his brows.

Still smiling, Dulce went to the freezing stream, settling at its shore to drink while thinking of a new wistful melody she wanted to try on the piano when she returned home. As she imagined a room full of ghosts from her favorite poem dancing to the tune, the shuffling of feet drew her out of her thoughts.

Reed crouched beside her and handed her a piece of bread with a tired smile. "I miss Vesta's cooking already." He sighed, biting into his slice.

"It only takes one meal from her to grow accustomed." Dulce laughed. She found she couldn't stop her gaze from drifting to those perfectly plump lips of his once more, as alluring and captivating as his deep brown eyes.

Reed brought a handful of water to his mouth and drank, unaware of Dulce's struggle not to stare. "Speaking of accustomed," he said. "Does the charming Ms. Bancroft know how to protect herself?"

"Me?" she asked, incredulous. "Have you not seen my disguises?"

"*Without* magic."

Dulce folded her arms and frowned. "Are you saying I can't throw a punch, Mr. Hawthorne?"

"Try it." He stood, spreading his arms. "I won't bite."

Dulce huffed while pushing up from her position. "Perhaps I will." She didn't prepare by stepping into a stance but threw her arm forward, hoping to catch him off guard, yet Reed easily caught her fist.

Spinning Dulce so her back was against his firm chest, he chuckled. "You punch like a *lady*."

She lingered a few seconds too long, feeling his warmth, as a flutter of butterflies flickered in her stomach. Finally peeling herself from Reed, she whirled to face him, her hands on her hips. "Teach me something useful then."

Reed smirked, leaning in until his chest was so very near to brushing hers. He trailed the pads of his fingertips down Dulce's arm while bringing his head closer to hers. "Like this?" he asked silkily. Instead of closing the distance left between them, he inched back and held up her black pearl bracelet.

Dulce snatched her jewelry from him. "How did you accomplish that without me feeling it?"

His eyes grew hooded. "A little flirtation."

"A *lady* is taught manners."

"Mmm, then toss your Moonglade manners aside." He cocked his head and shrugged. "Now, reach into my pocket."

"I'll do no such thing," she hissed, her cheeks growing hot.

"My *coat* pocket," he explained.

"Oh..." That was certainly more reasonable. Yet why did she feel a twinge of disappointment?

Reed gently grasped her hand and placed it against the hard planes of his chest, the butterflies in her stomach turning to hummingbirds. "Lean forward. Say something to keep my attention focused on you and carefully reach into my pocket."

Flirtation, indeed... What words of flirtation had she ever spoken to Cornelius? She hadn't ever. They had only discussed things like the weather, inquired after the health of his family and friends, meals, and his work. She would just have to come up with something from the forbidding poems she'd read, or the amorous stage plays in town.

Dulce's pulse raced faster the longer she kept her palm against Reed's chest, as she felt the *thump-thump* of his heart. She edged her face closer, mirroring what he'd done to her, only she veered her mouth to his ear, a hairsbreadth from brushing his skin, before whispering, "Ever since we met, I've been curious to know what your lips taste like."

His breath hitched, and Dulce nimbly drew out his wallet, then proudly backed away from him to wave it in his face. "How was that?"

"See?" Reed grinned, placing the wallet back into his pocket. "I almost believed what you spoke to be true."

Because it was, she realized.

Dulce cast her gaze to the carriage before he could see the truth.

"So how did you learn how to do all this?" she finally asked.

"One learns many unsavory things growing up in the Glen. I've found that hunger and necessity are the best teachers."

"When we return to Moonglade, will you teach me how to fight?" she asked. "I'll pay you, of course."

He lifted a tendril of her golden hair and twirled it around his finger. "If I don't see another ghost on this journey, I'll teach you for no payment at all."

"A fair trade indeed."

As they resumed their journey up and over the hills, Alder Bay finally crept into view. Black, white, and gray stone buildings dotted the town, and when they eventually passed through a bustling market, Reed's eyes widened. "Not everyone here is human."

"It's the result of the abuse of magic centuries ago," Dulce explained, smiling sadly, "Mother told me stories of Alder Bay, and how a quartet of witches sacrificed their families for wealth, but the magic went awry, throwing off the balance. Magic is sacred. Its power is meant to be respected. To do otherwise is to play a very dangerous game indeed."

Reed turned to her in alarm. "Why is every story about a witch appalling?"

Dulce grinned. "I'm not so terrible, am I?"

"You're certainly my favorite witch." He winked.

Her cheeks grew heated, and she hurried to put her mother's spell book inside her satchel.

Outside the carriage, plenty of humans milled about, but they weren't alone. Creatures that would appear otherworldly in Moonglade or the Glen were ordinary here. Fur, scales, and horns could be seen in wide variations. Some folk had protruding teeth, others were towering or smaller than cats. A furred orc kissed a human girl's hand while she giggled, offering her a flower that bloomed in sparkling blue.

"I'm such a fool for only believing in what my eyes could see." Reed's voice drifted through the carriage, full of wonder.

"No, not a fool," she said. "Just human. But now you're a successful merchant who's traveled the world, so try not to look too surprised."

"That one has *wings*," he hissed. "I apologize if I'm not able to look sufficiently bored."

A single brow rose up her forehead. "You have a few moments longer to practice then, Mr. Jones Taylor."

After passing a flower shop, its windowsills blooming with pots of dark purple petunias, Lucas drew the carriage to a stop in front of the White Cat Inn, its walls ivory marble.

Dulce placed a velvet bag of coins in Lucas's hand for him to venture to the servants' quarters before she entered the establishment with Reed.

The scent of roses permeated the air, and black and gold filigree lined the cream damask wallpaper along the mirror-adorned walls. Plush crimson chairs around a glass table decorated the center of the room atop a fur rug, and beyond that, a desk behind which a faun-like creature stood, his spectacles dangling at the edge of his snout, his horns curved.

Reed gawked at the creature, and Dulce elbowed him in the ribs.

"Ow," he groaned.

"Exude at least *some* boredom," she murmured.

"I thought I was."

"What you were doing was more like an exceptionally surprised blowfish when it's been pulled from the water."

Reed's shoulders shook with laughter, and Dulce bit her lip to keep from falling into a giggle spell herself.

The faun glanced up as they approached his desk. "Welcome," he spoke in a deep voice. "How may I help you?"

"We'd like your finest room." Dulce placed a handful of coins on the desk. "I'm unsure of the length of our stay, but this should cover a week, I'm sure. My husband and I are on our honeymoon, you see, and are traveling across the territories."

"This is the perfect place for you then." He drew open a drawer and passed her a golden key once she signed the registry *Mr. and Mrs. Jones Taylor* as Reed had at the Black Fox. "Second floor. Room 214. Our dining room is available to guests at all hours, and on the third level, you will find ballrooms and gardens, and in the lower basement level the gambling spaces, if you're looking for more entertainment. Before I forget, here is an invitation to the Duke's annual party. Everyone is welcome."

"Oh! Thank you," Dulce exclaimed. "Sweetheart, look! A festival, what fun."

Reed didn't have to feign surprise this time. "It

sounds grand.”

Dulce walked beside Reed down a long hallway, where black and scarlet masks hung. Some full faces, others only half.

They descended a curving staircase and found their room as soon as they took the last step. Inside, the enormous space held two lavish beds draped in dark silk blankets, gossamer curtains covering glass doors leading out to a balcony draped in vines. A wardrobe stood in one corner across from a writing desk.

“I like this place better already,” Reed announced, placing their luggage beside the bed.

“Are you sure something isn’t lurking down there?” Dulce said, and when he glanced uneasily at the furniture, she added, “I’m only jesting.”

“I’ll owe you for that.” He winked.

She could only imagine what he meant by his response and changed the subject to more pressing matters. “So, I’m contemplating where we should start. Any ideas?”

“Easy answer.” He ticked his finger in the air. “The gambling room. It’s a place where gossip slips from the tongue and questions can be asked without appearing suspicious.”

“See?” She grinned. “It’s most advantageous having you here as my dear husband.”

Reed slowly trailed a finger across his lower lip. “I take it you don’t know anything about cards?”

“Not a thing.” That was something she’d never been taught by her mother, but now Dulce wished she’d learned a game or two herself. The only cards she knew were the ones Vesta used for fortune-telling.

“Come on, pretty wife.” Reed offered her his arm

with a grin. "Let's go downstairs, and I'll teach you a round."

She folded her arm around his, the sense of familiarity with this gesture already becoming.

He opened the door, and she followed him through the establishment and down to the basement, where a smoke-filled tavern was already crowded.

At least twenty tables took up the area. A middle-aged woman served drinks in silver steins behind a bar, and the musicians playing drums of painted skins and flute-like instruments sat in gnarled branches, their music drifting through the room. It was an experience she'd never witnessed in Moonglade.

Reed stopped before a table where one chair stood vacant, and two older men and a young creature with three small horns occupied themselves playing a game of cards.

"Hello, gentlemen, may we join you?" Reed asked, already sliding the lone chair back.

"If you have coin to lose," one of the older men with a long gray beard grunted, and they all laughed.

Dulce glanced around to find a spare chair, but Reed drew her into his lap as he sank down, settling an arm around her waist, making her heart beat merrily like bat wings. "My wife wants to learn to play."

At least Dulce wouldn't have to pretend ignorance at the game. Draping her arm around Reed's shoulders, she declared, "After a few rounds, perhaps I won't be as abysmal."

"You'll get the hang of it," the creature said with a smile. He shuffled the cards before passing them around the table to each person. "Or not!" and they all laughed again, including Reed.

"Oh, I see how it is," she pouted in a teasing manner.

Reed's thumb caressed her hip bone as he nuzzled into her neck. "My wife will do just fine."

As the men played, Reed bought the trio more drinks, explaining the rules to her, and Dulce easily caught on. Mostly she knew when Reed was bluffing because she could see his hand, but the other players had their own tricks too.

Once they completed their fifth round, Reed winning four hands, he asked, "Have any of you ever heard of La Bisou Morte, a witch who works for the Duke? I was told she might live here. My new wife has an ailment we're hoping to find a cure for while on our honeymoon."

"I have these dreadful headaches. Ever since I was a child," Dulce murmured, forcing her voice to sound somber as she pressed her fingers to her temple.

"I suggest finding another witch to help with that," the bearded man said, grabbing a card from the top of the pile to add to his hand.

"That witch's bargains aren't worth it," the second older man grumbled. "She'll ask for ten years of your life or something far worse in exchange."

Dulce cradled her cheek. "Oh, dear…"

"But she can cure my wife?" Reed pressed. "I would do anything to ease her suffering."

The horned creature lifted his stein, scowling at the loving couple. "Even if her price doesn't alter your decision, La Bisou Morte doesn't stay in Alder Bay."

"I was hoping not to hear such news." Dulce sighed.

The bearded man clucked his tongue. "If you want to find her, you'd have to get the answer from the Duke himself."

This was met with uproarious laughter, and Reed tossed his cards down, winning another hand.

The horned creature met Dulce's gaze. "Fair warning, the Duke's bargains are worse than his witch's."

Reed

Though the men playing cards had no knowledge of the ruby-haired witch's whereabouts, at least Reed and Dulce had a lead on La Bisou Morte. Except it involved the fobbing Duke. Reed continued to act as if this were an everyday occurrence as Dulce sat in his lap, though his pulse raced dangerously. With each minor movement, he wanted to pull her closer against him and trail his lips up the soft curve of her elegant neck.

"I'm going to get some rest," she announced. "Will you be much longer, sweetheart?"

"A few more rounds and I'm all yours," he purred.

Dulce beamed, leaning toward him to pretend to kiss

his cheek, her lips just shy of touching his skin. "Good luck, then."

"A very lucky man, indeed," the horned creature said as Dulce walked away.

Reed laughed, nodding to his cards. "That I am, gentlemen. That I am."

After a couple of rounds, in which Reed won a good deal of money but learned nothing of any value from his companions, he returned to his room. He was disappointed to find Dulce asleep atop the blankets, still dressed, her spell book open against her chest, as though she'd fallen asleep waiting for him to return. Or else determined to remain prepared for any unforeseen danger…?

Lifting a folded fur blanket from the end of the bed, he gently placed her book onto the night table and covered her.

Her eyes opened briefly as she murmured, "Sleep here," before she drifted off once more.

Reed was tempted to slip under the blanket with her and hold her close, but he shook his head at the idea. She had been much too deep into sleep when she'd spoken.

"Goodnight, Highness."

He settled onto his bed, his gaze drifting to her beautiful face more often than it should've before sleep finally took him.

Now that he had coin of his own winning, Reed decided to surprise Dulce with a gown for the Duke's annual festival, which, the invitation informed them, was to be held that very evening.

Friends could surprise friends with gifts. Besides, didn't husbands buy gifts for their wives all the time?

"I'll just check on Lucas then," he called through the suite's bathroom door. "Take him to eat breakfast."

The sounds of water splashing along the copper tub, falling against the room's glass tiles, echoed. Reed tried not to imagine Dulce free of her clothing, the water caressing her delicate skin, and failed miserably.

"I have a list of herbs to purchase," she answered, her voice magnified against porcelain and glass. "The wonderfully extensive apothecary two doors down must be explored. Should take a few hours, at least."

"Take as long as you need."

Reed was grateful for the cool morning air as he left the White Cat in search of the stables. Toffee stood in a stall, blissfully eating alfalfa, ignoring his presence, but Lucas was nowhere to be found. He had no doubt already joined the other coachmen for a meal.

A four-winged creature with eyes like glowing full moons glared down at him from the rafters, and Reed arched a brow at it as he backed out of the stables.

Distracted by the wonders along Alder Bay's central avenue, Reed searched for the shop he'd ventured by on their way to the inn the previous day, with its wide windows displaying gowns he'd never imagined could exist, their fabrics seemingly made of magic. Everyone he passed was preparing for the annual festival, the trees being strung with bright-colored lanterns. Garlands of flowers hung across the lanes creating a canopy of petals along the route to the Duke's palace. A majestic structure that stood proud on the hill overlooking the bay, its water sparkling in the morning sun, and even at this distance Reed could see that the preparations in the gardens for the festival were in full swing.

"Welcome to Geschmackvoll." A scratchy voice sighed as Reed entered the shop.

An apparently bored man who appeared to be human but for his robin's egg blue skin and glowing cerulean eyes looked him up and down. Reed felt distinctly as if his clothing had somehow failed a test.

"Yes, hello." Reed straightened, drew back his shoulders, reminding himself he was a successful merchant. "Could you kindly direct me to where I might find attire for this evening's festivities?"

The man regarded the shop's ceiling as if life itself pained him. "You *do* realize you have mere hours."

"Yes, I'm aware." Reed busied himself with the sleeve of the nearest draped garment, its texture like liquid. How was such a thing possible? "My wife and I are just passing through, and she insists on attending. I would rather not spend an exorbitant amount on clothing we will wear only once, I'm sure you understand."

The man narrowed his eyes. "I'm sure I do." Beckoning Reed to follow him with a lazy wave, he sauntered further into the boutique. "All of our best festival pieces for this season have been purchased, unfortunately. But we do have a few, uh, *discounted* items just here. Riffle through them, if you must."

Reed knew what he wanted for Dulce the moment he saw it, and was surprised to discover the gown's price was well within his range. The blue man—with dramatic reluctance—helped him to match it to something for himself and explained how to wear the clothing. The ensembles required headdresses and then shoes.

As he was leaving, his pockets nearly empty of coin, the man finally smiled, his eyes glowing vividly while he waved goodbye. "I recommend fasting," he called after Reed. "And don't forget to sleep. The festival begins well before sunset and continues all through the night!"

Reed planned to wait for Dulce to return to the inn, but with the street outside devoid of any carriages and no longer any merchants shouting their sales, he soon found himself drifting off.

He woke to the sound of the key in the door—the sunlight streaming through the window turned a warm afternoon glow, highlighting Dulce's delicate features. Reed swallowed deeply when he recalled the day before, her warm body against his as she sat in his lap, how his fingers had brushed her hip.

"I got you something while I was out." He tilted his chin in the direction of the boxes on her bed.

Holding an embroidered sack he presumed was full of herbs, Dulce's eyes lit up like a child's at a fair, and she rushed to open the boxes.

"A gift?" she said, her smile bright. "For me? Really?" Pointing to the embossed symbol along the wrapping, she chirped, "Oh! From the boutique down the street, the one with the—Reed, it's exquisite! It's… What is it?"

The forest green material unraveled to the floor in gentle shimmering folds, red and gold embroidery of delicate leaves sparkling in the sunlight.

"Don't worry, the surly creature at the shop showed me how it's worn," Reed drawled, producing his ensemble. "You wrap, tuck, and fold. Simple."

Dulce's lips parted like a fish, which somehow made her still appear adorable. "Wrapping and tucking? What am I supposed to *tuck*? Yours has trousers."

Reed held up the antlers, their tips covered in gold. "Good question. I'm sure we'll figure it out."

Dulce's cheeks pinkened. "I think I'll find one of the inn's maids." She took the antlers from him and gathered up the clothing, preparing to leave the room.

"It can't be that difficult!" Reed called down the hallway after her.

Dulce muttered something that sounded suspiciously like a curse he was surprised she knew, then frowned over her shoulder at him when he laughed.

"Says the man who gets to wear clothing that's in *no* danger of unraveling!"

Closing the door, Reed changed into the trousers in question, finding them tighter than his liking, and next attempted to wrap his shirt over his torso and arms. He soon understood something of Dulce's trepidation. The fabric slipped through his fingers and seemed determined to fall from his limbs, giving no resemblance to the elegantly draped garments displayed in the shop. After three attempts, Reed gave up and called one of the inn's stewards to help him.

As the boy was finishing his task—which he made look as easy as skipping rocks along Dogwood Glen's flooded lanes—Dulce returned.

"Ah," she said, crossing her arms when the steward

left, her emerald eyes glittering with mischief beneath the headdress of antlers atop her artfully twisted blonde curls. "It wasn't difficult, I see."

Reed was speechless. Dulce looked radiant, exquisite. Breathtaking. The gown, reflecting the deep greens of the forest, fell in gentle pleats from her hips to the floor. Its golden and ruby embroidered panels hugged her torso in opulent folds, ending in a knot of fabric where part of it draped over one shoulder, leaving the other bare. Her skin was like smooth ivory in the golden light of the setting sun.

He knew he was gawking, but he couldn't stop. "You look…"

"I don't think I have ever worn such a luxuriously comfortable garment in my life," Dulce exclaimed, twirling. The fabric fluttered in graceful waves, its embroidery flashing like embers. "Even my night clothing is more restrictive. It's positively indecent!"

She appeared to notice his full attire for the first time and stilled.

"You're staring." Reed arched a brow. "Is there something on my face?" He touched his cheek and inspected his hand. "The antlers are a bit much, of course. If anyone in the Glen saw me in this getup, I'd never survive the beating I'd—"

"You look very handsome," Dulce whispered, stepping forward to take his arm. "It's what a wife would say to her husband, of course." She bit her lip. "Anyway, we have a duty to fulfill. After we eat. No use approaching greedy dukes on an empty stomach."

Reed recognized they were the plainest dressed at the night's festival the moment he and Dulce entered the Duke's gardens. But that did nothing to change the fact that, to him, Dulce was the most beautiful woman there. The festival was in full swing along every section of the tiered gardens, each tree-lined space decorated in bright lanterns, flowers, food and drink, winding its way gently downward to where the copper and ivory palace faced the glittering waters of Alder Bay.

Attire made of every element twirled around him in a kaleidoscope of colors beneath thousands of floating lanterns and drifting petals. Gowns that flowed like glittering water and sparkling ice, costumes of dancing flames, the fabric leaving sparks in their wake. Dresses decorated in leaves and blooms, garments of soft clouds, their shape changing with each movement of the wearer, rainbows and lightning reflected within their misty folds. Those present held the widest variety of creatures Reed could have never imagined in his wildest dreams.

Music filled the air, its sound coming from everywhere all at once, drums that seemed to beat within his very chest.

Tables of food lay in front of them, and Reed trailed his finger across a buttery roll before sampling every dish he encountered. He thought of home, of his brother in the Glen, and a pang of guilt passed through him at the decadent luxury surrounding him. He ventured to guess that no one present had ever gone to sleep hungry a single night of their lives.

Dulce picked up a dessert that looked like a lotus flower, covered in cocoa and hazelnuts. Reed then lifted a pastry drizzled in blueberry glaze. "Try this one." As she reached for it, he pulled it back with a grin. "Tut-tut, remember you're my wife."

She rolled her eyes before slowly parting her mouth. As Reed placed the delicacy against her tongue, his index finger brushed her velvety soft lips.

Her gaze lit up while she chewed, her stare not once wavering from his. "Another. Or no, I shouldn't be greedy." She grasped one from the table. "Your turn."

He didn't hesitate to open his mouth, thoughts of what it would be like to taste her lips filling his mind— what a delight it would be to discover the flavor of the pastry from her tongue. Her hand stilled when she glanced past his shoulder.

"Those enforcers are watching you," she said in a low voice that only he could hear. "Do you think it's possible they might recognize you?"

He peered at the enforcers, not remembering a single one. "No." He shrugged. "Not with the *marvelous* job you did with my hair."

The crowd shifted, and as the moon's silvery glow illuminated a towering tree at the center of the garden, he cursed. The bristlecone pine was much like the one at Dulce's manor in size and shape, except its bark mirrored tar with gray speckles, its leaves changed from green to spiked flowers of red and ash-deadened white.

"One of the Trees of Life is here!" Dulce's breath hitched, her eyes becoming wide, her skin growing pale with what had to be fear. Reed wanted to draw her near, promise her that the world would be all right. But who was he to promise such an impractical thing?

The music faded, and Reed turned to find the Duke had arrived. Surrounded by at least twenty enforcers, he descended the palace stairs, his arms spread wide, his attire reminding Reed of a thunderstorm at sunset, dark clouds lit by gold. He looked no more than fifty years of age beneath a crown of curled horns, and even from this distance, Reed could see something of the insatiable greed in his vile face.

"Welcome!" the Duke called theatrically, his voice carrying across the crowd. "Welcome one and all. Eat. Drink. Dance. Enjoy the night away!"

The crowd cheered, the music swelled once again, and the Duke was swallowed by the crowd to attend from a pavilion set above the largest pool in the garden. Its billowing curtains moved in the gentle breeze as a throng of revelers joined him, their silent laughter swallowed by the music.

Dulce's gaze returned to the Tree of Life, and Reed no longer felt like eating the delicacy still grasped in her hand as her eyes filled with sorrow. "It looks far worse than I ever could've imagined."

"I won't leave your side until we find an answer." Reed took the pastry from her and set it on the table before offering his hand to her. "For now, dance with me until we can get closer to the Duke?"

She smiled softly, as if she understood his intention of lifting her spirits. Understood his desire to be of some use to her, no matter how unworthy his qualifications.

Dulce placed her hand in his.

Reed rested a palm against her lower back, pulling her close as he swept her into the crowd of twirling dancers, the Duke still unreachable.

When his gaze met hers, the world disappeared in a blur. With each subtle touch of her hands along his shoulder and neck, his blood grew hotter, the reason they were at this celebration slipping away. It was only Dulce, her eyes, her warmth, her alluring lips.

Reed lost track of time as the music played, gravity itself deprived of all meaning while they continued to dance, to float, with Dulce in his arms. He forgot he was being hunted by enforcers—he forgot he had no home, nowhere to go. All there was, was this moment.

"I have something that belongs to you," Reed said when he knew he couldn't selfishly dance with her any longer. He needed to help her get answers, and so he steadied Dulce as she caught her breath. "I should have given it to you before, but…"

She looked up at him, her cheeks flushed, her smile turning quizzical.

Making certain no one else could see, he reached into his pocket for Dulce's ring and gently took her hand. He then placed it onto her middle finger, watching her expression turn to awe.

"Mother's ring," she gasped, quickly disguising the piece of jewelry's color and shape to silver and amethyst with her alchemy. "I thought it was destroyed in the fire!"

Reed shook his head. "I stole it back for you." He then leaned closer and whispered in her ear, "It was this ring's magic that brought the enforcers to my door, and that same magic brought me to you once more."

His mouth was close to hers now, and Reed swore his heart would soon tear his chest open. His fingers made their way up her back, to her neck, until they were entwined in her hair, and Dulce, instead of pulling away from him, inched closer, her eyes never leaving his. Her lips were so near that he could feel their beguiling warmth.

That was when the screaming began.

Dulce

Dulce broke away from Reed and whirled around as the screaming grew louder. Thick smoke filled the air in gusts of black, accompanied by yellow flashes of light streaking within the night, illuminating faces, their skeletons visible through their skin before their bodies collapsed to the ground.

"Don't tell me the world's ending *now*," Reed said, his eyes wide.

"I should hope not." Yet Dulce had no idea—there was nothing she'd read in her mother's book that illustrated this, whatever this horror was.

A woman near a collection of rose bushes shrieked in

pain when crimson flames shot from the smoke and caressed her flesh, leaving boils bubbling across her arm.

Dulce struggled to think of a conjuration to help dispel this nightmare, but she didn't have anything in her satchel that could combat this.

"Why is this happening?" a bald man screamed in confusion as the wind snapped like a whip around them, snuffing out the row of lanterns and overturning a table of food.

Lightning cracked, its veiny glowing web illuminating the fright across the crowd's faces. Reed grasped Dulce by the hand and drew her out of harm's way when a large branch snapped and fell from a gnarled oak.

The Duke stepped forward to stand before the ailing Tree of Life and held up his arms, a stone glowing an iridescent hue at his throat within a glass orb on a golden chain. He closed his eyes, moving his lips, and the stray magic stilled. Soon, the crowd quieted except for the sounds of heavy breathing and a few cries.

"All is well," the Duke bellowed, lowering his arms to his sides. "As you can see, I have been granted the power to protect Alder Bay."

Dulce gasped, and Reed pulled her close, his gaze full of concern. "La Bisou Morte isn't working for the Duke," she whisper-shouted at him. "The Duke works for her!" She recalled one of the passages in her mother's book about stones of pearlescent crystals and how only witches could produce them. A wearer who wasn't a witch—such as the Duke—meant they belonged to the maker.

"Does it matter who works for who?"

"Yes," she hissed. "It means the witch is much more dangerous and powerful than we thought."

Reed frowned. "And so I imagine that he most definitely will not tell us where she is."

"We don't need him to tell us." Dulce smiled. Finally, they would have a clear plan. "If we can get that necklace, we can locate the witch ourselves."

He arched a brow. "Locate her … how?"

"With the help of alchemy in my mother's book," she explained.

"Mm, so should you or I flirt with the Duke to steal it?" He smirked. "With so many enforcers lingering around his lumpish loutness, this could be challenging…"

The ground shook suddenly, the oak's roots lifting with an ear-splitting crack as the trunk smashed to the earth. A creak then stirred from a conifer as the flowers along the Tree of Life's bark moved, its gray-speckled roots slithering from the ground like tentacles. The crowd turned frantic once more. Fear stormed through Dulce at the thought that soon her mother's tree, if it hadn't already, could turn into this if she didn't find La Bisou Morte and make her undo her wretched spell.

A woman wearing lacy layers of sapphire fabric shoved into Dulce, tearing her away from Reed, and she fell to the ground hard. She gasped, trying to rise through the stampede of running guests, but there were too many. A pudgy man nearly stomped on her stomach in his clumsy panic before she was finally able to scurry back, her hands stinging with the effort, her dress unraveling, and she staggered to her feet.

Securing her gown around her, Dulce pushed through the sea of costumes, shoved helplessly along with the current of terror-struck bodies, her thoughts too jumbled to think clearly. Only one thought repeated in her mind.

Find Reed.

"Mrs. Jones Taylor!" Reed yelled off to her right, using her false name, and she sighed in relief.

Just as she opened her mouth to call for him, a callused hand grabbed Dulce's arm and yanked her backward.

"Unhand me!" she seethed, slapping blindly, and the grip on her slackened.

"You're not my wife." A middle-aged man realized, removing his arm from her, his expression dazed. "Apologies, she has hair just like yours." His eyes were frantic as he searched for his wife.

Dulce turned, a flash of golden hair near the stone bird baths catching her eye, where a woman stood alone, holding her middle, trembling in apparent fear. "Is that her?" she shouted, pointing in the woman's direction.

He didn't answer, only dodged through the fleeing throng of partygoers to reach the woman. Dulce focused on finding Reed, wishing he still had his ivory hair so he'd be easier to locate. No more wild magic erupted, but the crowd continued to depart, shaken, taking the injured along, and leaving the dead.

While the garden emptied of guests and the Tree of Life became still once more, Dulce's gaze settled on Reed, kneeling in the center of the garden near the fallen oak. And he wasn't alone.

Her heart sank as two enforcers held him up by the arms, three more standing guard proudly at his back. A bruise was already forming along one cheek.

She'd had a dreadful feeling that they'd recognized him.

One she certainly now recognized—he was the same

man who'd visited her manor to inspect her grave, the same enforcer she'd met when she'd disguised herself as her dead husband.

Dulce ducked behind a stone pillar just as Enoch barked at Reed, "Who knew I'd discover a coveted prize at the Duke's party."

"Why, thank you." Reed grinned, and Dulce stared bug-eyed. How could he remain so calm? "But that's not the first time I've been called a prize." He leaned forward, turning his head to look the man up and down slowly.

Enoch narrowed his eyes and started to kick Reed, but the other enforcer raised a hand, stopping him.

He seethed in frustration as he sputtered, "You'll answer to the Duke for your crimes, filthy swamp maggot."

The enforcers hauled Reed toward where the Duke lingered, not the least bit phased by the pandemonium of magic, the scattered dead bodies on the ground, the guests that had fled his gardens in terror, the fallen oak before him, or the Tree of Life's hysteria. In fact, he appeared positively thrilled, seeming to relish the chaos.

Not fighting back, Reed instead smirked at the Duke. "So we meet at last. The Grand Duke of Putrefied Pompousness, and the, what was it again? Oh, yes. The Coveted Prize of the Glen."

Dulce palmed her forehead, hoping Reed would keep quiet before someone ran him through with a blade. But she had to admit a part of her admired the way he didn't cower as most surely would've.

The Duke cocked his head, his crown of curled horns making him appear like a king instead of a witch's servant. Gray streaks peppered his deep auburn hair, and while

Reed was taller than the Duke, the man was much wider as his costume hugged his muscular form.

"Meet the criminal who started the fire at the prison," Enoch ground out, his hand still clamped around Reed's arm. "And stole your property."

"The fire wasn't me," Reed clarified. "One never takes credit for another man's work."

The Duke sneered, raking his icy gaze down Reed. "Why, he's nothing but a foul dog who can't stop barking."

"I take that as a compliment," Reed drawled, looking genuinely smug. "Hardly any compare to the dog in loyalty and affection."

"A sharp tongue," the Duke grunted. "I will enjoy cutting it out."

"How about a duel to make things even more entertaining?"

Be quiet, Reed. Dulce knew what he was doing—he was distracting the Duke so she could escape if she hadn't already.

Dulce's heart thundered against her ribs—she couldn't remain hiding uselessly and watch the Duke end Reed's life on this fateful night. She'd brought Reed into this, she'd been the one to give him her jewelry, then convinced him to come with her on this journey. He'd even given her back her beloved ring when he could've kept it.

And then, all at once, Dulce knew precisely what she must do.

To alter her appearance further, she didn't need a new batch of elixir, not when she'd consumed enough of the previous one for it to feed through her veins for days.

This would only take a toll on the magic thrumming inside her already, lessening its effects so her disguise would need the next batch of elixir sooner rather than later. It was a very small price to pay for saving Reed's life.

"I think we should start with removing a hand." The Duke unsheathed the sword at his waist. "See how that mouth of yours sounds with pretty screams coming out of it instead of impertinence. There's no need to inform me of which hand you use the most—we'll slice off both, as is the fitting punishment for thieving. How does that sound, yapping dog?"

Dulce slammed her eyes shut, focusing on the alchemy alight within her. She instructed her body's flesh to turn translucent, and she opened her eyes, observing as every fiber of her body became ghostly alabaster. Cuffs of vines wrapped around her wrists like bracelets that she could release as whips, and large blooms of spiky hellebores gnashed their razor-sharp teeth.

It wasn't just any ghost she chose to mirror, but the one who children and adults alike would fear, a spirit that had haunted the bedtime stories of every town near and far. Centuries ago, the story went, the ghost of the hanged widow Leski had returned from the grave to murder half of Alder Bay with her carnivorous flowers, taking all the children to her cave and feasting on them, before a witch banished her to the bottom of the sea.

Once Dulce's transformation was complete, she stepped from behind the pillar.

"Your magic called to me, Duke," Dulce cooed in a low voice, gliding her feet against the ground in his direction. She kept her gaze trained on him, showing no interest in Reed. "The magic here called to me, and I am here to answer it."

The Duke's wicked expression faltered, and he paled as his gaze fell upon her. "Who are you?"

"Don't be coy. You know my name," she purred and motioned him with a finger. "Come closer, or I'll devour all who live in your village."

The Duke did as told, inching toward her on quaking legs. Out of the corner of her eye, Enoch had released Reed, and she noticed the brute had even soiled himself.

When the Duke reached her, Dulce continued, "Speak. Say my name."

"Leski," he rasped, his shoulders tense, his demeanor more like that of a boy than a man.

"If you want to save your town, I will need a sacrifice. Just one," she crooned. "Give me that, and I will return to the depths of the sea. My flowers have gone hungry for much too long. They thirst for blood." One of her flowers drew forward and snapped its teeth near his cheek.

"Take him!" The Duke's throat bobbed as he gestured one shaking hand toward Reed, now kneeling in exaggerated fear.

"No!" Reed shouted, but when she glanced at him, Dulce discovered his eyes dancing with laughter for an instant just before he fell to theatrical sobs while the enforcers fled en masse. He clearly knew it was a farce. "Please! I'll do anything! Don't let her take me!"

"He is mine then." Dulce wrapped her fingers one by one around the Duke's neck and leaned forward. With her other hand, she reached behind him, undoing the clasp of his necklace as she whispered in his ear, "Do sleep well tonight, Duke. And remember, I know all your secrets."

The tactic was the one Reed had taught her, only now she discovered that fear worked just as well as flirtation to distract.

Dulce released the Duke, and he stumbled backward, his eyes widening. Now released from La Bisou Morte's spell, he appeared to comprehend fully the mayhem around him for the first time. He then fled through his garden toward the palace steps, taking them three at a time, his crown falling with a clank against the marble before he disappeared behind its doors.

No one remained in the garden now. Only Reed.

His gaze met hers, and he clapped his hands as he approached her with a grin. "Beautiful theatrics, *Majesty*. You put those other ghosts to shame, truly. They should take lessons from you."

"To my prison in the sea, shall we?"

14

Reed

Reed and Dulce kept themselves safely within the tree line as they circled back toward the inn, but by the time they sat to rest behind a large boulder not too far from the White Cat, it was apparent that no enforcers had followed them.

The night was almost over, signs of dawn already lightening the sky.

"Where did you get that?" Dulce asked as Reed studied the sword resting across his lap. The glow of lights from the town illuminated her terrifying features. Reed found it curious that he could still somehow see the beauty of her eyes beyond their sunken orbs, her skull illuminating beneath her ghostly white flesh, sharp teeth grinning through cracked lips. However, the cuffs of vicious flowers had faded.

"Took it from that mewling canker-blossom when he pissed himself," Reed told her. "Pretty sure he wouldn't have noticed if I'd taken every weapon he wore."

"You could've gotten yourself killed acting a fool in front of those enforcers!" Dulce hissed. "What would you have done if I couldn't have rescued you?"

"I would've figured something out." He smirked. "But I wasn't worried—I knew my knight in shining terror would save me."

"You're partially forgiven," she muttered. "But look at me. I certainly can't go back to the inn like this."

"Can't you just…"—Reed waved one hand through the air—"magic yourself back to normal?"

Dulce tilted her head, lost in thought. "No, the transformation seems to be stuck. There is the option to wait it out, or I could drink the elixir. Something which is not on my person, unfortunately."

"Are we talking minutes or hours?"

Dulce thought again. "Without sage leaves? Hours." She studied her arms with a frown, turning her hands over in the shadows. Bones still shone through deathly pale skin. "At least two, if I had to guess."

"Well, that certainly won't do…"

"When one saves the world," she sang, "one must make certain sacrifices, mustn't they?"

"Take this." Reed handed her the sword. "Though I'd love to meet the creature brave enough to face you looking like that." He rose. "I'll fetch the elixir from the inn and you'll be sleeping comfortably in your bed in no time at all.”

Letting his brown hair fall across his face, Reed turned to leave, but Dulce reached out and grasped his wrist.

“Wait,” she rushed out. Reed turned to find her eyes pleading, an expression oddly heartbreaking on such monstrous features. “I want you to send Lucas home.”

“Now?”

“Yes. While you’re at the inn, please find him and send him to the manor. He’ll protest the decision less with you. I will not break my promise to his grandfather. If exploding magic wasn’t horrendous enough, I knew this was too dangerous the instant I saw the Duke’s necklace. As long as we don’t wear the necklace, we’re safe.” Dulce peered down at the sword in her lap and murmured, “You can… You can leave as well, if you want to. My home is always welcome to you, uh, that is, at least until you can return to your brother, and you’ll be paid handsomely for the trials this venture has put you through…” She fell silent.

“Is your soliloquy quite over, Highness?”

Dulce glanced up at him, surprise almost comical on her terrifying face.

“I’m not leaving you on your own,” Reed promised, crouching before her. “What sort of man do you take me for? Do I strike you as one who would miss out on a grand adventure? Do not mistake me for that cowardly lout you married.”

“I meant no offense.” Dulce smiled softly.

“None taken.” Reed winked. “Now, wait for me here. I’ll return in less than twenty minutes.”

Reed arrived at the stables within five minutes, the sight of a man in costume running being nothing unusual on this festival night. The town's main avenue was still overflowing with a wide variety of creatures, injured and otherwise, each frantic to reach the safety of their homes, the panic ignited at the Duke's party not yet subsided. Reed still couldn't believe everything he'd learned about the magic of alchemy since meeting Dulce, but he was becoming accustomed to it much quicker than expected.

He found Lucas sitting on a stool outside Toffee's stall, nursing a singed arm, his legs outstretched, his boots unlaced. His ridiculous costume of red and purple velvet and lace was a burned and tattered mess. When his gaze settled on Reed, his face lit up with a wide smile.

"Did you see that, Reed?" he whisper-shouted. "Me and the other grooms snuck into the Duke's party just in time to see the entire place go absolutely fobbing full-gorged mad! Magic *exploding* all about, everything destroyed. One woman got her costume singed off, and I offered her my cape. It was a thing to behold, I tell you, the embroidery of a giant stag just—" He made a sound very like an explosion. "And I saw a man covered in spotted fur get a leg ripped clear off! Shame about all that food though…"

"What happened to your arm?"

"Oh, this?" Lucas shrugged. "A lantern fell on me— it's nothing."

Dulce would certainly not find that to be nothing.

"How much do you think you can get for the

carriage?" Reed asked, jerking a chin toward the vehicle in question.

Lucas stilled, narrowing his eyes. "Why?"

"Because you go home on the next caravan to Moonglade now."

"What?" Lucas stood, indignant. "It wasn't me who sent the enforcers to your room, if that's what you're thinking. You gotta believe me, Reed. They swarmed the whole place, searching for visitors from out of town, looking for a young couple, a woman with golden hair accompanied by a man with brown hair. They know you're with a *witch*. They must've seen the two of you together at the festival. By the time I went to retrieve Dulce's things, it was too late. There were at least five of those spongy louts already there, riffling through everything, and another two guarding the entrance."

If they knew he was with a witch, then it wouldn't take long for the Duke to figure out Dulce altered her looks to pretend to be Leski.

"You're still going home," Reed pointed out. "Sell the carriage for passage. We won't be needing it."

There was no way to return to their room at the inn. Even if he could get in through a window, Reed was sure their belongings would be gone by now. Dulce hadn't left everything she needed in one place, so there could be something of use in the carriage. They didn't have that much time to waste.

Crossing the stables to the alleyway, Reed reached beneath the carriage passenger seat to retrieve Dulce's second bag of alchemist supplies, hoping there was some of the elixir to disguise them within. Next, he placed Toffee's bridle over the sleepy Clydesdale's head and led the horse from the stall, ignoring Lucas's glare as he passed the boy.

"What should I tell Grandfather and Vesta?" he called.

"Tell them we know where to find La Bisou Morte," Reed said, halting. "Tell them not to worry, that Dulce has a plan. That this will all be over soon. Tell them whatever you want to help them sleep in peace at night."

"Is any of that the truth?"

"Of course!" He slapped the lad on the shoulder. "Safe travels, Lucas. I envy the meals you will soon enjoy."

By midday, Reed and Dulce came across an empty and dilapidated cottage in the forest beyond Lake Elara, and while Toffee grazed, he built a fire and Dulce read her spell book. An extra elixir hadn't been in the satchel he'd taken from the carriage, but at least she'd returned to herself from the vision of terror that she was. Unfortunately, his brown hair had also returned to white shortly after.

Dulce needed to get the location spell right soon or their travels might end up in failure. Reed watched her in the firelight as she pored over her book, her dark hair falling across her forehead in shimmering waves, her lips slightly pursed in concentration. Her skin perfect and smooth.

To think he'd almost kissed her at the Duke's party. His heart pounded at the memory.

Dulce's eyes met his, and Reed's blood turned hot. He rolled his shirt sleeve to his elbow before poking at the fire, avoiding her gaze.

"It's not the location spell, but I've found something quite useful." She slammed the book closed with a triumphant smile and jumped to her feet. "Stand here."

"What?"

"We can't travel in this clothing, can we?" Dulce asked impatiently and flicked her wrist in the air, her ring returned to its ruby and gold coloring. "For one thing, the cold is becoming unbearable. But fear not! Mother's book has just the thing. Stand here, and don't move…"

"What happens if I *move*?" Reed arched a brow, suddenly imagining green silk stitched into his skin. "I can remove it, cover myself in one of those moth-eaten blankets over the—"

A pretty blush crept up Dulce's neck and flooded her cheeks. "That won't be necessary." She blinked fast. "It's perfectly safe—I can … almost assure you."

Before he could protest further, she'd thrown some sort of powder at him and Reed coughed, the scent of it not unpleasant, like oranges and pine. When he studied himself, he magically wore much more suitable clothing. A long dark overcoat made of woven materials in wool covered a sturdy shirt and trousers, his feet encased in fur-lined boots. He noticed the blanket in question had disappeared from the rotting chair, as well as the animal head along the wall.

"Thank you," he said, and she bowed with a flourish. "I'll see to the fire while you…"

Dulce ducked into the next room, taking with her the remaining blankets, and when she returned, she wore similar clothing to his own, only layers of onyx skirts flowed from her much shorter overcoat. Lifting them, she raised a foot and presented Reed with a high black boot, fur peeking out of its top.

"If all goes well"—she laughed—"perhaps I'll open my very own boutique."

For the next few hours, Reed searched the surrounding forest for food and water while Dulce worked on the location spell that would direct them to La Bisou Morte. He found very little to eat, some clover and nettle, several bushes of wild raspberry, and a few handfuls of sorrel. A stream of icy water ran through a field of black poppies, and Reed gathered all he could in the canteen made of what he guessed to be the dried bladder of a cow.

Dulce's spell required fresh vervain, bay laurel, and rosemary, which he found easily, grateful that he succeeded in that at least, even if they traveled hungry as he stuffed his many pockets, making his way back to the cottage.

The fire roaring, Dulce raised the Duke's necklace. "I'm ready to perform the location spell." Soon the cottage filled with acrid smoke that curled in unnatural shapes, and, a flash of blue extinguished the fire before she opened her eyes.

"We must travel north," Dulce exclaimed. "The edge of Silver Birch Straits is where we will find the witch."

"You're becoming quite the fortune teller." Reed produced the map that Dulce had given him to study while she'd worked on the spell. "We must traverse something called the Forest of One Thousand Sorrows. How bad can that be, right?"

Dulce ate a raspberry. "That's to be determined."

They slept sheltered from the elements along the cottage's dusty cots and began their journey at dawn, taking turns riding the horse, saving their energy where they could. Around midday, they found more berries, and even a walnut tree, which they feasted on like ravenous squirrels, stuffing their pockets with as much as they could before continuing. When night fell, they rested sheltered between a boulder and a group of holly bushes, Toffee bound to a nearby tree. The darkness was soon filled with the sound of wailing, and as the wind picked up, Reed realized where the forest got its name.

Three days they spent crossing the forest, exhaustion sapping their energy, and he wished Dulce had a spell for that too. She lay secured in Reed's arms while she dozed in and out of sleep, and as he once again felt her against him, he was reminded of the gambling room when his heart had raced, and it took every ounce of self-control to remain a true gentleman.

"We're getting closer," she murmured.

On the morning of the fourth day, Reed slowly came to realize that the plant life surrounding them, once diverse with chaotic variety, had become made up of only one thing.

Birch trees.

Only their leaves, instead of a cheerful bright green, were bleached white. Endless rows of sticklike trunks obscured his vision on all sides, the scabs along their silvery expanse like dark mazes that tricked the eye.

"Dulce," he whispered, jostling her shoulder gently as Toffee broke into a trot. "I think we've reached Silver Birch Straits. I think we're almost there—"

"The witch's castle," Dulce breathed, peering just ahead. "Why, it's breathtaking."

His mouth formed a tight line as he followed her gaze. "By the looks of it, I'm certain she has *quite* the collection of ghosts there."

They broke through the forest, setting their sights on the castle of ebony stone beyond a sweeping field of grass, its twisted spires covered in vines. Toffee, distracted by the grass, hardly seemed to notice when her passengers alighted, and they left her just outside the castle gates to feed.

A bristlecone pine—a third Tree of Life—took up the wide courtyard. This one in an even more dreadful state than the last. At first glance, it seemed to be covered in ashes, but as Dulce approached it, she released a shaky breath. "It's stone." Cold inanimate rock slowly taking over the tree's bark, veins of marble winding along its branches. It was still somehow beautiful, but its beauty was catastrophic. Soon, it would be devoid of all life.

"It's eerily empty here…" she whispered.

No signs of occupancy halted their progress in the fading light as they entered the castle doors, which strangely stood open.

La Bisou Morte's home felt devoid of life, filled only with the stillness of misuse, and a thick layer of dust covering every surface. The silence was complete, as if the walls themselves held their breath, and it was clear that the witch had left this place long ago.

Dulce

"The witch isn't here." Dulce sighed and drew the Duke's necklace from her pocket.

Why had the stone led them to this place if La Bisou Morte was no longer at the castle? The spell was meant to locate the object's maker herself, not only a place she'd once been. The witch had clearly tampered with the Tree of Life here at some point, and she held back her fright, her anger, her sadness, not wanting her emotions to wear her down when she needed to focus on her strength to continue.

Perhaps the inside of the castle was a mirage, a spell cast upon its dark walls to make it appear empty, a way for intruders to believe they were alone, that dust and vines didn't cover every inch of the grand entryway.

Dulce tucked the necklace back into her pocket, then fished out a basil leaf from her satchel and placed it against her tongue. As she chewed, its sweet and savory flavor collecting in her mouth, she circled her hands around her eye, peering through the hole she created.

"You have quite the imaginary telescope there," Reed interjected while Dulce attempted to concentrate on the words from an old spell she'd learned on her tenth birthday when her mother had disguised a butterfly as a snake.

"An incredibly big one," she whispered. "Now hush for a moment."

Nothing within the castle changed as they searched its halls. Animals, still as statues, lined what must've been a sitting room. Two gray chairs and a glass table rested in the center of the room atop a bear hide. Crimson and black wallpaper covered the walls, along with every animal one could ever imagine. Some animals were only heads hung up, others remained intact, the full bodies of a giraffe and stag stood beside the chairs. Birds dangled from golden chains as though they were flying. Onyx benches were pressed against the walls, obscured by more animals, some in ivory cages.

"Everything is as you see it," Dulce continued, lowering her hands to her sides.

"Quite the warm welcome we're receiving here," Reed drawled. "Although, I do feel there are far too many eyes on us. It's like they can all still *see*."

"The eyes are generally not real in taxidermy." Dulce tapped her chin. "Although, these might not be taxidermy at all. Perhaps La Bisou Morte froze the animals in this state."

She pressed a finger to an opossum's eye, finding it to be glass, and grinned as Reed pursed his lips. "You're in luck. They're dead."

"Joyous news," he said sarcastically. "As long as we don't meet the same fate by lingering here, though."

Dulce nodded. "It's unsettling, to say the least. But while we're here, let's search for something that I can add to the location spell to divert it from here. I know I performed it correctly—however, the witch's magic is still strong here. It could've easily confused the stone."

"Onward with the search then." Reed extended his arm to her. "Upstairs, shall we? I may not be able to fight magic, but I'll guard your life with my fists if someone slips out of the shadows."

Dulce smiled, taking his arm. "That's a fair trade."

She quickly cast her gaze away from Reed's deep brown eyes as she thought about how they'd almost shared a kiss at the Duke's party. Since then, they'd been alone day after day, even her sleeping in his arms for comfort and warmth, but it seemed the moment had passed. They'd spent the hours traveling, and when they stopped to rest, they were too hungry and tired, spending their time eating what they could and sleeping or reading her mother's book.

"Must be nice to possess so much wealth—you leave a whole castle unlocked and falling into decay. Look at all this stuff, must've cost a fortune." Reed cast his gaze toward a painting of crows pecking the meat from a stag when they reached the top of the staircase.

"She was either in a rush to leave and hasn't been able

to return, or she left all this purposefully. But why?"

Except for the strange paintings and the questionable taxidermy down every hallway, the castle was quite exquisite. There were twenty large rooms on the second floor. They discovered one of them to be dedicated to taxidermy, where they found some of the answers to how La Bisou Morte acquired such pieces—she created them herself. Stacks of animal hides took up another room, followed by a painting area, and the grandest room of all, which Dulce assumed was the witch's own bedchamber.

A thick layer of dust enveloped everything, vines recovering the dark stone at every possible opening. Positively haunting. Why had the witch left this place? And why had no one else claimed it?

Dulce inspected La Bisou Morte's private suite. A majestic bed of carved ebony stood on a platform in the center of the room, its many pillows and quilts of fine quality, even under a layer of dust. She wondered if Cornelius had ever visited the witch's bed outside of Moonglade. It wouldn't come as a surprise if the fawning louse had, with all the secrets he'd kept.

Reed went straight toward the desk, leaving with nothing but blank paper, a quill, and ink. Dulce patted the floors, rummaged through the wardrobe, and drew out a white leather dress. She attempted to locate the witch by touching a piece of fabric, something that had belonged to her.

It was as though Dulce had hit a wall when she repeated the spell, her incantation low and steady. A failed attempt.

"We have more rooms to search downstairs," Reed said when he must've noticed her frown. "But for the moment, how about you rest on this luxurious bed? After nights in the woods, this would be superb.”

As he leaned over the mattress, Dulce caught a ripple like water within the silken blankets. A dark presence sewed its way through her chest, making her eyes flutter, attempting to lure her to the bed.

“Don’t!” she shouted and yanked him back, but her foot caught on the edge of a wolf hide rug, and they went tumbling toward the floor. Reed twisted to prevent himself from falling on her, and she landed instead on top of him. Dulce’s breath caught, and she could feel every hard plane of him pressing against her softest parts. She didn’t move, and neither did he.

“Or we can rest down here.” He chuckled. “But I warn you there were more spiders and beetles in the woods than there would be in that bed.”

“The bed is *rippling*!” Dulce whisper-shouted when she finally remembered what words were. “I would venture to guess it would swallow anyone who lies on it! Murder you, or send you to somewhere torturous.”

“La Bisou Morte must be fobbing mad to be that attached to a bed she discarded.”

“No, I don’t think it’s hers.” Dulce closed her eyes. “This doesn’t feel like witch magic as everything else here has, though I don’t know what it is precisely…”

“Another unpleasant mystery.” He tucked a lock of hair behind her ear. “You’re still sitting on me.”

“Oh! Sorry!” Dulce scrambled off him as though he’d scalded her. She’d gotten married less than a fortnight ago, and already she had begun to think of Reed in a way she had never thought of her dead husband. It was the strenuous journey was all—must be…

But the memory of Vesta's fortune for Dulce drifted into her thoughts once more. A most unfortunate and muddy circumstance had certainly led to her meeting Reed. Though as the days passed, Dulce was more and more certain that having him by her side was the farthest thing from unfortunate.

They left the room and descended the stairs to find that every single animal head was turned in their direction. Dulce's breath caught, her throat dry as she swallowed deeply.

"I think it's time for a little fresh air before we finish searching," Reed suggested, his jaw clenched.

Something wasn't quite right here in the least. "Lovely idea."

The castle doors, which they had left open, were now closed. Her heart pounded so hard she expected it to break free from her chest.

Approaching them with exaggerated calm, Reed and then Dulce tried to open one, but the doors remained sealed.

He surveyed the room, trying a window, to no avail. "A spell, I assume?"

Creaks echoed and Dulce whirled around to find that two taxidermy horses blocked the staircase.

A low growl reverberated from the corner where a deceased leopard lingered, slinking a step closer. Dulce and Reed could handle the rabbits, the birds, or the small critters, provided they didn't all attack at once, but the larger animals...

Reed unsheathed the sword at his hip, only it turned to ash, falling in a cloud of dusty gray to the floor before he could wield it.

"Come on!" he shouted, grasping Dulce by the hand and tugging her down the hall. "There's bound to be a room we can hide in to think!"

As though her mother were bestowing her a gift from somewhere otherworldly, another old spell she'd learned came to her. It had to be performed within an enclosed space where wind wouldn't stir. She ripped a white baneberry from her pouch, then a strand of hair from her head, and spoke the incantation, the one her mother had taught her to win against Vesta in marbles.

Everyone froze, including Reed. Speaking two magical words within her mind—*solanum dulcamara*—she touched his hand, freeing him.

Reed jolted forward, his chest heaving. "That felt … very strange, Highness. I would be much obliged if you never do that again."

Inches from his ankle, a snake sat reared to strike, unmoving, its mouth opened wide, exposing poisonous fangs.

"On second thought, much obliged." Reed chuckled, though fear shone in his eyes, fear matching Dulce's own because she knew they didn't have much time.

"This spell won't hold them long." She fled toward a dark brown door near the end of the hallway just past a dining room, Reed's hand in hers. "Let's hope that's the cellar with a way out of this cursed place."

As the door closed behind them, its bolt driven securely into place, dire growls and groaning pierced the air. Dulce trailed Reed down a shadowy narrow staircase, and when bodies suddenly slammed into the door, she jerked.

"At least we're safe." She sighed, her heart slowing a

fraction.

"A more polite word for *trapped*."

"Or that."

"But alive." He glanced back over his shoulder at her with a wink.

Yet for how long? If they didn't die within this castle's walls, then they would surely perish away with the remainder of the land if they didn't stop La Bisou Morte. Dulce didn't understand why anyone would do this. Once the world was nothing but darkness, where would the witch go? Wouldn't she die too?

They reached the bottom of the cellar, lighting candles by the dim light of a window barely large enough for a person to fit through. A spark of hope ignited in Dulce's chest. The place must've been a spell room once. Flowers rested withered in their vases, a cauldron hung in a corner, unfilled. A shelf where books might've once lingered stood without a single tome, abandoned cobwebs its only decoration now. Jars lined another, mostly empty or broken. Dulce could use some of the dried herbs for spells, but she didn't think any would help them escape the castle.

Reed opened the window. "Seems we have our escape route, if we want it."

Night was falling beyond the castle as a wolf howled in the distance. Dulce worried for Toffee, left outside to graze, knowing she would have fled by now.

"We might as well stay the night down here," Dulce decided. "Perhaps this room holds something the witch valued enough that it will lead us to her."

"We could go back to our original plan and question the Duke directly if we have nothing else to go on," Reed suggested.

"You would risk that?"

"Only for you."

Her heart raced at Reed's admission. However, with the elixir gone, she couldn't disguise herself to frighten the bastard into telling her anything. Not to mention it would take days to return to Alder Bay. It was time they didn't have to waste, especially provided that the Duke had worn the necklace and wouldn't know anything that La Bisou Morte didn't want him to know—he was one of her puppets, after all. No amount of money or bargains could get him to reveal any answers in that case.

"If I can modify the location spell soon, we can find the witch," Dulce finally said.

"And once we do?" Reed was watching Dulce carefully now. "I try not to pry, Majesty, but curiosity is getting the better of me, I must admit."

"Once we find her." Dulce bit the inside of her cheek, a pit forming in her stomach. "If she doesn't strip away the curse she cast, I will have to end her life with this. It wasn't easy to make, and it will only work on the most powerful of witches. That is, if I made it right. I followed the instructions in my mother's spell book back at the manor." She held up a vial of a dark purple liquid swirling within the glass.

"One thing at a time." Sympathy shone in Reed's eyes, and he took her hand, leading Dulce to the dusty sofa. "For now, let's eat the fine meal you have in your pocket." He smirked.

"Fine meal, indeed." She reached inside her overcoat pocket and fished out several nuts and berries. "Here you go, good sir."

Reed chuckled and sat beside her, opening the canteen of water and offering it to her.

"So, since you're quite the powerful witch yourself, can you turn one berry into a whole jar of jam?"

"If only." She tried to smile but failed. "I'm sorry things have gone much worse than I'd expected. I'm sure a more experienced witch could have…" Her mother could have.

"Hey, we found a way out of there—it's not all bad." He grasped her face, and Dulce leaned toward him, wanting desperately to close the distance between them, to think of anything other than her failure, when a deep croak came from the other side of the room, and she leapt to her feet.

Reed darted toward a cabinet hanging on the wall beside one of the shelves. As he opened the door, a raven burst out, the music of its deep gurgling croak filling the room.

Dulce gasped as Reed cursed and leapt back. "I would ask how it managed to remain alive all this time," he grunted as he grabbed a broom in the corner and lifted it, "but nothing about this place makes sense."

"Fair warning," the raven trilled. "My master doesn't take kindly to snooping thieves."

Her eyes widened. *It speaks.* "Do you know where she is?"

"If my master is what you seek, prepare to meet doom and defeat."

"You do realize your master has abandoned you," Reed pointed out, the broom in his grasp still raised, prepared to swing. "For quite a while, by the looks of it."

"My master would do no such thing."

"She's your new master now." Reed motioned toward Dulce.

What a clever notion, something she hadn't thought to try. "This is *true*," Dulce lied and held up the Duke's necklace. "Your master gave this to me so you would understand she wished you to follow our orders now."

The raven tilted its head, regarding her with one beady eye, then after a long moment, it at last bowed. "Master."

"Would you happen to know how to pacify the animals upstairs?" Reed asked, lowering the broom.

"Certainly. Is that a request?"

"Yes," Reed demanded.

The raven nodded and flew not out the open window but through the wall with an ear-piercing shriek.

Reed

Reed waited beside Dulce at the top of the cellar stairs, her ear pressed to the door. He was prepared to rush her down the steps and out the window if need be.

Growls and other wild animal sounds died until sustained and complete silence filtered through the door.

"It's safe, Master," the raven croaked as it flew through the door just above their heads this time.

It wasn't the most *peculiar* thing he'd seen thus far.

Reed wasn't certain if he trusted the, possibly immortal, bird, yet Dulce seemed to as she nodded to him.

With a heavy sigh, he reached to remove the bolt and

pushed the door slowly open. Before he could crane his neck forward, she passed him in a rush, and he drew her back to his chest.

"What are you doing?" Reed hissed in her ear.

"We heard the animals wander off."

"If growing up in the Glen taught me one thing, it's that you can't trust mere words. Especially a *talking* raven."

"You trusted me rather quickly," she indicated.

"It was your actions which earned that trust, Highness." Reed noticed his arm remained draped around Dulce's waist, and her addictive lily smell caressed his senses. Though his lips yearned to brush against hers, he wouldn't put her life at risk for a kiss. Reluctantly, he removed his arm from her delicate body, and she gingerly turned to face him—he could've sworn she was just as affected by their closeness as he.

"First things first," Dulce said, her voice breathy when she retrieved a torch from the wall and lit it with an accompanying flint and steel.

"Food?" Reed smirked.

"Food," Dulce agreed. "Every castle in existence is equipped with massive food storage, if I'm not mistaken."

"If there's any that hasn't rotted by now," Reed pointed out.

"I will not accept pessimism in my company," Dulce teased.

He placed a hand beside her head against the wall. "What do you accept?"

Dulce looked up at him, her golden-brown eyes wide, her lips parted, mere inches from his, banishing all thought but her from his mind. "Are you trying to get *burned?* You're standing a bit too close to my torch, Mr. Hawthorne." She smiled, and it illuminated her beautiful face, tempting him to close the distance between them.

"To be close to you, I'd gladly risk a few burns." He backed away from her with a grin.

"Well, then. That is risky indeed." Dulce's cheeks pinkened, and she walked at a brisk pace just ahead of him as if she didn't want him to see how affected she was.

Once they entered the main hall, Reed grew uneasy when they came face-to-face with the glassy-eyed animals, but they stood as before, disturbances in the dust around them the only indication they had moved at all.

As Reed and Dulce ventured down another hallway, he watched the taxidermy over his shoulder until they vanished from his sight. He stayed close to Dulce while they descended a dark marble staircase.

Vaulted ceilings in elaborate stonework of black and gray framed a kitchen the size of ten houses in the Glen. Chopped wood piled in every corner next to not one, but five fireplaces large enough for a man to stand in, dozens of steel rods to roast meats stacked at their sides. Worn wooden tables took up the center of the room, where a meal had been being prepared when its cooks must've left it. Beneath hanging pots and pans sat half-sliced slabs of rotting meat, vegetables unrecognizable below a layer of mold, and dough long since dried and covered in dust. More pots hung over ashes, their insides burned to charcoal. A rotted hog remained along a spit, and Reed grimaced.

"I hope you don't mean for us to eat *that*, Highness," he stated.

"Certainly not the feast I would welcome us with."

Dulce bit her lip and peered around the large space. "A-ha!" She grasped his arm and pulled him behind her through a half-hidden door, then down another staircase. She lit torches along a stone wall as she led them farther underground into a labyrinth of storage rooms, each colder than the next.

They discovered provisions kept fresh and crisp in fermenting vinegar and grape leaves—rows upon rows of pickled cabbage, turnips, carrots, peas, and even eggs, dyed pink in beet juice, lined the walls in glass jars. There were smoked meats and plums preserved in honey. Barrels of salt held citrus, fish, and meats of all kinds. There was even a cheese room, which smelled more fragrant than Reed cared to experience.

In one chamber, drying herbs hung from rafters, dill, garlic, and mustard chief amongst them, waiting to add flavor to the pickling jars.

Beyond a root cellar, they stumbled upon a wheat silo, the grain sealed in clay pots, kept safe from rodents.

"Please, *please* tell me you know how to make bread," Reed practically begged, his stomach growling. The meals he knew how to prepare were hardtack that lasted months and pitiful stews made of whatever meat and vegetables happened to be the cheapest at the market, when there was time to prepare anything at all. Most ingredients were too much for them to afford, so Reed usually worked at whichever tavern needed help in exchange for a meal.

"It won't be as fine as Vesta's," Dulce told him, her smile radiant with excitement at their find. "But I'm confident I've assisted her enough times that it should be edible." She pried open a pot of millet and inhaled. "They'd know the coming winter would be particularly harsh if the mice began to steal more than their usual share before the first frost, isn't that clever?"

"How do you know all this?" He found himself admiring how knowledgeable she was in different situations.

"Vesta's books. I didn't have many friends my age as a child. Or an adult. Besides my family, I mainly made friends with the moths, spiders, and beetles in our gardens," Dulce admitted with a shrug.

"Moths and spiders are more trustworthy than a lot of the people I've come across, so consider yourself lucky."

"At least I have a friend now." She grinned.

He tugged a lock of her hair. "A friend that won't let you down."

Dulce's expression didn't waver, even as she focused her attention onto the task at hand. "Look, see that shaft there? It's one of many that runs from the deepest cellar to the castle's highest tower, where the wind outside pulls air upward to create what's known as pressure differential ventilation. Genius, don't you think?"

"Yes, genius indeed." Reed couldn't stop smiling as he watched her.

Dulce collected food, stacking jars of honeyed fruit and sacks of wheat into his arms, and the two of them hauled provisions up the narrow stairways and into the kitchen, following the chalk-marks on the wall, left most likely by the previous cooks so they would never get lost.

Reed busied himself with starting the fires and clearing off the counters, using water from the kitchen's very own well to scrub them, while Dulce readied the ingredients, dusting the ceramic bowls and copper pans she would need.

The counters cleaned and the fires blazing, Reed drank his first proper glass of water in days, ate a honeyed plum, and fell back to studying Dulce. She hummed softly to herself, frowning in concentration as she kneaded dough. He caught her staring at him when she crossed the kitchen, and her cheeks pinkened once more while she returned to adding cinnamon, nuts, and fruit to the mix before fashioning it into a twisted braid, glazed in honey, then placing it into the oven.

Next, she melted sugar in a pan, letting the bubbling liquid cool as she retrieved slabs of meat and fish from a bowl of salt, sniffing tentatively at it.

"Dare we risk it?" she asked, peering mischievously at Reed from behind the haddock she held up.

"If you'd seen what happened after they served bad quail at Dankworth's," Reed told her around a pickled egg, "you wouldn't ask that."

Dulce dropped the fish back into the salt, her pout so adorable it took every ounce of Reed's self-control not to bring her face to his and kiss her.

Soon, the aroma of baking bread filled the kitchen, and by the time they had constructed the sugar into candy around fruit and nuts that would travel easily, Dulce declared the bread ready to eat.

Reed had never tasted anything so delicious in his life. He'd never had a meal so satisfying, though it was admittedly a strange mix. *Perhaps half starving is the answer to appreciating food*, he thought with a laugh.

With his stomach blessedly full, sleep pulled at him, the exhaustion of travel and the unwanted excitement of almost being killed by possessed animals taking its toll at last.

Dulce encased yet more food in sugar while Reed made two sheets of hardtack from flour, water, and salt, rolling out the tough dough, poking holes in it to ensure it baked evenly. Finally, he cut the crackers into squares once they had baked—they would be dry enough to last through next winter.

She placed her hands on her hips and nodded in approval at their loot. "Come morning, I think we should have enough sustenance to travel for days."

Reed hoped she'd thought of some magical solution to their witch-finding predicament when he asked, "How will we know where to go next?"

"Oh, I'm confident the raven can help us," Dulce answered. "It would be impossible for such a creature not to have *some* connection to the witch herself, her magic is melded to its entire being, after all."

"You don't plan to…" Reed arched a brow, running a thumb across his throat. He wouldn't fault her if that were the case, however.

"Of course not!" Dulce exclaimed with indignation. "The spell should be quite harmless. A little marjoram, some holly, and a touch of rosemary never hurt anyone."

Reed yawned. "No time like the present, yes?"

They found that the raven had returned to the witch's cabinet in the cellar, and the bird hardly seemed to notice when Dulce walked right up to it and threw a cloud of fine powder over its form. The raven simply blinked at her and slept, allowing itself to be lifted onto the velvet-covered table.

"Now comes the tricky part," she whispered, shooing Reed onto the sofa and instructing him to remain silent with a finger over her lips. She ground something in a mortar and pestle, murmuring words he couldn't understand all the while. Placing the ground concoction under her tongue, she rested her fingers on the raven's feathered back and closed her eyes.

Candlelight flickered across her features, and Reed held his breath as he watched, flinching when the bird's foot twitched.

"Beyond Nightmore Forest, La Bisou Morte resides at the northeasterly edge of the Crowmare Sea, where a fortress lingers and the sky is painted in blood." Dulce opened her eyes, triumphant.

"Blood sounds *promising*," Reed drawled. "I'll give you my Admit One ticket right now to go," he added with exaggerated cheer.

Dulce, whose eyes were clouded with worry, broke into laughter that spilled through the room, waking the raven as she shook her head at him.

She removed the folded map from inside her spell book and spread it across the table, then trailed a finger over it. "We need to cross the Rust Fields to reach Nightmore Forest."

"Before we begin that marvelous journey, and before we sleep, I have a surprise for you."

Dulce studied him with interest. "What is it?"

"Wait here, and I'll return shortly." He winked.

Reed ignored his exhaustion as he heated water in the kitchen and filled two of the castle's wide copper tubs, the thought of a hot bath and clean clothing motivation enough for him.

He fetched Dulce, who was flipping through her spell book, and led her to the first bathing chamber upstairs.

"You did this?" she beamed. "I could've helped you!"

"Without your knowledge, all we would've had is pitiful hardtack."

She grasped his hand and gave it a gentle squeeze. "Thank you."

Once she slipped into the bathing chamber, he flexed his hand, wanting nothing but to trail his fingers across her delicate skin.

Night was half over by the time they were finally able to retire. Standing outside the castle's first bedchamber, they paused, and Reed placed a hand on her arm as they looked at one another. They came to the silent agreement that neither of them wanted to sleep in that place alone. Reed found that, ghosts, taxidermy animals, and a witch's death bed aside, he had grown quite accustomed to having Dulce's company while he slept. And he would be damned if he let her sleep alone in a place where anything might harm her.

New clothing magically fashioned for them after their baths, sacks of provisions and full canteens ready for their journey, they dusted off the quilts and slipped beneath them, a fire blazing in the wide hearth as the wind howled outside.

Dulce's presence in the bed beside him kept his heart hammering until he finally found sleep.

The first light of dawn crept through the row of narrow windows beyond the bed's gray and black curtains, and Reed knew instantly that something was wrong. The castle's silence, which he had thought to be complete before, was now so absolute that it was almost deafening.

As he drew back the covers and sat forward, he stilled. On the floor between the beds lay the witch's raven, dead atop a pool of blood, its eyes burnt-out cavities.

"Dulce." Reed leapt from the bed and touched her shoulder, his voice a shout in the silence. "We have to leave. Now."

17

Dulce

$\mathcal{A}$s Reed spoke, Dulce couldn't make out what he was telling her, her focus trained on the dead animal on the floor before her. She studied its broken feathered body, the crimson blood pooled around it. The raven hadn't been a living taxidermy thing like the rest. Under some magic spell, it had survived years inside a cabinet in the castle cellar. Had La Bisou Morte returned home and slaughtered the bird for helping her and Reed?

Dulce knew that wasn't the case as soon as lightning cracked outside, thunder booming. She hurled herself across the room and thrust open the balcony doors, a heavy gust of wind nearly knocking her backward.

Emerald sparks flashed within a light purple mist cloaking the gardens and forest.

Reed circled his arm around her waist and pulled her to him. The roots mimicked the movements of the last dying tree, which lifted like tentacles from the ground. Only this time, the Tree of Life slammed them along the earth, rattling the castle.

The bristlecone pine screamed in agony, piercing Dulce's ears as she gritted her teeth against the harsh sound.

"We can't stay here," Reed rasped, tugging her back into the bedchamber.

"We can't leave yet," Dulce breathed. "At the Duke's party, he stopped the tree's wild magic with this stone." She held up the necklace. "Perhaps I can do the same now without putting it on. The Trees of Life are linked to my mother's, and the sooner they turn to stone, the sooner the world ends."

Reed's jaw tightened as though he wanted to argue, yet he relented with a nod. "As long as you don't get yourself killed."

"Have I made such an impact that you would miss me?" she cooed.

"I think you know the answer to that, Highness."

Dulce tore her gaze from his and plucked up a silk blanket, then wrapped it around the bird's frail body, cradling the fragile creature close.

She finally passed the raven to Reed. "Once I finish with the tree, we can bury the raven. It's the least we can do after the creature helped us."

"If I have to dig a hole with my bare hands for you, I will," Reed promised.

As they rushed down the stairs, the castle continued to shake. Nearly reaching the bottom of the steps, Dulce's breath caught, and her chest tightened.

No longer did taxidermy animals stand across the sitting room—instead, they rested on the floor in awkward heaps, their black sockets empty of the glass orbs that now lay in front of them.

"But do please hurry so we can get out of this nightmare," Reed groaned.

Dulce took out the book from her satchel and flipped between a couple of spells she had in mind to try. She would combine them—she was almost certain what to do. A spell to help flowers bloom and another to rid someone of a fever. While the tree was a plant, there was a possibility that mixing it with what would be considered giving life might slow its death.

Together, they stepped out the now-unlocked castle door, and another heavy breeze rustled her hair.

"Wait here," she told Reed.

He looked as if the very thought of leaving her alone was utter madness, but he didn't stop her. "Remember. Don't die."

"If something doesn't go as planned, save yourself." She then walked through the light mist toward the Tree of Life, thankful it wasn't the poisoned fog spoken of in her mother's letter.

If Toffee hadn't already disappeared, she certainly would've after this. No carcass lay on the ground, which was a good sign that the horse was on her way back to Moonglade.

Dulce clutched the orb encasing the stone, the way the Duke had, as she approached the bristlecone pine.

The tree's shrill cries became louder, its roots snapping the earth harder. Just as a root lifted above her, moments away from crushing her, she hurriedly spoke the incantation.

The tree stilled, the root frozen, listening to her long and lyrical words. She approached the wide trunk and pressed her other hand to its unnatural stone bark.

Taking a deep breath, Dulce chanted louder, letting the magic weave within her and pour into the Tree of Life. She watched as the roots slowly lowered and sank back into the ground. The tree's stone didn't improve—however, the wild magic had ceased, and the world was quiet once more.

When she peered up, Dulce noticed along one of its branches, pearlescent flowers bloomed, and she took that as a sure sign she'd given the tree a little more time.

The fog hadn't dissipated, and she couldn't see Reed through its thick layer, so, clutching her skirts, she rushed through it until she found him waiting in the spot she'd left him.

"You survived." He grinned, his tense shoulders relaxing.

"You doubted my talents?" She beamed.

"Never."

Before burying the raven, Dulce took two of its feathers and placed them into her satchel for a future incantation. They then buried the raven near a sunflower bed in the castle's courtyard, Dulce saying a few words of gratitude. A wave of melancholy washed over her at the thought of the poor creature's life, wondering if it had ever known a moment of freedom.

Once Reed dropped the last handful of dirt on the

grave, he rubbed his chin. "Travel is going to be hard without Toffee. Do you think you can revive one of the taxidermy stallions?"

Necromancy wasn't something Dulce had any wish to dabble in, not when her mother had warned her, *we don't know what the dead want.* But she did know how the spell was performed. "I would first need the heart of another stallion."

He pursed his lips. "No horse for now then. Let's gather our things and leave this wretched place by foot, shall we?"

While their travels would be temporarily slowed, at least they had plenty of food and water to keep their hunger at bay for a few days.

After collecting their traveling bags in the upstairs bedroom, they pushed open the heavy castle doors and returned out into the fog before stilling.

Four men stood before them in the morning light.

Clearly leading the other three was perhaps the largest and most repulsive man Dulce had ever seen, his width nearly measuring his height, and as he grinned rotting teeth, she noticed open sores covered his bald head.

"The Leper, I presume?" Dulce whispered to Reed, having heard rumors of what the offensive man looked like.

"In the corpulent flesh," Reed answered, stepping in front of her.

"Nothing personal," the Leper hollered gruffly. "But there's quite the bounty on that pretty white head of yours. I knew you'd want a friend to be the one to tell you."

"Very considerate," Reed said as the three men in

black moved steadily closer. "But if it's all the same, I have somewhere I need to be, so if you'll excuse us."

"There's been a mistake." Dulce's voice remained steady as she peeked out from behind Reed. The men must've sensed something in her beyond courage because they halted. "I'm clearly not dead, am I, gentlemen?" She held up her hand and flashed them her family ring. "I gave Reed the jewels myself as a reward. He never stole anything. It's vitally important that you let him go since he never should've been arrested in the first place."

"Vitally important, she says," the man with greasy long hair and a wide scar across one cheek sang.

"Oh, well, if it's *vitally* important," a second man, his nose twisted, answered, and they all laughed.

The trio turned to the Leper then, waiting for his order.

"Elevated company for a swamp rat." The Leper's grin widened, exposing his rotting gums as he slowly raked his overt stare down her form. "The fleshmonger needs fresh workers in the Glen. How's about it, moppet?"

Her? Disgusting bastards. She spat on the ground. "That's my answer. Now leave."

"Or is it *witch*? Rumor has it my boy Reed is traveling with one. A witch can perform quite the pleasure, I hear." the Leper's gaze turned slitted.

The three men's eyes lit with a darkness and hunger that sent a chill through Dulce, and they edged closer toward her.

The fog lifted beneath sulphury sunlight, revealing four horses tied to a tree.

"Thank you in advance for the horses," Reed purred

with a mock bow, producing one of the kitchen's many spit rods she hadn't realized he'd taken. Before Dulce could blink, he lunged forward and swung it with vicious force into the nearest man's head, who went down like a collapsing bridge.

"You've really saved us a lot of trouble," Reed continued, spinning to catch the second man with the end of the iron rod in the stomach. He made a terrible choking noise as he doubled over, and Reed kicked him in the head, leaving him sprawled along the grass, still.

Dulce would step in with magic if she needed, but at the moment, it was much more entertaining watching Reed fight with incredible skill.

The third man looked wary, but he rolled his shoulders, inching closer to Reed, daggers in each hand. "This is the day you die, Reed. Once a mangy Glen dog, always a mangy Glen dog."

"That was always your problem, Fowles," Reed said calmly, as if he hadn't a care in the world. "Thinking you're better than a dog."

The man lunged at Reed with a wild cry, swiping blindly at Reed's face, but in a blur of steel his knives flew from his hands, and he screamed in pain, falling to his knees, cradling badly broken wrists. Reed didn't hesitate to swing his weapon across the man's throat, and despite the viciousness the vile man's eyes had promised, she winced.

The Leper stood still, studying Reed with apparent indifference. Dulce knew the man could never outrun or outfight Reed. He would be foolish to attempt even a sliver of violence.

"You won't get far, swamp rat." The Leper clenched

his jaw. "I have eyes everywhere. I will find you, and I will collect my reward in exchange for your head. Consider that a warning from a friend."

Reed took Dulce's hand and led her toward the waiting horses.

"Much obliged," he called over his shoulder. "But sorry to be the one to tell you, you have no friends. Only those who fear you."

He untied two of the horses and slapped their withers, sending them cantering off across the field toward Silver Birch Straits and home. The next horse, he helped Dulce to mount, untying its reins and placing them in her hands. And finally, he unbound the fourth horse and mounted it himself.

"We should have dinner sometime," he shouted to the Leper. "You know, after Ms. Bankroft and I save the world and everyone knows you tried to stop me from helping her. For profit."

"You'll regret this!" the Leper screeched, the sores across his forehead oozing as he turned beet red. "I could've helped you out of the mess you've made for yourself. You could've *lived*. Now"—he shrugged his massive shoulders, struggling to collect himself—"it's out of my hands."

Reed smirked, kicking his horse into action. "Out of your hands is just the way I like it!"

Reed

By the afternoon, the endless rows of birch trees had blended into a blur of black and ivory, the music of their ghostly white leaves rustling in the wind like gentle waves. Rocked by his horse's movements, Reed followed Dulce as they continued their journey north, exhaustion pulling at them.

Fingers going numb with cold, Reed smiled to himself at how easily the Leper's men had fallen, how spectacularly they'd failed in capturing him. The Leper should've kept his trap shut about Dulce bringing anyone pleasure—he'd brought it all upon himself.

"You fight incredibly well." Dulce grinned, glancing

over her shoulder at him as her horse led the way. "You could join the royal guard if you wanted."

"There's only one woman I want to call Majesty." He smirked.

She laughed just before her smile slowly fell. "Once we return to Moonglade, I'll get everything sorted for you. There will be no bounty on your head, I promise."

"And you? Won't the villagers discover you're a witch if gossip spreads further?"

"Rumors are easy to manipulate."

"They'll regret the day the Great Alexandra Josephine Bancroft intervened." Reed winked, making her laugh once more, which was precisely what he wanted.

They would have to return from facing La Bisou Morte first, however. Anyone without magic would've been a simpler threat. When Dulce went alone through the fog to halt the wild magic of the Tree of Life, he'd wanted to believe she would be fine, but a part of him had worried she wouldn't be. That the magic would turn against her and kill her in some horrific, unimaginable way. And there would have been nothing he could've done to save her.

They fell silent, carrying on through the endless rows of birch trees as weak sunlight peeked at them through their leaves from farther along the western horizon. At least it wasn't raining. They had that in their favor.

Reed, lulled into a half-slumber, wondered what his life would be like if he'd made different choices. Would he have avoided ever meeting the likes of brutes like the Leper, Nickolas 'the Pikeman' Davies, and the many men of questionable morals who worked for them? Would he have ever, like so many young boys before him, begun training to fight, to finally enter the arena hidden away in the Glen's swamps, with its stench of blood and fear, and use violence to earn coin?

Would he have ever met Dulce?

The thought of never meeting her disturbed him more than he cared to admit. Especially knowing she could've easily fallen into death if he hadn't dug her up when he had.

What was life but a collection of crossroads, each action taking destiny onto a different path? If Reed thought about it, the trajectory of his life could be determined by a single decision he'd made one winter day five years ago.

It was the first time he'd known true hunger. Fear of not eating the next meal. Reed and his brother found themselves down to the last of their dead parents' savings. Despite his brother Philip working at the blacksmith's and Reed himself doing what little he could to earn coin, the savings had slowly dwindled like sand falling through an hourglass, until coin for only one more month of rent and one more meal remained.

Philip unable to leave work until late into the night, Reed was tasked with taking the payment to the landlord and going to the market to buy whatever rations he could by using the rest. The lanes of Dogwood Glen had been covered in slushy mud that day, a steady curtain of snowflakes floating from the washed-out sky to cover every surface of the maze of crooked hovels all around him in snow, and Reed held his tattered cloak close to himself as he tried to avoid the trampled path's deepest puddles.

That was why he hadn't noticed the small boy until he

collided with him, knocking Reed off his feet while he was thrown out a door two huts down from the landlord's larger one.

"And *stay* out, you mangy bastards!" a deep voice bellowed, adding another and still another child to the last, the final victim hitting his head on the ground with an alarming crack.

Reed struggled to sit, ignored as the largest of the three helped the other two to their feet, frantically brushing snow off their clothing, and the youngest cried in earnest. None of them wore shoes, and their cloaks were threadbare in the bitter cold. Their appearance was so pathetic that it made Reed, who donned his father's tailored cloak, look like a wealthy boy by comparison.

They all had the same bright blue eyes and freckled cheeks. Clearly siblings.

"What will we do now?" asked the third boy to the eldest. "What chance do we have if we can't—"

A girl rushed from the alleyway and joined them, taking the youngest into her arms. She was older than the rest, her expression furious as she turned identical bright blue eyes from her brothers to the locked door of the hut they'd just been thrown from.

"Leave," she finished. "Now, today. Before they come back with more men."

"He took the rest of our coin," the eldest boy told her, staring at his bare feet in abject misery. "I tried to stop him, but…"

The four children stared at each other, pale and terrified, already trembling in the cold, and, as if the sun shone through the dense clouds above him, Reed knew what he had to do. Even if it meant moving into a smaller hovel, even if it meant taking a job at the butchers, which smelled vile and gave him nightmares.

"Take this," he called, holding out the bag of coin he carried as the four spun to face him. "It should be enough for passage south on the next caravan. Enough food for four days. Maybe even … some shoes."

The four gawked at him in disbelief, the girl's expression filling with distrust.

"Why would you do that?" she demanded. "Why would you help us?" The girl stepped back from him in horror, her arms wrapped protectively around the two smallest boys. "I warn you—we'd sooner die than work in the Leper's brothel."

"Oh, this is nothing," Reed lied, shrugging. "Me and my brother, we have more than enough coin to live on comfortably. We have a rich uncle with no children of his own, and Father works in Moonglade for a grand duchess. My cousin Alfie is even the personal stable boy for a baron."

They didn't look convinced.

"Trust me, no one will even notice it's gone," he insisted, dropping the bag of coin at the eldest boy's feet. "I was on my way to the market to buy the latest sled— you know, the red one, with the extended brackets and the new drag pads? But in truth we already have several of last year's designs."

Reed walked away, leaving them to watch him in stunned silence. Sometimes his lying skills were a little too good, but he generally only told untruths when it came down to survival.

He thought Philip would be angry at him for losing the last of their coin, but when he told his brother what he'd done, he only embraced him warmly in understanding.

"Don't worry, Reed," he'd said. "We'll figure something out. We always do, don't we? You did the right thing, helping those children."

But when they couldn't pay their next month's rent in full, even after taking one of the smallest, most miserable huts available in the Glen, the Pikeman's men had come sniffing around, looking for fresh recruits. They were only too happy to add desperate boys to their workforce, especially those rumored to be foolish enough to help those more unfortunate than themselves…

"Reed, *look!*" Dulce cried, pulling him from the past. He raised his head to find that the endless sea of haunting trees had cleared, leaving a meadow of southern marsh orchids, their wine-red blooms spreading out to the base of a waterfall, the liquid like milk on black stone to meet a pool of deep green, lilies and sea campions decorating its shores in silvery mist surrounding them.

Tossing her reins to him, Dulce bolted from her horse's back, and, skirts gathered in each hand, she ran across the meadow, her laughter filling the warm afternoon light as a flock of magpies took flight in a cloud of wings.

The horses, eager to drink, followed along as Reed dismounted and went to catch up with her. By the time he reached its shore, Dulce removed her boots and dipped one foot into the lake, clearly longing to enter the water as she hesitated. "It's warm," she breathed. "Do you think it's safe?"

"It doesn't seem to bother the plants or birds," Reed pointed out. "Unless they're an illusion and in actuality we're surrounded by death and decay."

"Ah, not the worst it could be then." Dulce removed her cloak and untied her skirts—Reed spun from her to face the meadow.

"I'm not removing everything!" She laughed, and Reed glanced over his shoulder to find her cheeks flushed a deep pink. "My mother taught me a drying spell on rainy days years ago, when the washing was forgotten on the line."

His throat bobbed as Dulce stripped away all but her thin black chemise, and he looked toward the meadow again while trying not to imagine what she looked like beneath the fabric.

"You can keep all of your clothing on," Dulce called. "But I can't promise your overcoat's fur lining will thank you."

Reed turned to find her wading into the pool until she lay floating at its center, her chemise clinging to her curves, a wide smile painted across her pretty features. He bit the inside of his cheek harshly to control where his mind was veering off to.

Once he gathered his wits, Reed chuckled. "You seem to be enjoying yourself."

"If this is an illusion, I'll enjoy it before it fades!" she shouted at the blue sky above her. "Who knows when the next opportunity for a hot bath will present itself!"

Shedding all but his drawers, Reed entered the water, petals of flowers he'd trampled on his way swirling around him as he swam beneath the falls, his sore shoulders luxuriating under the force of the cascading water. He wondered absently if it was safe to be enjoying this astonishing place, or if the world was ending the closer they journeyed across this cursed land. But as he watched Dulce, her joy so contagious, Reed decided that even if he died tomorrow, he would never regret coming with her on this mad adventure.

The horses grazed along the meadow, and Reed distracted himself from Dulce while he observed them, their tails swishing lazily in the fading afternoon light. As the water fell around him, Reed's worries drifted away.

Exhaling, he let himself sink beneath the water, his body weightless, the current lifting him slowly back to the surface. Pushing his hair from his brow, he opened his eyes to find Dulce standing before him, close enough to touch, her golden-brown eyes shining like a million stars, her raven hair falling around her perfect face, water dripping to her parted lips.

They looked at each other in silence, Reed's heart pounding, his blood scorching.

"Would you mind terribly if I kissed you?" Dulce whispered.

Reed blinked, certain he had misheard her. Was this some haunting ghost, trying to deceive him again? No, this was real, this was Dulce. He had almost kissed her lips twice before, yet here she was, asking *him* to? It seemed impossible that such a thing could be true. He knew he was nothing but a swamp rat compared to this beautiful creature—however, Reed inched nearer to her and lifted her chin with his forefinger. He brushed his lips along her warm cheek, and she arched toward him as he dipped his other hand to her lower back, closing the distance between them. And then his lips, *finally*, captured hers.

Dulce sighed against his mouth when he drew her into

his arms, and she tasted of the sweetest nectar of any flower. While time seemed to stand still, Reed thought of nothing but this utopia of wanting. Wanting nothing but Dulce, more of her, all of her.

19

Dulce

A kiss that could light up the darkest skies. A kiss that could ignite a million stars.

That was the only way to describe kissing Reed.

Dulce kissed him as though this were her last chance, which it very well could be if she didn't get the witch to break her ghastly spell. As the lake's water swished against her, her breasts pressed against the hard planes of Reed's chest, her chemise and his drawers the only layers of clothing between them.

She threaded her fingers in his ivory hair and knew with certainty that if she didn't end the kiss now, she wouldn't leave this lake with him until morning.

Breaking apart from Reed, she bit her lip and fought a smile as she drew back. "Well, Mr. Hawthorne, you truly know how to sweep a lady off her feet."

His lips were handsomely red and swollen, his chest heaving in sync with hers. "Why, Ms. Bancroft, I do believe you were the one who asked to kiss me, so it's you who knows how to sweep a man off *his* feet," Reed drawled.

Dulce laughed softly and waded through the water to the fall's bank. Byzantium marigolds decorated one edge of the field, and she added cloves and cinnamon to the mix, invoking the element of fire in one of her mother's favorite magical tricks until her chemise was dry. Next, she turned it on Reed, keeping her gaze strictly trained on his deep brown irises instead of his drawers.

The sun had begun to set by the time they were both dressed, and Reed tugged a lock of her hair as he said, "I'll start a fire."

The horses slept soundly while he gathered twigs and leaves, and she unpacked their provisions, determined to make them last the longest they could.

Dulce watched him light the kindling, his hands gentle and delicate despite the scars across them. She marveled at the thought that she'd never once been so exposed with any man as she was with Reed in the lake. How easily she had removed her clothing. Her behavior would be considered unladylike, scandalous for a woman of her station. Yet, instead of feeling ashamed, she found it to be rather liberating. After months of tiptoeing around Cornelius with barely so much as a few chaste pecks, her kiss with Reed was the one she'd wished had been her first.

They warmed their hands by the fire, and she ate dried fruit and hardtack accompanied by one of her poisoned berries.

The corners of Reed's mouth curled up. "I really enjoyed kissing you."

"Me too," Dulce murmured, a kaleidoscope of butterflies swarming in her stomach.

"Perhaps we can do it again sometime."

"Perhaps." She grinned.

He bit into a candied plum and placed his hand atop hers. "You mentioned you played piano. What else do you like?"

"Poetry."

"Ah, lovesick fools, heroes rescuing helpless damsels in distress."

Dulce laughed. "No, not even close. Dark poems that speak of death, agony, and *ghosts*."

"I should've known." He smirked, then settled on the grass and patted the spot beside him. "But do tell."

"If you *insist*." Dulce settled next to him, and they both lay on their backs, peering up at the stars for a few moments. She hoped her mother was somewhere up there, watching over her, always there to continue giving her guidance, assisting her on how to overcome the obstacles she would soon face.

"Let me recall one of my favorites…" Dulce began, "When twilight petals droop upon their stalks. Death whispers in my ear. When the herd returns at day's end, trudging along on tired legs. Death steals into my home. I cannot understand his words, spoken through a garland of smiling skulls. Yet his dark infinity, it fills my heart. And silently, at night's long last end, I am swept away by my lover. To join the dead…"

Dawn brought another gray sky and a cool wind that nipped at their skin as they traveled, inching closer and closer to La Bisou Morte's location. Still, it would be days until they reached her.

To stay awake, Dulce told Reed more poetry at his request, and their conversation fell into easy banter or comfortable silence. The landscape, after the isolated summer falls, slipped back into nothing but rows of silver birch trees, and she wondered if this forest would go on forever.

By late afternoon, though, the ground beneath them changed to vast hills, and Dulce was able to see into the distance for the first time since entering Silver Birch Straits.

As the valley below was bathed in shadows, she discovered that all along it were torches burning with bright orange flames. Her legs ached from being on the horse throughout the day, and the thought that they approached a town, bearing an inn where she might sleep on a real bed, filled her with the kind of excitement that only comes from experiencing the alternative.

When they drew nearer, it wasn't homes the torches illuminated, but a massive black and red tent surrounded by a number of silver and gold caravans and wagons. Dulce was reminded of the carnivals that came through Moonglade each spring, but when a songbird of a voice, accompanied by graceful piano music, drifted through the air, she knew at once that this was one of the performing operas.

She slowed her horse, and Reed's dapple gray trotted up beside her. He waggled his brows at her. "I'm sensing you want to stop here for the night."

Dulce hurriedly nodded. "I've always wanted to see the performing opera. The opera in town doesn't have acrobats as I've heard they do."

"Then"—he dipped his head, dismounting, and helped her from her horse with a twirl—"it looks like we have an opera to attend."

They secured their horses' reins to a tree and approached the entrance with a red and silver sign in a language she didn't recognize.

A young woman eating an apple held up her hand at them and shouted over the singing that emanated from the tent's interior. "We're not open for a few more days."

"Oh." Dulce's shoulders slumped. Perhaps experiencing the magic of the artists wasn't meant to be.

"Could we perhaps pay to watch the performers practice?" Reed asked, his voice alluring as silk.

The woman combed her fingers through her thick brown curls and took another bite of her apple. "Six coins."

When Dulce reached into her bag, Reed stopped her. "Three," he purred. "And three more for accommodations."

Dulce arched a brow at him as the woman grinned. "Fine." She pointed to her left, where a silver wagon with golden swirls painted along its side rested. "You two can sleep the night there. Steal anything, and I'll know. Also, since you want to watch the performances, you're in luck, they just started, and they'll be practicing for most of the night."

"Thank you," Dulce said, handing her the coins.

Making their way toward the tent, they passed a group of people sitting near a large fire, drinking and eating, laughing uproariously, and several talking in a language she didn't know. Some wore large colorful dresses and suits, and others were attired in checkered jester or sequined acrobat costumes, beads sparkling in the firelight. A strikingly handsome man with long black hair to his waist winked at her, and Reed glared.

"I prefer men with ruffled white hair." She took his arm, and his shoulders relaxed.

They entered the tent to find rows of makeshift benches that took up the space in front of a stage, where hundreds of paper crows and moths hung over the source of the magical song, and at last Dulce's gaze locked on the woman singing. She wore a braided crown, and an onyx butterfly mask covered half her face—a sapphire and silver gown fell around her figure in gentle folds to pool at her feet. Besides two young adolescent girls sitting in one of the middle rows, no one else watched the performance.

Dulce and Reed sank down on the bench behind the two girls, enraptured in wonder as the performer sang her heart out, perfectly conveying every emotion and happy heartache through song. It was the most beautiful sound she had ever heard, one her mother would've adored. The song spoke of fighting for love, no matter if death came for one in the end.

Tears gathered in Dulce's lashes as a mixture of sentiments coursed through her at the lovely melody. No matter how much she loved the piano, she knew with certainty that she would never master it as beautifully as the performer playing this piece. She glanced at Reed to find he wasn't focused on the performance but instead on her. She elbowed him in the arm. "You're missing the act."

"Am I?" He grinned and studied the performance while pirouetting dancers entered the stage, twirling silk streamers. Two jesters soon joined in, raising the singing lady into the air, stealing her away from the man she loved as she continued her mournful song. Next, a man wearing a dark suit, a golden owl mask covering the upper portion of his face, added his voice to the song, his baritone deep and melancholic, complaining of heartbreak before rescuing her.

They sang to one another, lifting the mask from the other, until finally, in a crescendo of passion, they kissed, the piano music fading.

It was just the right amount of emotional strength Dulce needed on this journey. She stood, clapping loudly, and the two young girls turned to look at her with wide smiles. As another performance began, one of the little girls, missing her two front teeth, squeaked, "We're going to eat candy apples if you want to join us. My mama won't mind."

"Who could refuse candy apples?" Reed said, and the two girls giggled.

The two young girls led them toward a middle-aged woman dressed in a brown wool skirt. She placed her hands on her hips as she peered at the two girls. "Are you bothering strangers again?"

"No, Mama," the one with braids huffed. "They're

hungry. And they loved our performance!"

"I can pay," Dulce offered, opening her bag.

The woman waved her off. "Certainly not. There's plenty of food for everyone. It'll only go bad if we don't share it, am I right?"

Seeing—and smelling—the hot meal brought out, Dulce didn't argue, and they each ate a bowl of ham and carrot oat porridge and delightedly accepted candy apples from the little girls, who were named Yunis and Thyme. They watched the performers practice fire juggling until they could scarcely keep their eyes open, and, thanking everyone they passed for their hospitality, Dulce and Reed made their way toward the wagon to retire for the evening.

A thick knitted blanket lay folded in the middle of the wagon—Dulce knew one of the performers must've left it for them. These strangers had been nothing but kind, and they didn't know about the curse, what would become of their beautiful opera if La Bisou Morte got her way? Her heart ached at the notion.

Reed plucked up the blanket and held it out toward her. "You can use it."

Dulce thought about their kiss, how close they'd been to one another throughout the journey. "I have a much better idea. We share it."

"As you wish." He smiled.

Dulce set her satchel on the floor beside Reed's to use as a pillow, then they removed their boots before settling beneath the blanket. She stared up at the ceiling, where a sliver of the moonlight shone through a small rectangle.

Minute after minute ticked by, and when Reed adjusted himself beside her, she turned to face him.

"I can't sleep," he said, pushing up from the floor and resting his back against the wall.

"Me neither." Dulce sat beside him and swept back a lock from his forehead. "Is everything all right?"

"I'm thinking about my brother." Reed sighed. "I know he's blaming himself for my disappearance…"

Dulce didn't know what it was like to have siblings, but as she thought about it now, she could see that it would've been nice to have the company, someone close to share childhood with, someone with whom to grow and support each other. "You two seem to be very close."

Reed nodded. "We were all each other had growing up." He shrugged. "Even before my parents died, it was always Philip, looking after me, sharing everything, even when we had hardly enough food for one."

"I can help you both find work outside the Glen," Dulce promised.

"Your generosity is already too much, Highness."

"Not when you're risking your life to help the world. Not when you saved my life, Reed."

He studied her a long moment before relenting, "Perhaps for my brother I will accept it, but not me. I'll owe you though."

"You owe me nothing."

"I know you were close to your parents. When did you lose them?" Reed asked.

"Fourteen, my father, and sixteen, my mother. Both succumbed to illnesses. My father was the one who taught me piano, would make me laugh. My mother was outgoing, everyone loved her, and she was giving, creative. When she died, my world fell apart, and I pretended as though the witch in me didn't exist because everything with magic reminded me of her, of what I'd lost. I only continued the poison tradition each day since I knew how important that was to her. Thankfully I did, or I'd truly be dead."

Reed wiped away a tear streaming down her cheek that she didn't realize had fallen. "I'm glad I found you and not a real corpse."

She couldn't help but laugh, and he bit his lip, his eyes drifting toward her mouth. Her pulse thrummed, and she couldn't stop herself from leaning forward and pressing her lips to his. He instantly reacted, his mouth coasting deliciously across hers as his hand cradled her cheek, and the kiss deepened, his tongue slipping between her lips to savor hers. This was a new kind of kiss, one that made her breath catch and her body yearn for more.

Here was the affection, the *hunger* for another that she'd read about in poems, that great songs sung of, that men died for.

Dulce arched into him, and Reed's hands trailed down to her waist to lift her into his lap. With each kiss, each subtle shift of their bodies, she hoped for more. Her head dipped toward his ear, and she whispered, "Touch me, Mr. Hawthorne."

"Where?" he rasped.

"Beneath my dress." Her voice came out breathy, desperate.

In answer, he slowly pushed her dress up her legs, and he guided her undergarments aside while continuing to kiss her, to kindle every fiber within her. His warm, callused hand touched her flower, and she gasped, whimpering in pleasure when he stroked her. On instinct, she rolled her hips forward, riding his hand as he deftly brought out a ravenous part of herself that she didn't know existed.

This was the sweetest poison she'd ever felt, because she knew she was starting to fall for him, that Vesta's tea leaves had been accurate in their prediction—Reed Hawthorne was who she was meant to be with. She feared confessing to him about the fortune, that such a thing might frighten him, make him feel powerless against his own fate. So for now, she relished the feeling building up in her heart, something wonderfully new as a wave of euphoria washed over her and she moaned.

Her breath was ragged when she peered up at Reed beneath thick lashes. He kissed her forehead and tucked her against his chest before drawing the blanket over them both.

"Perhaps we can sleep now, Majesty," he whispered.

"I do believe so." Dulce blissfully sighed and closed her eyes. She would cherish this temporary haven for the remainder of the night.

In the morning, they would have to leave it.

20

Reed

Dulce slept on, her lips slightly parted. Reed recalled the night before, and the desire to remain with her in this wagon, to feel her quake beneath his touch once more, intensified.

Reluctantly tearing himself from her side, Reed left the wagon and took in his surroundings in the light of day. The expanse of Silver Birch Straits loomed above the wide valley, the tree's white leaves like snow-covered mountains at this distance. To the north lay the barren wasteland of the Rust Fields, its wide canyons resembling open wounds along the reddish earth for as far as the eye could see.

Looking to the west, full of green life, where towns crowded with people waited to venture out to watch the opera performers, the temptation to avoid danger dragged at his heart, and Reed pushed it aside.

Everything would be destroyed anyway, if they failed to reverse the witch's destruction.

"You headed north?"

Reed started, surprised to find an ancient woman sitting in a chair outside the neighboring wagon, watching the sunrise as she smoked a pipe, its bluish smoke joining the misty air with the cloying aroma of cloves and tobacco leaves.

"I wouldn't pass through the Rust Fields again," she stated, coughing. "Not if you offered me the world's weight in gold."

"That bad, huh?" Reed found that rather than filling him with dread, her words only served to awaken his curiosity.

"Worse."

"Really?" He sat next to her stool, the cool grass beneath him as the sun rose farther into the sky, the mist along the valley dispersing like smoke from her pipe. "What if one has no other choice?"

She squinted toward the Rust Fields, exhaling smoke. "Then you'll die if you don't have enough fire. Fire is the key to keeping the warped away."

"The warped?" At that, Reed had to admit to some measure of unease. Yet perhaps it wasn't as grim as it sounded.

"Decaying magic has twisted the creatures of that place," the old woman said. "They are no longer as they should be. They have become something of nightmares.

They hunger. Only their fear of fire keeps them at bay."

That most definitely sounded *grim*.

"How did you survive the journey before?" Reed asked. "That is … you mentioned you wouldn't pass through it *again*."

Dulce, her cloak wrapped firmly around her shoulders, joined them in silence, her eyes filled with concern as she studied the woman carefully, clearly having heard every word the crone had uttered.

"We blindfolded our horses." The woman nodded. "And we brought as much fire as we could. Alchemists' fire works best. Those who held ordinary torches, well…" she sniffed. "They died in the darkness, didn't they? I still hear their screams in my dreams."

Reed glanced at Dulce, the blood drained from her face.

"Can one traverse it in a day?" she asked. "To avoid the darkness, I mean."

The woman burst into laughter, a high-pitched cackle that sent a chill along Reed's spine, before falling into a coughing fit.

They waited for her coughs to subside. "There is no avoiding the darkness in the Rust Fields," the crone replied. "Its canyons are so deep and narrow, sunlight has hardly a chance to wink down into its red dust before it's swallowed up in shadow. And those foolish enough to believe they could pass along its surface soon find that their only choice is retreat or fall to their deaths."

Footfalls at their back, Reed turned to discover a group of performers crowding around them. The little girls, Yunis and Thyme, held pitchers with carved stoppers and thin necks out to Dulce.

"We heard you're passing through the Rust Fields," Yunis chirped.

"Yes." Dulce stood to face them, her determination leaving no room for argument, and Reed felt a swell of pride at her bravery.

With a nod from their mother, the girls handed over the pitchers. "We thought," Thyme said. "That is, you will need this oil more than us. We can purchase all we need in the village. Once tickets begin to sell…"

Dulce pressed gold coins into their hands. "Please," she insisted. "For all of your kindness."

No one spoke much during breakfast, stealing sympathetic glances at Reed and Dulce as they ate. He was certain they were all sure they watched the condemned.

Afterward, Dulce excused herself to pore over her spell book and collect mysterious things from a nearby field, while Reed accepted amulets from the elderly of the troupe, trinkets they insisted kept evil away.

The fire jugglers sold Reed four of their ropes, the tallest one mournfully informing him, "We're not sure how long the flames will last. We've never used them for longer than a few hours."

They then instructed him how to best use the oil along their weighted ends. Reed overpaid them, but under the circumstances, it was only fitting. After today, they may not need coin ever again.

A few of the men offered to lather their horses in a clay, alum, and salt solution, explaining that this would act as a heat shield along their coats and tails. They also tied sacks of the same mixture to their saddles.

"I suggest you cover yourselves with it as well," the

man with long black hair told them as Dulce returned, having fashioned blindfolds from leather she attached across the animals' bridles.

It was three hours past dawn by the time they departed from their new companions, and, looking like painted warriors about to enter battle, they crossed the valley and faced the Rust Fields alone.

Sweeping his gaze across the expansive waste as far as the eye could see, Reed reached for Dulce's hand, reminiscing the night they'd spent together in the wagon once more, their easy conversation, the taste of her lips, the feel of her soft flesh against his hand, the sound of her moans.

"No regrets," he said. "No matter what happens."

She nodded, blinking back tears. "No regrets."

The earth was dyed the rusty brown-orange of oxidized iron, its crevices like giant mud cracks. Reed believed he mirrored a small insect in a vast desert as they wound their way downward into the looming shadows of the canyon. Their map indicated in no uncertain terms that there was but a single passage through the Rust Fields, all others leading to death, no end to their twisted mazes.

"Luckily alchemists who traveled before us have lined our path with rocks painted in a photoluminescent coating," Dulce pointed out as the first of a neat row of skull-sized stones came into view.

When the shadows deepened, the stones held a light of their own, glowing in the gathering darkness.

Reed peered at them. "They aren't … skulls, are they?"

One of her black brows perfectly arched. "Do you

really want the answer to that question, Mr. Hawthorne?"

Reed thought about how many men would've had to die in order to line leagues of canyon floor with their bones and decided it was better to remain a mystery.

Movement along the sheer cliff caught his eye then, vanishing as he turned. Reed held his reins tighter, urging his horse closer to Dulce's.

"Your spell book has answers to our fire problem, yes?" Though she'd told him creating fire would pose no significant hindrance to them. "Shouldn't *now* be a good time to maybe, oh, I don't know, implement said measures?"

Dulce seemed unbothered by the increasing movement around them, even as the unmistakable sounds of scratching echoed from above.

Reed refused to look, focusing instead on exuding calm for the sake of his horse, whose ears pinned when the animal's gait moved from a walk to a trot.

"Ah, but fire still requires fuel," she noted, leaning to unhook one of the jars from her saddle while she rode, lifting the length of rope soaked in a mysterious concoction she wore around her shoulders into her right hand. He mimicked her movements until he held his rope, prepared to light its end with hers and swing it above his head as they'd planned. "Alchemy and magic assist us, but if we aren't careful, our fire will run out of fuel."

He made the mistake of glancing to his right as blood-tinged sand fell in sheets from a ledge, to find a row of glowing eyes.

"It's … rodents," he said, frowning. "How dangerous can they really b—"

"Those aren't rodents," Dulce murmured, concentrating on her task. "I take it those are the warped creatures the performer mentioned."

Of course they were... Reed's brow furrowed in the gathering darkness, wondering if they may have once been common stoat, hare, or marmot. Could there be warped humans within these vast canyons? He tightened his fists at the thought.

A dark cloud moved over the narrow horizon, swooping toward them at astonishing speed.

Dulce gasped and ignited the end of her rope, where a weighted pouch burst into unnaturally wide flames, sparks dancing along its base in purple and blue.

"Warped locusts," she hissed, reaching across the space between their horses to set off Reed's flame as the cloud descended on them, the insects crashing into the narrow cliffs at their sides. Dulce kicked her horse into a canter, a halo of fire above her distracting them while she swung the rope.

Reed followed suit, his pulse racing as the warped locusts screeched around them, the sound of their fury filling his ears until he thought he would go mad with it.

They continued like that, awakening the slumbering, warped creatures while they went, the glowing stones guiding their way, the flames above them keeping the monsters at bay.

And then Dulce's horse tripped, stalling to a trembling standstill. Reed watched in horror as she flew from her saddle, mud-covered skirts sailing around her as if in slow motion, to land in the rusty sand, her flame guttering out to darkness.

Snapping his reins, Reed skidded to a halt, one leg

over his saddle and to the ground, he gathered the two horses' in one hand, flames circling above him in the other, and rushed to Dulce. Creatures swarmed her from all sides, biting and tearing at her clothing as she frantically swatted them away. Seeing them this closely, Reed recoiled. Warped was exactly the word to describe them. Where once they had been fur-covered harmless creatures of the desert and mountain planes, now they were twisted abominations. Magic, rotted and dying, had transformed them into hideous, carnivorous shells of their former selves—rows of teeth, jagged claws, and biting tentacles along their spines, eyes crazed with hunger as they screamed beneath Reed's flame, falling back into the shadows.

Dulce scrambled to retrieve her rope, reigniting the flame at its end with shaking hands. Meeting her gaze, Reed's heart leapt to his throat at the fear he saw painted there. He wanted nothing but to wash the expression from her face.

"Think of the stories of great adventure we'll be able to tell," he professed.

"Oh yes." Dulce smiled, and Reed's pulse raced at the sight. "We'll leave out the heroine falling gracelessly on her face though, please." She clasped his hand, and he pulled her to her feet.

"That will be *our* little secret."

When the sky far above them matched the shadows of the canyon, they stopped to feed the horses and give them water, taking turns keeping a steady wall of spinning fire above them. Reed's arm ached, though he switched from left to right when the pain became too vexing.

How much longer could they keep this up? Surely,

they must be almost through this torture by now.

"You should eat," Dulce uttered, handing Reed something he hardly bothered to look at before he stuffed them into his mouth. The sweet nuts and dried fruit instantly drove his strength up.

There was nowhere to tie the horses, surrounded only by sand and smooth rock, and so they had no way of stopping to sleep, even if Dulce's talents allowed them to surround themselves with a protective circle of fire. The thought of holding Dulce in his arms again, kissing her lips, touching her skin, was enough to push him to keep going.

"It can't be much farther." She met his eyes as if she'd read his thoughts.

An especially large boar lunged at them, startling the horses. Reed swung flames at it until the creature retreated into the shadows, its ribs exposed beneath rows of fangs.

"How could anyone do this?" Dulce asked, studying the moving shadows beyond their circle of firelight. "What purpose does this cruelty serve? I don't understand…"

Reed brought his horse close to hers, and he lifted her chin with his forefinger, wishing he could throw down the torch to embrace her instead. "We'll find the light in the darkness. I promise I won't leave your side."

"A perfect line to add to our adventurous story, Mr. Hawthorne." The grief in her expression slowly gave way to determination.

Their flames replenished by the significantly lighter pitchers, they continued their way, keeping the horses at a slower pace, letting them walk for spells. Reed ignored his exhaustion as the night wore on, his arms long since going numb by the time the sky above was painted in struggling light. They had gathered an enormous crowd of creatures by then, keeping pace with them along the canyon floor, maintaining their distance from the flames, waiting for the moment they would flicker and go out.

Waiting for their meal.

By midday, when a moment of sunlight shone down onto them, illuminating the sand beneath their horses' hooves in bright red, Dulce came to a halt before him, her head down.

"Reed," she whispered, shaking the pitcher by its delicate neck. "We're down to the last of it."

He peered ahead, seeing no end to their passage.

"We need to divide it between us…"

"You mean…" Reed swallowed. "Do you mean what I think you mean?"

"We need to ignite the mixture on ourselves when our ropes begin to die out and gallop the rest of the way."

He cocked his head. "We won't burn?" Flames licking away his skin wasn't the *loveliest* way to spend the day.

"We'll soon find out." Dulce poured the last of the alchemical oil onto their ropes one after the other as they took turns keeping flames spinning endlessly above them.

"We're dead if we don't try, regardless." Reed winked at her, one side of his mouth curving upward, as he prepared to kick his horse into a canter. "No regrets, remember?"

Dulce

Adrenaline surged through Dulce's veins as fire cloaked her and Reed, heat raging around her in brilliant orange. She held her breath, praying they would survive.

Covered in flames, the horses galloped for their lives toward the edge of the Rust Fields, just barely slipping past the canyon walls into a rushing river. Their flames died out to sparks while the screams of frustrated monsters lingered in the distance, their prey escaped to safety, and Dulce could finally breathe again.

She sank beneath the water, ensuring every flame was extinguished before breaking through the surface. Reed grasped her arm, their chests heaving as the flowing water washed away the smoke, dirt, and grime from their exhausted bodies.

"That is something I don't fancy ever doing again, Majesty." Reed smirked, raking a hand through his soaked hair.

"Certainly more challenging than ghosts." She smiled, though her heart still palpitated.

"Not a lie in the least."

Dulce and Reed pulled themselves from the river, and she used magic to dry their clothing. They then trekked a little farther to a nearby cave where they were too tired to eat a full meal.

Exhaustion swept over Dulce and she rested her head in Reed's lap as he leaned against the granite wall, his eyes already shut. When sleep overtook her, she dreamed that her mother's tree would no longer turn to stone.

As soon as morning light spilled into the cave, rousing Dulce and Reed, they left the comfort of rest behind, continuing their travels. Although the journey throughout the day didn't involve being chased by monsters, still, the world around them grew more grim with each passing second, each thump of her heart.

Lavender magic that belonged safely within the earth's embrace was now siphoned from the land, cut astray, its power floating around them like aimless buzzing bees. The hairs on Dulce's arms stood on end, not from fear but rather as a result of the strange enchantment.

The deeper into Nightmore Forest they traveled, the

grayer the world surrounding them turned. The trees, at first appearing to suffer pox-like blemishes of stone along their branches, became more consumed by their disease as the leagues passed, until life in all its vibrant green dwindled completely away to gray. They stood as nothing more than silent stone statues, their life frozen.

Dulce hoped the wildlife had fled, but that hope was dashed as they rode past stone creatures. A stag, its neck stretched toward the stone leaves of a mulberry tree, stood motionless in rock. A flock of birds, the detail of their feathers awe-inspiring but for the fact that they were not created by the hands of a sculptor. Rabbits, immobile in mid-run.

"Don't stop!" she called to Reed. Her lungs tight, she urged her horse on, faster, fearing if they lingered too long that they too would turn to stone, two horses and their riders preserved in rock forever, their mission never seeing its end.

Reaching the northern edge of Nightmore Forest, the sea of stone trees dissipated to wide expanses of rolling valleys, the hills beyond it their destination at last. They had passed through the stone mausoleum unscathed, but Dulce knew that eventually, the sickness of dying magic would creep across all the land. She thought about the kind strangers of the opera, the gamblers in the Duke's town Reed had played cards with, and her friends at the manor. She had to make certain they didn't succumb to such a terrible fate.

"Over there!" Reed shouted over the buzzing of magic, pointing.

Dulce followed his gaze to a small wooden hunting cottage near a lake of unnatural blue.

The cottage's roof and sides covered in overgrown vines, it appeared as if it hadn't been inhabited in decades. Her bones ached with exhaustion—the thought of relaxation inviting. This would be the perfect place to rest for the night before they reached La Bisou Morte the following day.

Though she knew they could reach her faster if they continued, it would be foolish not to regain their strength before they would face the witch. Besides, she didn't want to put Reed in more danger than she had already. There was also the question of how the witch would receive them. Would she be willing to discuss the possibility of removing the curse, or would a fight with magic ensue? Would Dulce have to kill to save the land?

The breeze blew, and the crackle of magic sang its untamed melody while Dulce and Reed dismounted their horses.

"It seems today is your lucky day," she sang. "You're about to have a little witch blood pulse inside your veins."

"That sounds rather forward." He winked.

Dulce laughed softly and watched as the horses fled, happy to be rid of their tack and riders, eager to explore the wide valley with its strange blooms.

"I'll make sure no one's hiding in the cottage," Reed said as they approached the crooked door. It was locked, so he kicked the door in with his boot.

After a moment he craned his neck out and waggled his finger at her. "It's all clear."

Dulce stepped over the threshold, her gaze sweeping across the simple room. The air held a musty smell of stillness that wasn't too unpleasant. A bed took up one corner, a chest of drawers opposite it, and a wood-burning stove beside a fireplace.

"It's cozy." She opened the three small windows and picked up a jar of cinnamon sticks, using it to freshen up the room before gathering bark, dirt, and dry leaves from the long-neglected garden outside. Reed carried two large pails to collect water from the lake, the muscles of his arms drawing her eye as he hauled them back to the cottage.

Dulce sat across from him on an old wool rug in front of the unlit fireplace—she didn't want chimney smoke to alert anyone of their presence.

"Sit still," she instructed. Leaning forward, Dulce grasped one of the longest strands of Reed's ivory hair and plucked it.

"You could've warned me, Highness," he teased.

"I'll remember that next time." She smiled, then opened her mother's book, flipping to the page she sought. As Dulce pored over the two spells to create her own, she yanked out one of her hairs and measured the two strands until they were the same length. She tied them together at the top, winding them around one another, then binding them at the opposite end. Grabbing a poisonous yew berry from her pouch, she placed it into her mouth, letting its bitter juice coat her tongue when she chewed. "You might not be able to perform magic tomorrow, but after this, you'll at least be protected. If you're struck with magic, this will save you from death. It won't last more than a couple of days though."

"Sounds enticing indeed."

Dulce shifted closer to him, her pulse accelerating, and placed her palm atop his. "Kiss me?"

"You know I'm always more than happy to oblige."

Reed arched a brow and studied her as though she were mad. "But you did just eat a poisonous berry."

She rolled her eyes. "It won't kill you. Not with this spell in place." She raised the two strands of hair laced together. "Do you trust me?"

"With my life, Highness." He kept his gaze on hers, and Dulce wanted to drown in Reed's brown irises as he drew her into his lap so her legs straddled him. "If I die, at least it will be a gratifying death."

"I promise you won't die." Dulce entwined her fingers in his hair and tilted his head back as she pressed her lips to his. He smiled against her mouth, then parted his lips for her, and she flicked her tongue against his, allowing the poison to seep into him just enough before she pulled back. "See? You're still alive."

"Some poisons' effects take longer, I'm sure," he said gruffly.

"True." She grinned. "It's a good thing you trust me."

Reed's gaze grew hooded as he gently tucked a lock of hair behind her ear. "You're beautiful."

"If you only trust me because of my face, then we might need to teach you a few things." She laughed.

"Mmm, teach me anything you wish." He brought her face closer, his mouth so very near to brushing hers once more.

"When was the last time you courted someone?" she murmured, curious as to how many women had fancied him in Dogwood Glen.

"Courted?" He chuckled, his breath warm against her lips. "Never."

"Never?" Her eyes widened. Reed was the most courageous, kindest man she'd ever met—it seemed impossible no woman had fallen in love with him. It didn't matter to her his station in life, what he'd had to suffer to survive, or how much coin he carried in his pockets.

"I was always too busy surviving." He shrugged. "Why? Would you be happier if I'd married my own lumpish pignut?"

"I have forgotten such creatures exist. Banished from my memory."

"Outstanding," he drawled. "I shall banish them from mine as well."

Before she could speak, he cut her off with the pleasantest of kisses. He pulled her closer, the kiss deepening, and as a savage heat spread through every fiber of her being, she couldn't stop from thinking of the last time he'd touched her, the raw, blissful emotion he'd brought her. It didn't take long before the heat turned into a blazing inferno, and she wanted more—she wanted to feel every inch of him against every inch of her.

Dulce's fingers reached the buttons of his shirt, and she freed them one by one, running her palms up his firm chest before removing the garment.

Reed loosened the buttons of her dress, peeling the fabric down her upper arms to trail a spark of scorching kisses along her jaw and to her bare shoulder.

"I want you like I've never wanted anyone, Dulce Bancroft," he said, his voice gruff. "Ever since I first laid eyes on you, I thought you were the most alluring girl I'd ever seen."

"When you thought I was *dead*?" she mused.

"Yes, even dead," he admitted with a grin.

Dulce placed her palm on his warm chest. "It was

your splendid, unselfish heart that I admired. From the very beginning."

"Oh, I'm very much selfish." Reed lifted Dulce in his arms and brought her down against the rug to settle between her thighs. "But not with you."

She swallowed deeply as her gaze locked on his glinting eyes. "I want you to know that Cornelius and I … we never… That is, I never have … with anyone."

Reed's face softened. "I haven't either. Perhaps we can learn together—if you'll have me, that is. I'll kiss you until the stars dim if that's what you wish."

"Until the moon sleeps." Her fingers skimmed down to the button of his trousers, and she unfastened it.

With eager hands, they removed the remainder of their clothing, their bodies bare, his delicious skin like silk pressed to hers.

"You're as perfect as any faerie queen." Reed's heated stare drifted down her form, and she couldn't hide the blush that warmed her cheeks. He softly kissed her collarbone, the valley of her breasts, before taking a peaked nipple into his mouth. Dulce bit her lip at the sweetest of sensations.

As he released her and strayed from her breasts toward her stomach, lowering between her legs, she blinked in wonder, anticipation.

He placed a kiss on her inner thigh, driving her positively mad, curious as to what would come next, when, finally, his mouth caressed her core. She arched in pleasure, never experiencing anything so exquisite, so wonderful, when he licked and kissed her. He circled her pearl, making her feel as though she were walking on air.

And then wave after glorious wave of pleasure she

didn't know was possible arose. The same growing bliss she'd experienced from his touch bloomed within her, only bolder, more feral, and Dulce couldn't fight back the moans that left her lips, her body quaking beneath his delectable tongue.

As she fought to catch her breath, Reed found his way back up to her lips, capturing them sublimely. Exposing the dauntless part of herself, she reached between them to grip Reed's flawless length. A deep groan escaped his throat when she stroked him, his skin like velvet. It was the first time she'd touched a man like this, and while her movements were unpracticed, he still appeared to relish her touch.

"Reed," she murmured. "Make me yours."

He tenderly took her hand from his manhood and brought her arm around his neck. "It would be my honor." His mouth claimed hers, drinking her in as she savored him. She felt his hardness just before he slowly buried himself inside her. A sharp pain pierced her, and she gasped.

Reed stilled. "Are you all right?"

"More than all right." She glided her hands down his back. "Don't you dare stop."

"I'm at your will."

"And I at yours."

Reed moved against her, and with each gentle thrust of his hips, the dull ache subsided until only pleasure took root. She could tell by the trembling of his shoulders that he was restraining himself, lost in the same pleasure as she. Dulce wrapped her legs around his waist, allowing the blissful feeling to deepen. She grasped his hair, pulling his mouth to hers as something like wild magic alighted within her. It was as though the stars were illuminated brighter, the sun ignited in the night sky, and the world shook while pure euphoria unraveled through her blood, seeping into her bones, and she could've sworn her nerves crackled with untamed lightning.

Reed emitted a guttural groan against her lips, his body shuddering as he found his own pleasurable release, and he relaxed into her, his forehead kissing hers.

"Ms. Bancroft," he whispered. "Though our paths crossed under the most unfortunate of circumstances, I'm delighted they did."

Dulce had only one thought as her heart continued to thunder:

Vesta's tea leaves were right.

# Reed

Beneath a knitted blanket, Dulce's warm body lay against Reed's chest, and in that moment, he felt like the wealthiest man in the world.

Part of him wanted nothing but to live out the remainder of his days pressed to Dulce, his lips claiming hers. The rest of him knew that was impossible. It would only serve his own selfish desires. Peace could never come from cowardice—he knew that all too well. And even if running could bring happiness, it would never last, not with the destruction of their world inching ever closer.

Reed had to face the fact that Dulce could be taken

from him at any second. Before they were turned to stone or destroyed by some other twisted form of magic gone awry, they had to do whatever they could to prevent this curse from spreading further.

Dulce's hand brushed his cheek, and there was a smile in her voice as she said, "There are no ghosts here, so why are you frowning?"

His mouth formed a crooked smile.

"You're thinking of what could happen to us, aren't you?"

He tugged a lock of her silky hair. "Aren't you?"

She nodded. "Yes, but let's not, shall we? Let's think only of the present..."

Eventually, though, they left the warmth of the cottage, pulled from their bliss and thrown back into the cold reality of their journey. Neither spoke as they gathered their things and saddled the horses, the animals having wandered back to them in the night, perhaps sensing it was these humans, and Dulce in particular, who could protect them from whatever mysterious magic was destroying the world around them.

Soon Dulce would face La Bisou Morte, would try with everything in her to convince the witch to reverse the havoc she'd created. Reed vowed to do all he could to keep her safe, and with the kiss she'd given him after eating the poison berry, he hoped the spell would be enough to combat the witch's magic if need be. The thought of Dulce's life being endangered in any way made his chest tighten. Was this what it meant to love? Anguish at the very thought of another's unhappiness?

Dulce rode in silence, her dark hair streaming behind her like silk ribbons, the landscape around them continuing to grow more devoid of life as they rose out of the valley to pass over endless rolling hills.

They stopped only to rest the horses and eat, determined to keep up their strength, knowing they would need all the advantage they could get.

The day wore on until at last, in the distance, their destination slipped into their view for the first time.

A fortress, as large as ten of the Duke's palaces, lay like a giant's discarded crown along the cliffs of the Crowmare Sea, its water reaching out beyond the horizon in midnight blue waves. Here was not an abandoned castle. There would certainly be guards protecting its walls.

Halting their horses within the shelter of a row of stone oak trees, they looked on in gloomy silence, Reed's heart galloping against his sternum.

Dulce's lips formed a tight line as she glanced up. "The sky isn't painted in blood. That could be a good sign… Possibly."

"Please tell me you have a plan of entry, Majesty," Reed said, imagining an army of guards with giant spears, eager to impale any unwanted visitors.

"As a matter of fact, I do." Dulce turned to grin at him, and Reed stared, the desire to kiss her overwhelming his every thought. "But I must warn you, it will be somewhat disorienting."

"Expound on *disorienting*," he uttered. "Do you mean disorienting like seductive, murderous ghosts, rabid taxidermy animals—or disorienting like fireballs falling from the sky?"

"Disorienting like … you may not be able to feel your limbs properly." She patted his shoulder.

"Oh, just that?" Reed arched a brow. "Sounds like every successful fight night."

"You may experience nausea."

Reed nodded. "Mmm, enticing." His voice came out laced with sarcasm.

"And dizziness," Dulce added.

"I survived the fever plague as a child," Reed confessed. "How much worse can this be?"

Hopping from her horse, Dulce retrieved her satchel from where it hung and searched through it. She placed worn utensils and mysterious ingredients along the rocky ground as she consulted her spell book, muttering to herself, an adorable frown of concentration on her face while she mixed and stirred ingredients.

"The horses will be spotted from miles away." She sighed, grinding something crunchy into a small bowl with a rock. "But I hesitate to feed any horse this. Did you know so many things are poisonous to them? Alsike clover, ivy, yellow star-thistle, foxglove, oleander, hemlock, yew—the list goes on and on. I cannot in good conscience make them consume it."

"So we let them go." Reed dismounted his horse and placed a hand on her shoulder. "They'll find their own way back home."

Dulce's eyes were wide as she turned to look up at him. "What if they're turned to stone? What if—"

"If we fail, they die along with everyone else anyway." Reed crouched to face her and kissed her softly on the cheek. "Nothing matters more than breaking this spell."

A smile played along her lips. "Nothing…?"

He watched her, his lungs unmoving, as Dulce brought her lips to his. She'd begun this journey a stranger to him, yet how quickly that had changed. Now she was an integral piece of him, and he would give up his life to make certain she was still alive in the end.

"If La Bisou Morte doesn't want to play nice, you will defeat her," Reed whispered. "I know you will. This whey-faced assassin strumpet has no idea what she's about to encounter. Truth be told, I almost feel sorry for her."

Dulce laughed as tears filled her eyes, the sound an alluring melody. She brought her lips to his once again, soft as feathers.

"Truth be told," she started, "I have no idea what I'm doing, Reed. My mother said in her last letter to me that everything I need to know is already in my heart, but what does that even *mean*? Yes, she taught me alchemy, tricks, and I have her book. But, if I'm honest, most of what my heart contains is fear. Fear that I will fail, and everything we know will be destroyed…"

Reed lifted Dulce to her feet before brushing her tears away and taking her hands in his. "Then you'll make a spell like no other. Your mother believed in you. And so do I."

Dulce reached into her satchel and held up two dark feathers. "Let's hope the raven's feathers have enough magic left in them for this spell to work."

It was true that Reed could hardly feel his limbs as they flew across the open plain, but he soon became accustomed to the strange sensation while they soared toward the looming castle in the distance. Dulce warned him that to shift into animal form through alchemy was to be at one with the elements around him, and seconds after following her instructions—wrapping a strand of his hair around a feather and adding a drop of his blood to the drink she offered him—he merged with his surroundings. Which were mostly rock. The trees, their shape stuck in a perpetual summer, turned to stone, their branches heavy and blooming stone fruit in the warm light of the sunset. Even the wheat stalks had become stone, frozen in time, leaning in wind that once blew across the land, the air now fallen still but for the fog swirling against the ground like ghostly fingers, purple smoke moving with each footfall.

While he moved his wings beside Dulce, gliding through the air, it was a peculiar thing. Natural. As if he'd flown his entire life.

Closer to their destination, the details of the castle became clearer. Its doors were entirely swallowed up by one of the ancient Trees of Life, this one larger than all the others. Bleached white, its branches spread out like twisted bones across the front of the castle. Its carved trunk opened without a sound and a line of shining carriages passed through, traveling west along a winding road, and Reed and Dulce slipped inside unnoticed by the guards. Their white, black, and gold uniforms were pristine, their spears shining before feathered helmets decorated in an elaborate insignia he didn't recognize. As he watched the guards, he thought something about them seemed inhuman, their movements too precise, too coordinated, and when he passed within inches of one, he noticed their faces were obscured not by fabric but in swirling shadow. He concentrated on the wind caressing his feathers and followed Dulce.

She led him across a piazza of carved stone, and he knew she was being guided to La Bisou Morte by her location spell. Her wings fluttered faster, urgently, as they entered another courtyard, this one empty of guards, and glided over a garden of stone, its hedges, trees, flowers in full bloom, now nothing but granite and crystal.

"There," Dulce whispered, her voice just the same in her raven form. "Beyond this door…"

Reed knew from his view of only a few hours ago that the castle was a round structure, that the middle of it must hold something of at least practical value. He didn't expect what that would prove to be.

Cages hung in midair by some invisible force, filling the area like floating lanterns. Reed nearly flew into one, barely catching himself as he came face to face with a dour creature, its ivory wings folded beneath iridescent fur, curved horns shimmering like pearls. Its sadness was palpable, and as Reed gazed around, he was horrified to discover that each cage held a suffering magical creature.

A perfectly circular expanse of water lay beneath these floating cages, a liquid mirror, reflecting the twilight sky above the metal domes. And at its center, surrounded by equally spaced stone trees, stood an enormous golden cage, designed to house every comfort someone could ever want—a luxurious bed, a bath chamber of the finest marble, a sitting room filled with opulent furniture, furs and rugs that even at this distance appeared soft, a dining space dripping in crystal and porcelain, decorated in flowers made of shining silk.

But no door. No escape.

And in the center of this cage, gazing up at the sky, sat a ruby-haired woman—*La Bisou Morte*—dressed in a gown of all white.

Dulce and Reed flew over the water and landed just outside the bars.

Around the witch's throat, she wore a stone very much like the Duke's, but no ordinary necklace—its chain was attached to the top of the cage far above her.

The witch stirred, and sniffing at the air, she rose.

"Who's there?" she demanded, her bright blue eyes flashing as she held up a hand, and Dulce gasped.

The witch wore a ring identical to her own.

23

Dulce

Time stood still for the briefest of moments as Dulce studied not only the stone mirroring the one that had belonged to the Duke, but also the ruby ring resting on La Bisou Morte's middle finger.

Why did this woman have such a ring? For a moment, Dulce believed the witch might've stolen her own, taken it from her, even while Dulce remained cloaked in magic, her ring as hidden as her human form, though she still felt it in her possession.

The witch slowly approached the golden bars, her sapphire eyes lingering on Dulce, a line settled between the woman's brows while she continued to peer at the ravens before her. Reed cocked his head, edging closer to Dulce. The young witch was beautiful, her hair, the shade of the brightest red rubies, falling in shining waves to her waist. Dulce easily understood how Cornelius could fall in love with such a woman, not only for her striking beauty, yet also for the mesmerizing power that emanated from her.

But something was certainly amiss, because a witch this powerful would never willingly allow herself to be locked in a cage, a gilded bird, shackled by the neck.

The creatures dangling from the cages floating above the water garden whimpered in the fading light, their cries creating the saddest of songs.

This wasn't what Dulce expected to find at all. So many questions whirled in her mind, she hardly knew where to begin. But before she could question the witch, the woman spoke, "You look like a raven I once had."

"The one you left trapped inside a cabinet at your abandoned castle?" Dulce supplied. "The one that died because of the curse you brought to our land? Yes, I suppose I do look like that bird."

The witch blinked, then narrowed her eyes, demanding, "Who are you?"

Dulce knew better than to transform into her human form, not with so many guards lurking about, and especially not while the witch was clearly being held prisoner. Held prisoner by whom, though?

"Who is responsible for your confinement?" Dulce asked.

The witch smiled sweetly, unfazed. "Answer my question first."

"You may recognize my husband's name," Dulce said.

"Cornelius Alastair Hale? Your lover. He attempted my murder. All for you."

"Ah, I see. Dulce Bancroft. Fascinating." The witch showed no remorse, not a flicker of guilt. Dulce wanted to feed her poisonous berries one by one until the woman's veins turned black.

"I saw you that night," she snapped, barely controlling her temper. "You poisoned our tree with your abhorrent spell."

The witch shrugged. "Your land, it was warded against my particular flavor of magic. I had to be invited by the rightful owner. Men are often weak-minded. Cornelius was the easiest way."

"He's dead now."

She shrugged again.

What was one more death to a witch who would destroy the whole world?

How was she to reach this woman? She seemed completely devoid of empathy, lacking all sense of remorse. There had to be some way to convince her to help them, to rid the land of her curse, before everything perished. Dulce looked at La Bisou Morte's ring, so exactly like her own.

She had to try.

Closing her eyes, Dulce spoke the words written in her mother's book, willing the matching ring into view, and the jewel shone along her clawed raven foot like a bracelet. This reached the witch at last. The moment she saw the ring, she gasped, straightening, her indifference completely vanished.

"Where did you get that?" she demanded, kneeling and reaching through the bars for Dulce, who leapt back from her grasp.

"It was my mother's," Dulce said.

"Your mother…" The witch blinked, paling. "She was Waverly Brewer?"

"You knew her?" Dulce studied the woman, who trembled with emotion.

"I know she is dead," the witch whispered. "I felt it the moment she departed." She gripped the bars, her face twisted in first sadness, then fear. "I would tell you to leave this place, but all of our lives are forfeit now."

No. No, they couldn't give up.

"Remove the curse," Dulce pleaded. "I know you can. You cast it—you can *uncast* it. Please. We can help you escape this prison."

The witch clenched her jaw. Her skin going impossibly pale in the gathering darkness, she nodded, seeming to settle on a decision as she reached out to them. "Come. See the truth through my eyes."

Both Dulce and Reed shrank from her touch, exchanging a glance. By his narrowed gaze, Reed didn't trust La Bisou Morte in the least. She bobbed her head in encouragement to him, and he reluctantly hopped closer, allowing the witch's hand to rest along his wing. What choice did they have? Here was the only person who knew how to rid the destruction spreading across the land.

The moment the witch's hand touched her, Dulce gasped, transported in time. Plunged into La Bisou Morte's memories.

A building carved into a mountainside, lined with rounded windows, full of winding underground corridors and assembly halls slipped into her mind. Young girls carrying books and wearing matching clothing in furs and wool walked in groups and lines past one another through a courtyard, laughing and arguing.

A school. For those with magical abilities.

Dulce nearly cried out when she recognized one girl in particular. Her mother. She looked to be around twelve or thirteen.

"My name is Marguerite," the witch said, her voice echoing in Dulce's head, calm and comforting, as though she were about to read a children's bedtime story. "Your mother was once my dearest friend. We were sent to the same boarding school, a school for girls born with magic. When mine overflowed and threatened the lives around me, which it often did, I was severely punished. Starved. Shocked. Submerged in ice water. Anything our teachers could think of to bring my power under control. It was your mother alone who would bring me food, fire-warmed clothing, a comforting song, though she risked being beaten for it. It was she who showed me kindness when all I had known was cruelty. She told me on many occasions that our teachers were only envious, that I held more magic than all of them combined, that I would be truly great someday. She was my only family, a real sister to me...

"I studied hard, learned some measure of control over my power," Marguerite continued, and Dulce watched the scene change. The girls went from children to young women arm in arm as they skipped through the dark corridors, ignoring the scowls of the others. Her mother's laughter echoed along the stone—a sound Dulce thought gone forever, almost forgotten.

"When the time for the binding ceremony came, of

course we chose to tie our fates together." Marguerite played with the ring on her finger, her eyes filled with sadness. "Few had ever mustered the courage for it, but your mother and I, we had known for years that we wanted to be more than sisters. We would gladly sacrifice our lives for each other. And so we made the blood bond. We would be there to help one another, to lend our magic to the other, come what may. Everything was perfect, until…"

Dulce watched as the scene changed once again. Marguerite, appearing just the same as she did now, her youth and beauty in full bloom, stood alone in a field of berries, humming softly to herself as she filled her basket. Was she immortal, or was it magic that had prevented her from aging?

A young man of surpassing beauty approached Marguerite. Light shone around him in an enchanting halo. He was incredibly handsome, almost impossibly so, with golden hair framing his otherworldly features, falling past his shoulders, his eyes like silver moons, his smile hypnotic.

"When I met Aldrich," Marguerite said, "I felt as if my eyes were seeing color for the first time. Love, true love, was mine. There was nothing greater than his affection. Within a fortnight, I had become entirely infatuated with him. He was more than life to me, all I could think of day and night.

"No secret can be kept between the bonded, though, and Waverly knew. She told me she didn't trust Aldrich. That she sensed a great wickedness in him. That he hunted me for my magic as a tiger might hunt his prey. She implored me to never see him again, to protect myself and my power from his greed. But that was impossible. Unthinkable. I was already too far under his spell. Soon, perhaps sensing the disapproval of my bonded sister, Aldrich wanted to take me away, out from under the strict supervision and rules of our school. He told me he loved me with his entire heart and soul and wanted to give me the whole world, and fool that I was, I believed him. So I turned my back on your mother, using a dark spell with Aldrich's sorcery to fracture our bond, and I abandoned the only true friend I had ever known.

"I never saw her again." Marguerite sighed, her gaze turned to the sky. "The day she died, I felt it through our bond, even though I had believed it broken. And part of my heart died with her. But by that time, I had become infatuated with a new desire. The desire for a child of my own. Aldrich refused to give me one, no matter how many times I begged him. Yet I was a powerful witch, and I took matters into my own hands. It was not a difficult spell. When I became pregnant, that was when everything changed. That was when I knew your mother had been right about Aldrich…"

As darkness fell in earnest, flames came to life around them, glowing along the water's edge, lighting up the stone trees. Marguerite looked only more beautiful as tears fell from her sapphire eyes.

"Our son was born a monster," she whispered. "One so hideous and powerful, no man or beast would ever be safe as long as he remained free. And so he is kept from the world, locked away. Only on a full moon does Percy become human. Only on a full moon can I take him in my arms and embrace him as a mother."

"But why did you curse the land?" Dulce asked,

bewildered. "Will ending all life here free your son?"

Can you really be so selfish? Dulce wanted to scream at the witch, but held her tongue.

Another scene came forward then, one of a beautiful child with hair as red as his mother's. He sat huddled within a cage so small there was barely enough space for his tiny frame to sit. He raised his head, wiping his tears, then crawled into the darkness of a tunnel, his feet becoming elongated, talons curling from his toes while he disappeared into the shadows.

The images cleared, and Dulce was back in the present with a raven beside her—Reed.

"Having a child stripped away Aldrich's *precious* immortality," Marguerite sneered. "Though he was centuries old, he began to age. There was only one way to regain his youth: to continue to cheat death and hold onto his power. Take the land's magic for himself. But he cannot do that alone—he needs a powerful witch. He always has. You see, it was never me who he loved at all. No. It was only what my power could give him. When I realized this and tried to refuse him, to escape, he hurt Percy. You have no idea what it's like to hear your own child's suffering. I endured it for *months* before finally I could stand it no more. And I gave in to Aldrich. I did what he bid me to do, and I saw my son every full moon. I thought... I truly believed I could discover another way to stop him, a way to save Percy. But now I fear it's too late."

The sound of Marguerite's anguished sigh echoed across the still water of the lake.

"And once this world ends," Dulce snapped, "then what?"

"At least in death, we will be free of him."

"You can still take away the spell!" Dulce shouted, frustration welling in her. How could this woman be so selfish? What of every living thing around her? "The sorcerer is powerless without you. Defeat him and save your son yourself!"

Marguerite's laughter pierced Dulce's very soul as she backed away from them, shaking her head while she cackled.

"He is more powerful than any witch, don't you see?" she screeched. "His greed knows no bounds. He has been gaining magic for centuries! Long before I or your mother were born, long before our ancestors were born! This world is only one of many he has devoured."

The dark magic Dulce had felt in the witch's bedchamber at her castle had belonged to the sorcerer—that was why it had felt so different. "There has to be a way to defeat him," she murmured.

"Your mother could've managed it, perhaps," Marguerite admitted. "There was enough good in her. If only I had listened to her…"

Dulce held up her mother's ring. "Then listen to her now. She gave me this ring—I have to believe she knew I would find you. That I could help you. Let me try, Marguerite. Please."

Marguerite's gaze filled with torment. Dulce could plainly see that she longed to change her past, that if she could go back in time and alter her decisions, she would.

"You're still a powerful witch," Dulce insisted. "I've seen what your magic can do."

Marguerite fell to her knees, looking at her hands, grief painted along her features. "My magic doesn't work here.”

“Tell me what to do—let me help you!”

“You may have her ring.” Marguerite shook her head. “But you are not your mother.”

Dulce’s talons pressed against the ground as irritation coursed through her. She struggled to think of another way to convince the witch to fight, to stand up against her captor, no matter how powerful. But suddenly the cries of the creatures in the cages grew to a frenzy, and Marguerite peered at them, her eyes wide with panic.

“You need to leave, *now*.” Marguerite hissed. “He’s *coming!*”

“No.” Dulce would not run. She turned to Reed. “He may know I’m here, he no doubt senses my magic, but he doesn’t know you’re with me.”

Reed hesitated, yet seeming to realize there wasn’t enough time to argue, he pressed his feathered forehead against hers. “I trust you know what you’re doing, Highness.”

“I’ll signal when I need you.” Dulce longed to kiss him one last time, but it was too late.

As Reed flew to land atop a stone tree branch, golden hair caught Dulce’s eye when the sorcerer appeared on the opposite side of the water. He walked across the liquid as though he were gliding on air, just as alluring as the vision she’d seen of him in the witch’s memories.

“Marguerite.” Aldrich smiled when he reached her cage, trailing his forefinger across its gold. His gaze drifted in Dulce’s direction through the bars, his smile growing wider. “Mmm, I see a little birdy has come.” He snapped his fingers and she shifted, collapsing to her knees on the ground in human form.

"You thought you could trick me, didn't you?" Aldrich purred, sauntering before her. "It's a good thing you're here. I've been waiting for you to arrive."

Reed

The moment the sorcerer appeared, the creatures' shrieks fell silent, and they sat trembling in their floating cages, their eyes wide with fear. Aldrich's robes flowing behind him, their jailer glided across the water to stand at the golden prison's door. Before Reed could steady himself on the tree limb, the sorcerer had snapped his fingers and turned both Dulce and himself from ravens back into humans.

If the branch he rested on hadn't been made of stone, Reed would most certainly have fallen into the water.

Not a notion he particularly admired, after the realization that the lake was full of what looked to be *very* lifelike human statues, and what he guessed were not statues at all. Reed imagined falling, the cold dark water soaking his clothing, weighing him down, until he couldn't swim, the drowned coming to life, their stone hands pulling him to his death, preventing him from rescuing Dulce…

Reed knew he was no match for the sorcerer. The puking lout, aside from being completely deranged with power, was centuries old and apparently had years of practice vanquishing his enemies.

Aldrich was not yet aware of his presence. Reed's only hope was to use the element of surprise to his advantage and create a diversion. There would be only one chance to accomplish this. He needed to do something to distract this sorcerer clotpole long enough to give Dulce a fighting chance to use her magic against him.

She was no longer outside the cage but imprisoned *with* the witch.

Reed frantically searched around, finding nothing but floating cages hanging well out of his reach, stone trees even the leaves of which proved unbreakable, water he had no interest in touching, and flame in wide basins.

He had to do something *now*—or it would be too late.

Climbing silently to the ground, Reed moved like a panther in the shadows toward the largest basin. Aldrich's attention fixed not on Marguerite but solely on Dulce, who he looked at as if she were an enticing meal. Reed's hands balled into tight fists at that. They didn't have much time before the sorcerer made some sort of decision, and whatever it was, it would not be advantageous to anyone but himself.

Reed freely admitted Marguerite's life made his seem

luxurious by comparison, yet he knew where his sympathy would lie if it came to a choice between helping the witch or helping Dulce. Regardless of any hardship Marguerite endured, the fact nevertheless proved she was a woman willing to see the entire world destroyed as a direct result of her actions. While Dulce was determined to put aside her grief and trials and do everything in her power to save the world around her, even at the cost of her life.

"I've been waiting for a fresh replacement," Aldrich cooed, his voice resonating across the circle of water as if by some vaingloriously fashioned magic.

Though Dulce lingered inside the gilded cage, her expression remained resolute when she straightened her clothing and stood tall.

The sorcerer sniffed the air, his grin lascivious. "Your magic smells delicious. Fresh and young. You will do splendidly."

What a fobbing lout, Reed thought while reaching the basin of flame, its sides large as a carriage.

Surprising him, Marguerite moved to stand protectively in front of Dulce, her stare like icy daggers when she faced Aldrich.

"No." She gritted her teeth. "You will not harm Waverly's child. If you do, I will never execute another spell for you again."

The sorcerer's chilling laughter echoed across the water, and the creatures cowered within their cages, a few whimpering at the sound.

"Do you actually believe I still need your spells?" Aldrich drawled, inspecting his nails in apparent boredom. "Pathetic, really."

Dulce wasn't only resting her hands in her deep pockets—Reed could tell she was in fact studiously gathering some mysterious mixture from the many ingredients she always carried with her. He didn't know how much time they had before the sorcerer put a chain around her throat as he had Marguerite.

Her hands stilled, and Reed knew that now was his chance to perform a distraction.

He pushed on the basin, and it moved slightly beneath the force. So, the mewling malt-worm hadn't bothered to notice his garden wasn't as well-built as a Glen tavern after all.

Reed prepared to topple the flames, his overcoat draped across one shoulder, ready to ignite.

"Hey, spongy toad barnacle!" he shouted, pushing the metal basin to the ground, where it crashed to the stone with an ear-splitting *clang*. Aldrich turned, a comical look of surprise etched across his face, and Reed swung his overcoat into the fountain of sparks and guttering blaze, allowing the oil-soaked silk and fur to burst into flame. While the churlish canker-blossom stared in dumb surprise, Reed sprinted across the lake's submerged steppingstones and straight at Aldrich, spewing curses like a madman.

He planned on wrapping the sorcerer in his burning overcoat, but he didn't make it that far. Leaping at the man, Reed found that the sorcerer had vanished. The burning overcoat became nothing but a hoard of charcoal moths, their wings covered in dying embers as they fell in slow spirals to the ground.

Reed spun to find Aldrich smiling in apparent delight, clapping his hands in a slow, mocking fashion.

But at his back, Dulce had carried out her magic.

The witch's stone necklace and chain holding both her magic and her prisoner disappeared, along with the bars of the golden cage surrounding Dulce and Marguerite. As had all the rest above them, leaving the creatures sitting suspended above the water on mere platforms, free to fly to freedom.

They didn't seem interested in escape, though. One by one, they stood, eyes blazing wrath while they honed their gazes on the sorcerer.

"Nice try, *boy*." Aldrich curled his lip, sauntering toward Reed. "But your blood holds no magic." He lifted his hand, and in a flash of red, some invisible force struck Reed in the chest like lightning, making him stumble backward, his vision blurring.

For a moment, Reed thought he was dead, until his sight cleared. He remained in place and patted his chest, where there was only a tear in his shirt, not his flesh. Dulce's poisonous kiss, along with her spell, had spared his life.

"*So* you're protected," Aldrich purred. "No matter. I have other ways of ending your life."

Still unaware that right behind him, the sorcerer's captives had been set free, Aldrich stalked toward Reed, his robes billowing in the night breeze.

"Did a slobbering worm such as yourself actually believe you could fight *me* and win?" he said with a sardonic laugh. "Why, it's almost tragic…"

Reed raised his hands over his head as the sorcerer approached him, and, pretending to cower, he peered at Dulce from behind the safety of his fingers. She and Marguerite were frantically working on something between them, Dulce emptying her pockets onto the thick rug.

A crowd of magical creatures gathered on silent wings, their glowing eyes eerie over the rippling water as they alighted along the stone, prowling ever closer to their prey.

Reed needed to stall Aldrich, keep the craven barnacle's attention on him, give Dulce more time.

He lowered his hands and smiled up at the sorcerer, who halted, frowning at his victim's sudden change.

"I've been wondering since you arrived, is that robe drafty?" Reed asked, pointing. "Or have you got a bunch of woolen knickers underneath?"

The sorcerer blinked, opening his mouth, then closing it again. "*What?*"

"I mean, really," Reed continued. "I imagine wool undergarments are quite itchy, especially on your sensitive territories. Is that why you're so ill-tempered, and *crotchety?* I've heard a cold-water soak with white vinegar can do wonders."

"You seem to want to die slowly," Aldrich seethed, his fury distorting his features to comical levels. Reed grinned wider.

"Now, silk, on the other hand." Reed scratched his nose absentmindedly as he ate the dried fruit Dulce had lovingly placed in his pocket. "Quite soft on the bits and bollocks, isn't it? Though I daresay no match for the winters you must get up here. Fur lining might be a solution." He wiggled his hand around, gesturing. "Though it would hardly give it that *villainous flare* when you strut about, would it?"

With a roar, the sorcerer lunged at Reed, but like an

angry mob, the creatures closed in on him, their claws tearing at Aldrich's robes. Reed thought perhaps the fight was over, until he noticed the object of their disdain had dissolved into thick gray smoke.

Appearing on the opposite side of Reed, the sorcerer at last noticed Dulce and Marguerite. They stood side by side, whispering while mist filled the ground between them, blue sparks passing along it, mimicking a tiny storm. As the sorcerer raised his hands, light bathed the night, blinding Reed for an instant, and when he opened his eyes again, all three alchemists lay on the ground.

Half of the creatures had fled en masse, apparently deciding this fight wasn't worth their long-awaited freedom.

"Dulce!" Reed rushed to her, gathering her into his arms. She was pale and still but breathing. "You can't die on me now, Highness. Not after everything we've faced to get here. I still haven't heard you play the piano, you know." Forgetting everything around him, he kissed her lips softly. "Please, Dulce. You have to wake."

"I always wondered what it was like to be kissed awake," she whispered, her eyes fluttering open. "Just like in the storybooks."

Reed didn't hesitate to kiss her again.

"Aldrich's magic is trapped," Dulce said against his lips. "I don't know for how long…"

The remaining creatures closed in once more on the unconscious sorcerer, but in a flash of sparks, Aldrich roused, holding a stone above him while sneering in triumph, and they retreated in terror, fleeing.

"Temporarily taking away my magic will do *nothing*," he growled.

"What's happeni—" Reed fell silent as an otherworldly howl pierced the night. He stared, dread gripping his heart, when the sky above them glowed red as blood, akin to a distorted sun rising from the north.

There the blood is… This can't be good.

Marguerite was on her feet, her eyes wild with fear.

"No!" she screamed, rushing to Aldrich, dropping to her knees, and clinging to his robes. "Don't do this! Please!"

With a harsh kick of his boot to her chest, the sorcerer sent Marguerite sliding across the stone in a heap.

Reed didn't need to wonder for too long what she protested, because the next instant something crept out of the shadows.

A monster stepped into the light. It was the most grotesque thing Reed had ever seen, and he'd once watched the Leper eat a Paralithodes camtschaticus. Standing tall as two men, covered in matted hair and scales, the thing lumbered into the garden, its gleaming eyes wild above a cavernous hole for a nose and a mouth impossibly full of shard-like teeth. Numerous horns atop its scalp shone in the gathering light.

The monster opened its mouth, and it was as though death surrounded Reed when its jaw opened wide enough to split its hideous head nearly in two. Its knees a tangle of bones, it spread its arms wide, fingers like shining blades, and screeched, the sound sending a jolt of pain through Reed's head.

"Leave Percy alone!" Marguerite no longer lay on the stone but stood tall, focused solely on Aldrich. Reed had to admire her concentration as the monster leapt to its gruesome feet, the tentacles squirming like snakes along its middle, making Reed regret eating anything at all.

The witch held blades in her hands, each one magically replaced by another as she threw them at the sorcerer, who dodged them with easy grace. It seemed magic was not his only gift.

"Run, Reed," Dulce urged. "Go, while they don't notice you."

"Under the circumstances." Reed gathered one of the many blades falling at Marguerite's feet. "And because an actual horned beast is stenching up the place, I'll forgive you for saying that, Majesty."

"You're as stubborn as me." Dulce grasped the vial of dark purple liquid that she'd shown him once before. The vial he knew held the last resort against the woman who they had all once believed to be their enemy. The spell that would kill La Bisou Morte.

The piece of magic that was now their only chance at defeating the sorcerer.

The monster screeched, and they turned to face it, Reed's hope faltering while he watched it tremble as if against unseen bonds.

Aldrich's magic was coming back—it was plain to see. Knives slowed before him, easily caught, his smile growing. Reed never knew he could dislike someone as much as he disliked this fobbing codpiece.

And then, grinning lasciviously at Marguerite, Aldrich unleashed the monster on Dulce, a blur of fur and teeth surging toward her. Reed lunged forward, shielding Dulce in his arms as he shut his eyes, expecting to feel talons rip open his back.

But nothing happened.

Marguerite stood before Dulce, prepared to die in her

stead. For the daughter of her only friend.

The monster hesitated, trembling against its master's will, as some tiny spark of awareness shone in its gleaming eyes.

"Percy," Marguerite begged. "It's not your fault. You don't have to do his bidding…"

The monster shook its hideous head, inching back with a rumbling growl.

"Kill them!" the sorcerer bellowed. "*Now!*"

Reed watched in utter disbelief as, in spite of the pain the sorcerer's magic was clearly causing it, the monster still refused to obey, instead taking a further step back.

"You defy me?" Aldrich raged. "You defy *me*? Fine! I'll kill your precious *mother* myself!"

He flung a volley of knives at Marguerite as she continued to stand unmoving, a shield before Dulce and Reed, a shower of metal hurling toward her chest.

But there was the monster, moving so fast Reed hardly knew how it was possible. The sorcerer's knives pierced its grotesque chest even as its mother screamed louder than ever, collapsing to the stone ground to enfold the monster in her arms.

Reed didn't wait. While Aldrich still surveyed his handiwork with pride, Reed left Dulce's side and barreled forward to plunge his own blade into the sorcerer's heart.

He wasn't surprised when it didn't kill the magic-infested pignut. But Aldrich failed to notice Dulce, serene as an avenging warrior while she performed her spell. The vial she held emitted dark shadows that slithered across the stone like smoky serpents, finding their way to the sorcerer, disappearing beneath his robes.

"You again," Aldrich ground out, his breath as rotten

as the centuries he'd stolen when he brought his face within inches of Reed's. "I will enjoy slowly peeling the skin from your—"

His eyes widened, Dulce's spell taking effect, and the sorcerer screamed in utter agony as his life leeched from his body, indigo light flowing from his pores, his veins imitating lightning, his bones glowing in strobes while he stood rigid like the stone trees around him.

"How did you…?" he asked Reed, his eyes filling with blackish, rotted blood, his skin paling, sagging from his bones in deepening wrinkles until it flaked away to ashes, and he slumped to the ground, aged centuries. Dead.

"Ha!" Reed whirled to face Dulce with a wide grin. "The poxy giglet thought I killed him."

She smiled, tears filling her eyes, and Reed caught her as she stumbled forward.

A heart-wrenching wail filled the night.

Marguerite trembled with sobs as her son died in her arms, his monstrous form slowly melting away into that of a small child. A mother rocking her son in her embrace, kissing his glossy red hair while tears streamed down her cheeks.

Dulce

Marguerite held Percy as though he were the most precious thing in existence. Which Dulce knew he must be since the witch was willing to sacrifice every living thing for him, to halt his suffering to any extent in her power, to see her son every full moon until the end came for them all.

Dulce hadn't known if she could defeat Aldrich, but she'd had to try. All she'd had left was the spell she'd planned to use to kill La Bisou Morte, before uncovering the witch's story.

A few of the melancholic creatures still lingered in branches, their curious gazes on the humans below them.

The bloody sky slowly darkened to black once more, a crescent moon illuminating a circle of clouds, countless stars twinkling like tiny diamonds in the gloom.

"Look," Reed whispered. "He's not dead."

Dulce turned to Marguerite and studied the small child in the witch's arms. The boy's eyes, the same sapphire blue as his mother's, were no longer closed but *open*.

"Marguerite!" she gasped. "Your son is alive!"

The witch's breath hitched, and she drew back to peer down at her son. Percy wasn't turning back into the monstrous creature of nightmares but remained rather a young child of two, innocent and pure. With the sorcerer's death, the young boy was free of his curse and would no longer suffer.

Marguerite cupped Percy's cheeks, and this time joyous sobs escaped her as she kissed her son's forehead. "My dear, beautiful boy."

Reed nudged his shoulder into Dulce's and grinned. "See? You saved everyone."

"We, Mr. Hawthorne," she clarified with a smile. "*We.*"

"Mama," the boy croaked, his voice barely audible.

"Shh, you're safe now, Percy," Marguerite assured him. "Sleep." Although her shoulders were relaxed and happiness lingered in her expression, her eyes remained haunted.

The witch stood, cradling her sleeping son to her chest as her gaze settled on Dulce. "You saved my son. You, a woman who I didn't know was the daughter of my only friend, a woman who almost died because I lured her beau to infatuation. I know I have no right to ask it, but can you ever forgive me?"

Dulce shrugged. "I readily forgive you for Cornelius. In fact, I should thank you for showing me his true character." She could still taste the bitter poison planted in her tea, the way it felt to be trapped below ground in an enclosed coffin, certain that death would soon take her.

A line settled between Marguerite's brows. "For all the rest though… I understand. My actions remain unforgivable."

Dulce twisted her ring around her finger. "You have goodness in you, just as my mother did. None of us are unforgivable. Every heart has the capacity to change."

"I can name a few missing that capacity, starting that list with the Leper," Reed pointed out.

Dulce rolled her eyes. "Perhaps you're right, but still. *Most* do."

Marguerite glanced down at her son, then met Dulce's gaze. "I will never regret what I did. Because that would mean Percy wouldn't exist. However, I accept responsibility to heal the land from its curse." She flicked her wrist, and a bridge made of pearls unfolded like a royal carpet across the water.

The witch led them through the castle courtyard, where guards' armor and uniforms lay sprinkled about, dark sand spilling from their shells.

"Where are the guards now?" Reed asked.

"They were made from Aldrich's sorcery. With him dead, so are they." Marguerite halted before the great Tree of Life, its white branches of stone encircling the castle like some tentacled beast, its wide doors carved out of its prominent trunk. She pressed a palm to it, keeping

Percy close in her other arm. Shutting her eyes, Marguerite spoke words in an unknown language, and as she did, a soft glow of light flowed from her chest and into the tree. After a few more moments, she took a deep, shuddering breath and stepped back. "The devouring spell is relinquished from the land. Every tree and animal will be free, returned to thriving life, as they were." Her gaze shifted between the pair. "And now, you wish to return home, yes?"

"Yes," Reed answered quickly, rubbing his hands together in the growing cold without his overcoat.

"Is there a faster way than we came?" Dulce asked hopefully. Walking home, while it would be nice to spend days upon days in Reed's company, the mere thought alone made her feet ache.

"It so happens there is." Marguerite smiled. "I'll return you both to Moonglade by airship before I journey back to my castle. It's the least I can do."

"Airship?" Reed arched a skeptical brow.

Dulce had never heard of such a thing. "What is that?"

"Just as it sounds." Marguerite angled her head to the side. "A ship that sails through the air. Its magic makes it perfectly safe—I assure you. The airship was how Aldrich sailed through worlds and across the sea when I needed to gather hard-to-find ingredients for spells."

"Sounds much more preferable to a horse." Reed smirked.

Dulce had never been on a ship, let alone one that could fly through the air like a bird, but it certainly sounded faster than trudging along the land, even if they did manage to find their horses again.

"Follow me." Marguerite motioned them forward.

"Why did Aldrich have the creatures in floating cages as prisoners? Where are they from?" Dulce asked as they wandered through the garden.

"From far and wide across every sea. Aldrich was drawn to the power of magic, collected it. He could take from any creature who held it in their blood," Marguerite said.

The trees surrounding the island in the lake had already begun to show signs of life, as if their stone had been ice and it was melting from them, revealing green leaves in the glow of the fire's light.

The fortress loomed above them as they passed between a row of pillars, opening to a wide clearing, where a massive object stood—a ship, but not a ship at all. Painted in a deep sapphire, its hull decorated in gold, silver, and ivory, various-sized spikes protruded from its sails, its deck.

The airship.

Its keel appeared to belong to any other ship that could cross the seas, but instead of masts and sails, its port and stern were fashioned as if great iron balloons had landed upon them, gears and clockwork gadgets covering their sides, stars painted on their blue surfaces.

"Welcome to the *Velvet Noir*." Marguerite threw a door along the ship's forward deck wide and led them inside what proved to be a luxurious home, broad windows on every wall, where Dulce could only imagine the spectacular views of sunsets over the vast land beneath them. It was like a dream.

Marguerite indicated two large sofas before an ample table of rose pink stone. "Eat. Rest. The magic inside the ship will give you anything your heart desires."

"*Anything?*" Reed drawled.

"Perhaps not *anything*. But any destination. Any item of clothing, fire or water. Any food and drink." She adjusted Percy in her arms. "The washroom and bedroom suite are just through there. I suggest you don't tinker with the airship in any way."

"Thank you, Marguerite." Dulce hardly knew what to say—a part of her was grateful the witch was rid of Aldrich, while another part knew she'd brought misery upon herself by forcing a wicked sorcerer to father a child. But now, perhaps she could find her own way in the world, be given a new beginning.

Dulce took Marguerite's hand in hers, and the witch's eyes filled with tears as she looked down at her son. "I hope the memory of his past won't linger in his mind forever. He's still young."

"Shower him with love," Dulce replied. "I'm certain he will grow to inspire affection in all who meet him."

"I vow to teach him to wield his magic for good."

"Please visit us," she offered. "I can teach Percy some alchemy tricks, and you and I could remember Mother together."

"Perhaps. When I'm worthy of rejoining society." Marguerite sighed. "Now, let me show you how to manage the *Velvet Noir*."

She informed them that it would be only twelve short hours before they reached their destination while she showed Reed how to decipher the numbers along one windowpane.

As the witch turned to leave, Dulce remembered something. "Wait!" she called. "May I ask a favor of you?"

"Only for you will I dabble in favors without cost."

"Will you make certain there's no bounty on Reed's head with the Duke or anyone else?"

Marguerite smiled brightly. "Easily done." Before parting ways, she added, "I may even fix a few more things."

Dulce hardly noticed the moment the airship rose from the ground, but as the night through the windows along the easterly side of the ship painted the sky in glorious dark blues and wispy clouds, she realized they floated high above the land.

She sank into a chair across from Reed, her exhaustion finally catching up with her. As she lifted a cup of tea to her lips, she found him smiling at her.

"This is an experience I wasn't expecting." Reed winked.

"Quite the story to tell." The tea's chamomile flavor perfectly held a hint of honey and vanilla.

They simply spoke what they wished to eat, and the food appeared before them. Reed was quite entertained by this notion, demanding all sorts of strange combinations—bletted medlar with auroch and dried whale blubber—though they thoroughly enjoyed a hot meal of fresh vegetables and bread still warm from the oven, as they bantered about the memories they'd shared during their journey.

The night wore on, and Dulce opened the window to the moon's silvery glow illuminating the landscape below while they glided over it. She stared at it all through a spyglass, purely ensnared by the world from this height. No longer was the land blighted by stone and desert, but rather bursting in emerald greens, herds of animals surging toward glistening rivers. A colony of fruit bats descended toward the foliage to fill their appetites.

Dulce thought of Moonglade and what would come next for her. She would simply get the marriage between her and Cornelius annulled, seeing as they never consummated it. The town would continue to believe he disappeared, but now out of madness for poisoning his bride.

"Are you going to stare out the window the entire ride home?" Reed asked, his voice echoing from the other side of the room.

With a smile, Dulce closed the window and peered at him. He lay on the bed, his boots tucked neatly beside a cabinet, his dark eyes shining mischievously beneath his adorably disheveled ivory hair.

She placed the spyglass on the table, and the corners of her lips lifted. "That bed does look rather tempting. Especially with the handsome man lying in it."

"Would you like to sleep?" He bit his lip, and any exhaustion she held dissipated.

"Perhaps later." Dulce boldly stepped toward the bed, unfastening the buttons of her dress. Reed's hooded gaze never wavered from hers as she peeled the fabric from her shoulders, letting the garments pool to the floor one after the other, until she stood bare before him. "Do you prefer to remain clothed, Mr. Hawthorne?"

Reed smirked, hurrying to remove his clothing, her heart pounding faster.

They studied one another's forms, learning each line, each curve, each lovely flaw before he rasped, "I do believe we have a bed to share."

Dulce laughed, then crawled into his lap, her legs cradling Reed's strong thighs. His delicious hardness pressed against her, and he sat forward, bringing his lips to the curve of her neck. She moaned, rolling her hips forward as his hands drifted to her hips.

Breathless, needing more of him, she raised slightly and slid down over his manhood, making them both gasp with pleasure.

Reed's lips found hers, and as they gave and took, she never felt so beautiful and powerful as she did in that moment, sitting atop him, in control, both ravishing one another in exhilarating kisses.

Once bliss had conquered them both, Reed held her in his arms, and Dulce cozied up against him. She could hear the comfortable sound of his still-pounding heartbeat, feel the rise and fall of his chest.

Dulce lifted her head and pressed her lips to Reed's. "Goodnight, Mr. Hawthorne."

"Goodnight, Highness."

Dulce awoke to find the airship floating downward to land. She and Reed hastily dressed and stared out the open window. Before the *Velvet Noir* came to a rest on the meadow just behind her home, she caught a glimpse through the spyglass of Sylvan and Lucas outside the front of the manor in the gardens, and she was thankful the young servant had returned home safely. Majestic as ever, her mother's tree—perfect, whole, and alive. Every fiber of her being became fully relieved at the sight.

Reed raked a hand through his rumpled hair. "I'm sure the villagers are wondering what kind of magic this aircraft is.”

“Something they’ll write stories about, I’m sure.” Dulce laughed.

Once they entered the late morning light, they didn’t retreat to the manor just yet—instead, they merely stood there, gaping at the airship as it lifted. It was one of the most extraordinary sights Dulce had ever seen.

Eventually, the flying machine disappeared from their sight, and she turned to face Reed, when he asked, “Is this where you tell me we should part ways, Highness?”

Dulce grasped his hand and smiled. “This is where I ask you to stay, Mr. Hawthorne.”

He tilted her chin up with his forefinger so their gazes held. “As your servant?”

“As my suitor.” There would be no other man in all the territories who she would want to court other than him.

“Ah, a pauper courting an heiress. How will the villagers of Moonglade take such news?” He grinned.

“You’ll be the town hero!” Dulce told him. “You would do well to prepare yourself now for the onslaught of your adoring public.”

“Nonsense.”

“After saving the world, it’s fact!”

Reed’s dark eyes became serious as he brought his face closer to hers. “I vow to court you in the way you deserve,” he promised. “I won’t take a single coin from you. I’ll find respectable work. And I will make certain to take you to the performing opera again.”

Dulce’s heart grew to the point she thought it would burst from happiness. “I have a secret,” she admitted.

“I love a good secret.” He rubbed his hands together

in apparent anticipation. "Do tell."

She laughed softly. "Last spring, Vesta foresaw a fortune for me in her tea leaves. She said the man who will own my heart entirely, and I his, is the one who will lift me from a most unfortunate and muddy circumstance."

His grin grew wide, and he tugged a lock of her hair. "So you *liked* me before we even met."

Her cheeks heated. "I kept it to myself because I didn't want you to think fate was choosing for you."

"Fate can choose for me all it wants as long as it leads me to you, Ms. Bancroft." Reed surprised Dulce by sweeping her off her feet and placing the most perfect of kisses against her lips.

EPILOGUE

Word quickly spread across Moonglade that the newlywed heiress hadn't died, but rather she'd been poisoned by her lumpish pignut of a husband, who fled the village before the truth of her survival came to light.

But the heiress had a secret. That foiled murderer himself was no longer alive.

She kept his rotting corpse in her cemetery garden, where it remained beneath a thriving black baccara rose, a reminder to the heiress not to ever take anything in this life for granted. That tomorrow is promised to no one. It served as a remembrance to love and cherish those she held most dear, including the man whom a tea leaf fortune predicted would someday come to be her true love.

The man who was now her beloved husband.

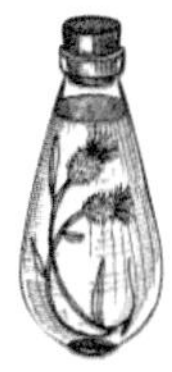

Did you enjoy Poison Nights & Twilight Alchemy?
Authors love reviews whether long or short!

Want to read another book by Candace & S.G.D.?
Try In the Haunts of Goblin Men.

Esther and Kitty grew up hearing tales of the goblins who live in the woods bordering their town. Stories they believed were nothing more than silly superstitions, fables meant to scare children into good behavior.

Until the people they love most are brutally murdered.

With only a bowl of goblin fruit left behind, the sisters are about to learn that the wicked creatures are all too real.

And The Goblin King has a vengeful appetite that must be sated.

ALSO FROM CANDACE ROBINSON

Wicked Souls Duology
Vault of Glass
Bride of Glass

Marked by Magic
The Bone Valley
Merciless Stars
Her Cruel Dahlias

Cruel Curses Trilogy
Clouded By Envy
Veiled By Desire
Shadowed By Despair

Untamed Darkness
And Then There Was Silence
Dearest Clementine: Dark and Romantic Monstrous
Tales
These Vicious Thorns: Tales of the Lovely Grim
Savage Delights: Two Dark Tales

Faeries of Oz Series
Lion (Short Story Prequel)
Tin
Crow
Ozma
Tik-Tok

Vampires in Wonderland Series
Rav (Short Story Prequel)

Maddie
Chess
Knave

Once Upon A Wicked Villain
Spindle of Sin
Tower of Shadows

Cursed Hearts Duology
Lyrics & Curses
Music & Mirrors

A Slice of Love
Hearts Are Like Balloons
Bacon Pie
Avocado Bliss

Charmed by a Spell
Bewitched by the Headless Horseman
In the Haunts of Goblin Men
Between the Quiet

ALSO FROM S.G.D. SINGH

The Infernal Guard
Emergence
Descent
Severance
Forsaken
Ravenous

Dracula Retold
In the Heart of Babylon
Exiled to Freedom
In the Haunts of Goblin Men

ACKNOWLEDGMENTS

Thank you so much to the readers who chose to step into our gothic and flowery story!

To our families and friends, you mean more to us than the biggest cottagecore flower bouquet. Amber H., thank you for finalizing all the last-minute fixes! Hayley, Amber D., Ann, and Jerica, you guys are the best proofreaders that anyone could ask for!

Hannah, we adore the map, Christina, you brought Dulce and Reed to life in your art, and to Jamie, Trish, and Alexis, thank you for letting us be a part of this multiauthor series!

And to those who find a portal to Moonglade, don't forget to visit the family cemetery at Dulce's manor where the single black flower lingers today!

ABOUT THE AUTHORS

Candace Robinson spends her days consumed by words and hoping to one day find her own DeLorean time machine. Her life consists of avoiding migraines, admiring Bonsai trees, watching classic movies, and living with her husband and daughter in Texas—where it can be forty degrees one day and eighty the next!

S.G.D. Singh lives in New Mexico and Punjab with her husband, two daughters, and various extended relatives and animals.